Prais

"5 MILLION STARS!!!!! ... My new all-time favorite [series] ... Heart-stopping ... Jaw-dropping ... You need to read these books." -- Megan, i fall in love book blog

"Every time I thought I had figured something out, the story took yet another twist and I was left re-thinking everything I had come to believe! ... This is a series that I will definitely be re-reading ... I cannot recommend it enough!" -- Ashleigh, Goodreads

"AMAZING is such an inadequate description of this series ... It teaches you how to breathe all over again." -- Tiffany, Goodreads

"It is rare and special when you come across an author who writes like Lynne. If you like dystopian novels ... you'll love this." -- Stephanie, TeacherofYA's Book Blog

"It's been years since I read a story that kept me begging for more. [The Sky series] did just that." -- Lindsay, Goodreads

"An awesome series. Intense. Creative. Highly recommended." -- Denise, Goodreads

BEYOND THE SKY

J.W. LYNNE

To Ashleigh, Denise, Doug, Erica, Hanna, Jaime, Lois, Lynn, Mark, Megan, Peter, Shannon, Sharon, Stephanie, and Tiffany for your invaluable help on this journey, from the beginning to the final chapter.

* * * *

BEYOND THE SKY

MONDAY, JULY 4
2141

SEVEN

We sail deep into the black ocean. Above us is a tiny sliver of moon and billions of stars. Other than that, the only illumination is the dim red light of the gaping room behind us—the ship's hangar. Panels in the ceiling and stripes on the floor glow crimson. Sleeping aerial drones form neat rows, flawlessly aligned with the stripes in the floor.

In the center of the hangar are fellow evacuees from the military base. Some are sprawled out on the ground, trying to get some rest. Some pace tensely. Some stand, ready to act at an instant's notice. The robots have remained down below, organizing our salvaged supplies.

I stay close to my family and friends, by a gigantic hangar window, where we can see the sky. I squint against the forceful air that pushes against us and try to detect anything in the darkness ahead, but nothing is forthcoming.

My baby is strapped to my chest in an infant carrier, a cloth sac that holds her against my body, facing forward, almost as if she is part of me, as she once was. Ten is beside us. The three of us together, one family. Nothing is comforting me more now than this.

Steps away are my parents and my little brother, Forty-one, as well as Ten's father and little sister, Forty-seven. I'm not quite sure exactly where Ten's mother is now, but I know for certain that she will never be among us again.

Ryan is also with us, standing very close. He has been my protector—and Ten's—ever since Ten and I first arrived up here, although it wasn't until slightly less than a year ago that I learned that he is my father's brother. Jackie is with us too, at my invitation, although I remain wary of her. I had once thought of Jackie as my protector, like Ryan, but today I learned that she was a spy for the Outsiders. She put many of us in danger in order to try to help her people. Her plan backfired, though, in a horrible way. Our military ended up destroying Jackie's entire community. Few of her people survived.

Another family joins us here, one that I barely know: Maria—a former warrior who was, up until recently, a prisoner of the Outsiders—and her four children: Jose, Katrina, Stacy, and Noah. In an infant carrier on Maria's chest is a tiny infant, just a few weeks old. Maria isn't the child's mother though. She is caring for the baby because his mother is dead.

Suddenly, Forty-one points at the ocean. "What was that?" he asks, with more awe in his voice than I've ever heard. I look down just in time to see a streak of light shoot past us, heading back the way we came. The other children rush over and join him in gazing excitedly at the water.

"That was a squid," Jackie says.

Forty-one stands on his tiptoes, peeking further over the top of the railing that separates us from the dark ocean. "What's a squid?" he asks as if he is expecting the ocean itself to answer.

Ryan wraps a protective hand around my little brother's left shoulder, urging his small feet back flat on the floor. "It's a type of animal that lives in the ocean," he answers, but it sounds as if his mind is far away.

"There's another one!" Katrina shouts, pointing at the water.

"It was glowing!" Forty-seven remarks.

"Squid are bioluminescent," Jackie says. "We used to see them all the time at night from the undersea windows at the base ..." Her voice breaks.

"Is the new base similar to our old one?" I ask Ryan.

He exhales. "Not really. It sits on land rather than in the water. It hasn't been occupied for years, except by security drones. Apparently it's fairly rustic."

"It'll be fine," Ten says quickly.

"Yes," I agree. "Everything will be fine." I'm not sure of it though. I can't help considering possible threats that may await us. My mind seems trained now to seek out worst case scenarios in any situation. Of course, in this case, there are plenty of reasons to be concerned.

I sense unexpected movement behind me. I spin around and see a stone-faced woman wearing a dark-gray jumpsuit. She brings her right hand to her temple and holds it there. Ryan does the same, before swiftly returning his hand to his side. The woman finally drops her hand back to her side and speaks, "Lieutenant Commander Ryan, your presence is required on the bridge, sir."

Ryan turns to us. "I need to go," he mutters, almost too quickly, and then he walks off fast with the woman in the gray jumpsuit.

I look to Jackie. "Where is she taking him?"

Jackie points upward. "To the ship's control center."

"Why would they need Ryan in the control center?" Ten asks.

She shakes her head. "I have no idea."

MONDAY, JULY 4
2201

SIX

The navigator on my wrist is dead. It displays no date.
No time. Nothing at all. I'm not sure exactly why or when it
died, or if it will ever come back to life. One thing is
certain: from now on, nothing will ever be as it once was.

My only comfort is that I am with my family and
friends, including people who, as of just this morning, I
never dreamed I would see again. I stand apart from them
though, as if I am outside a window, looking in.

My best friend, Three, lightly brushes my arm with hers.
Back home, a touch like that would be forbidden unless it
was accidental, which I'm fairly certain it was not.

"I understand if you want to stand closer to your
family," she says. "I don't want you to be far away from
them because of me."

I hadn't felt like I'd made a decision about where to
stand because of Three, but maybe I did. Or maybe it's that
I wanted to be far away from Jose.

Jose and I once knew each other well. We spent three
months together, back when I was prisoner of the Outsiders.
It seems he and I grew quite close, but I don't remember
how close. The military wiped my memory of all but the

first few weeks of my imprisonment. Jose could fill me in on what happened after that, but I don't know if I want him to. Besides, even if I did want to talk to him about our past, I can't. I'm not supposed to be the person who was his prisoner. After I escaped, Seven and I traded identities, and so it is Seven that is supposed to know Jose, not me.

I take a few steps closer to my family, far enough from Jose that I don't invite any interaction with him, yet close enough to my family that I can participate in the conversation, even though I don't feel much like conversing right now.

"Those are *real* stars," Seven is saying to Forty-one and Forty-seven as the three of them gaze up at the sky. Her tone is far too happy to match our situation. Our father's voice takes on that same quality whenever something is bothering him. Seven must be nervous. Of course she is. She knows the dangers of Up Here as well as I do, maybe more.

"What do you mean 'real stars'?" Forty-one asks Seven.

"The ones back home are just bright spots of light on a tremendous screen," Seven explains. "The stars above you now are glowing balls of heat far away in outer space."

Ryan taught me all about stars and planets while we were being held captive by the Outsiders. He relayed this information to me in stories. He said that the stories were to entertain us, to keep us occupied during the long hours of captivity, but his ulterior motive was clear to me. His stories were true. The purpose of those stories was to educate me about Up Here.

"Are real stars dangerous?" Forty-seven asks softly.

Before anyone can respond, a thunderous male voice

fills the air, "Ladies and gentlemen, this is your captain speaking. We are currently in transit to Santa Monica, however we will be remaining at sea for the night. We will disembark to the base after sunrise. Crew members will collect you presently and direct you to your quarters."

Forty-one's eyes widen. "We're going to stay on the ship all night long?"

"I guess so," our father responds, trying hard to sound upbeat. His worried gaze shifts to something behind me.

I turn and see an approaching man in a gray jumpsuit. When he is about three feet away, he stops walking and speaks, "I'm Petty Officer Delgado. I will be escorting you to your quarters."

Without waiting for a reply, Delgado spins around and starts marching away from us. He doesn't look back to see if we're following him, but of course we do follow. None of us wants to spend the night in the chilly drone hangar.

As we traipse through the narrow, red-lit hallways, Forty-one and Katrina pepper Delgado with questions:

"How long have you lived on this ship?"

"Five years."

"Do you like it here?"

"I enjoy being at sea."

"Have you seen any squids?"

"Millions of them."

Delgado leads us down a metal ladder that lies below an opening in the floor. Once we've all assembled in the hallway at the ladder's base, he gestures to the right. "Heads are at the end of the passageway on the starboard side." Then he points to a row of open doorways on the left. "You will sleep in the berths. Each berth is designed to accommodate six individuals, but there are enough to allow you to sleep singly if desired. Mess deck's directly above. Breakfast is at zero five hundred hours."

Forty-seven peeks inside one of the doorways. "What about all the people who work on the boat?" she asks. "Where will all of you sleep?"

"Of all of us, only the captain requires sleep," Delgado says.

It is only then that I realize that Delgado is a robot. He is so incredibly realistic, in both appearance and manner of moving and speaking, that his statement is the only hint that he isn't human. That fact makes me extremely uncomfortable. It is comforting to be able to tell the difference between humans and robots.

The robot looks to Jackie, the sole member of the military in our group. "Do you require any additional assistance?" he asks.

"No," Jackie says. "Thank you, Petty Officer."

Delgado turns and climbs the ladder, leaving us all alone.

"This boat is amazing!" Forty-one says. "Can Forty-seven and Katrina and I go exploring?"

"No," my mom says, her voice gentle. "We all need to get some rest. It's time to say goodnight to your friends."

Forty-one sighs and bids goodnight to the other children. "Goodnight, Forty-seven. Goodnight, Katrina. Goodnight, Stacy. Goodnight, Noah."

"Goodnight, Forty-one," the children reply.

"Goodnight, Baby Zander," Forty-one whispers to the sleeping infant strapped to Maria's chest.

The families file into the empty rooms. My parents

follow Forty-one into the first room. Ten's father leads Forty-seven into the adjacent one. Jackie enters a room alone. Maria ushers Katrina, Stacy, and Noah into the room next door.

"See you in the morning," Seven says to me.

I smile. "I'll see you in the morning." Up until very recently, I never thought I'd be able say that to my sister ever again.

As Seven and Ten disappear into a room with their baby, Jose turns to me. Without hesitation, he takes me into his arms, confirming my concern that Jose knows the difference between Seven and me. It is our first embrace, or at least the first one I remember. Strangely, it doesn't feel weird, until I look over and see Three staring at us.

Back home, an embrace between two adults who aren't paired would be absolutely forbidden, and so it must appear shocking to Three. Oddly, it doesn't seem so to me. I suppose after he nearly lost his life trying to save mine, an embrace seems appropriate.

"Goodnight," he says as he releases me, and then he swiftly disappears into one of the rooms.

Now only Three, her baby, and I remain in the hallway.

"I guess this is goodnight," I say to Three.

"It doesn't have to be," she says quietly.

She's right. There are no rules here. Three and I can share a room tonight if we want to. There is nothing to stop us. I inhale, trying to keep from going insane with excitement. "You want us to sleep together, like a paired couple?" I ask.

"If that's okay with you," she says timidly.

"There is nothing that would bring me greater pleasure,"

I say.

Three cocks her head. "We'll see about that."

MONDAY, JULY 4
2231

JACKIE

For the first time since I left my quarters this morning, I am alone. No one can see me here, and so I can finally let my face match my feelings. I pull the zipper of my jumpsuit partway down my neck, loosening its grip on me, and I stretch out on one of the six beds that are stacked in sets of three on the sides of the room.

As soon as I close my eyes, the tears come hard. Tears of relief. Sadness. Pain. I have lost everything I have ever known. Both my old life as an Outsider and my recent life as a spy against the military have been obliterated.

And my secret is out. This afternoon, when we went on the mission to rescue what was left of my people, I revealed to some of my fellow soldiers that I am an Outsider. A spy. No doubt they will share that secret with others. Soon, the fact that I am an Outsider will soon be known by all, and I will be forced to face the consequences. Will the others accept me? Or will I always be considered a traitor, someone who can never be trusted, who must be carefully watched for signs of duplicity? I suppose if it is the latter, I can't blame them. Although I believe my motives were good, my actions were a threat to these people. If they can't or won't trust me, I must accept that. I have no choice but to live among them. There is nowhere else in the world I could safely go, now that most of my people have been murdered by the people who are now my fellows.

A tap at the entrance to my quarters makes me jump. *Is someone there or is it my imagination?* I wipe the tears from my face. *I hope no one is here to see me. I don't want to be seen right now.*

There is another tap. A definite purposeful one this time. *Someone is knocking.*

I rise to my feet and zip up my jumpsuit, wishing there were a video monitor to prepare me for who I will find on the opposite side of the door, but the spot in the wall where the monitor should be has been vacated.

I steel myself and press the button on the wall beside the door.

The door slides open.

Standing in the hallway is Ryan.

"I need to speak with you privately," he says, his face stoic. "May I come in?"

There really isn't any other answer that I can give. And so I say what I must, "Yes, sir."

MONDAY, JULY 4
2236

FORTY-ONE

Today is the best day I've had in the entire nine years, three months, and eleven days that I've been alive. I'm inside a boat so big it could fit a hundred plaza atriums within it and still have space left over. It could be that this is all just part of one big spectacular dream, but I've never had a dream nearly this spectacular.

Boats are supposed to be made-up things. There are drawings of them in books, but only in *fiction* books. Out of the hundreds of books on my tablet, there were no *nonfiction* books about boats, or oceans, or almost any of the things that there are up here above the sky.

Up Here is like a storybook come to life. In storybooks, there are good things, but there are always bad things too. I know there are bad things *here* because all of the adults are nervous, even though they keep saying everything is "fine."

I am nervous too because I haven't seen The War yet. Seven said there isn't *exactly* a war up here. But if there isn't *exactly* a war, that means there is something *like* a war. I want to know more about it, and if it's dangerous, but nobody will answer my questions, and so I'm going to have to try to figure out things for myself.

My mom and dad are asleep.
It's time to get started.

TEN

I unzip the backpack that was given to Seven by one of the nurses on the beach. She said it contains everything we need to care for our baby for the next forty-eight hours. Inside the pack, along with infant formula and diapers, is a flat plastic rectangle labeled "Infant Sleep Box." The nurse said the baby should be placed on her back in that box at night and whenever we're unavailable to hold her. The nurse said the box is just as safe as the infant sleeping areas in the bedroom capsules back home.

When I pull the labeled tab on the top of the flattened box, the sides rise and snap securely into position. At the base of box is a cloth mattress striped pink and blue. Atop the mattress is a note. Quietly, I read the first words, "Congratulations on your new baby!"

Seven looks over at me, and then she sits down on a nearby bed. "I guess that's appropriate. Tonight is the first night that she's *ours*."

Like a jolt, it hits me. *My baby is now mine. Mine to raise from child to adult. Mine to watch over. Mine to protect.*

I shake my head. "I'm not putting her in that box. Not

tonight."

"The nurse said it's the safest place for her to sleep," Seven says softly.

"Only when we're not able to hold her," I say. "I'm able to hold her tonight."

"But when you go to sleep—" she starts.

"I won't be sleeping tonight."

MONDAY, JULY 4
2245

FORTY-ONE

I don't have to scan my arm to make the door to our ship domicile slide open. I only have to push a button. When I look into the hallway, I see a man walking to the "head"— which is what they call lavatories here. I wait a second and then check the hallway again.

There's nobody out there. Now's my chance.

I step into the hallway and press the button to make the door close behind me, then I walk fast into an open domicile and close the door.

I made it! Now I can explore.

My mom and dad wouldn't let me explore our domicile. My dad took me to the head to wash up, and then I was told to get straight into bed. My parents are not usually so firm with me. I hope their new behavior is temporary. It's probably because they're nervous about being above the sky.

Inside a small compartment near each bed, I find a floppy yellow u-shaped thing labeled "life vest." The printing on the life vest says to push the red button to make it "inflate" or blow into the tube. I push the red button. That doesn't do anything, even after a few times, so I blow into the tube. Nothing happens, so I try again. And again. And then I see that something *is* happening. The life vest is trapping my breaths inside itself. I decide to stop, because I'm not sure how to get the breaths out again, and if I put more breaths in, the life vest won't fit back into its compartment anymore.

It looks like there is some kind of compartment hidden underneath each of the mattresses. I pull the mattresses off one of the beds and lift up a heavy metal lid that is almost as big as the mattress. Sure enough, there is a compartment, and it is full of stuff, mostly clothing: dark green shirts and pants, white underwear, and green socks. Next to the socks is small paper box of short skinny brown things that look a little like old-fashioned pens but, when I try to pull one out, it disintegrates into darker-brown crumbly stuff. The stuff smells interesting, a bit like a strange-smelling flower.

I put the box back where I found it and remove a book with yellowish paper pages. The first few pages have drawings on them, but the pictures don't have any colors. Even so, they are just as nice as the ones in fairy tale books. The first drawing is of a house, with flowers around the outsides of it and a boy sitting on the stairs in front of it. The next picture is of the same boy maybe, but he looks older. It is just the boy in that picture, nothing else. He looks happy. His hair is very curled up, the way my mom's is in the morning, before she secures it properly. On the next page is a picture of a woman sitting on a chair. She is wearing a dress, like girls sometimes do in fairy tales, and her hair is unsecured. Even though she is just a drawing, I feel like she is looking right at me. It makes me uncomfortable the way she is looking at me, like she is trying to ask me a question, but I'm not sure what the question is.

I put the book aside and continue exploring the compartment. I can't identify most of the things that are in there. Some things crumble into pieces when I touch them. One thing has strings on it that make sounds, like music, when I touch them. That is my favorite thing that I find.

At the very bottom of the compartment is a thick envelope that contains images on small pieces of thick plastic, but these aren't like normal pictures. The images appear as if they would feel like three-dimensional objects rather than pictures, but when I run my finger over the plastic, it feels as flat as glass. It is as if the images are located deep *inside* the plastic, deeper than the plastic is thick. And those images look completely *real*, like real people in real places all frozen in miniature, as if by magic. I think they are images of people, rather than robots, because in one of them there is a woman holding a baby and she is touching her face against the baby's forehead. I don't think robots do that with babies. In another, there are two men and they both look like they are laughing. I've never seen a robot laugh.

What is in this compartment doesn't belong to a robot. What is in this space are the kinds of things that we keep in our personal drawers. *Belongings.* Robots don't have belongings like that.

Delgado said that everyone on this ship—except for us and the captain—doesn't sleep. If they don't sleep, they must be robots. If the captain is the only *person* who lives on this ship, who do all these belongings belong to? Where did those people go? Why didn't they take their belongings

19

with them when they left?

Maybe the people who used to live here left in a hurry, like we did when we left our box.

But if they left, where are they now?

MONDAY, JULY 4
2301

SIX

Fifty-one looks so peaceful in his little box, his body limp with sleep. "Your baby is beautiful," I whisper to Three as she sits down beside me on one of the beds.

"He's the most amazing person I've ever met, next to you." Three's left hand goes to my hair, brushing it from my forehead. A shiver of excitement runs through me. "I've missed being alone with you," she adds.

"I've missed that too." Three and I haven't been alone together for months. After I gave Ten's tag back to Forty-one—the tag's rightful owner—there wasn't any private place for us to be alone together. Plus, as much as I enjoy being alone with Three, the thought that we could get caught and sent to isolation was a lot to handle. Adults who are sent to isolation sometimes never return and, if they do return, their personalities have changed. I wonder if isolation could destroy the love that Three and I have for each other. If isolation is anything like the amnesia that was induced in me after my imprisonment by the Outsiders, I suppose it could do anything.

Three raises her eyebrows at me. "What are you thinking about?"

I don't want to ruin what could be the only night we will ever spend together, and so instead of telling her my thoughts I say, "I can't wait to sleep with you." These beds are much narrower than the one in the bedroom capsule I shared with Nine, even narrower than the one in the capsule I slept in as a child. When Three and I sleep together in one of these beds, our bodies will overlap a little. The thought of sleeping like that with Three fills me with excitement.

"Perhaps we should get started then." Three walks over to the door and pushes the light switch. Instead of extinguishing, the lights take on a shade of red—like the lighting in the drone hangar and the ship's hallways—giving the entire room an eerie glow. She pushes the button again and the lighting turns off.

The dark is too dark. I want to see Three in my arms. "I like the red," I say.

She switches the lights back to red and returns to me, but rather than sitting beside me, she reclines on the bed. I recline next to her with a sense of wonderful anticipation, the kind of feeling that I imagine some people get on their Assignment Day night, the first time they join the person who they were paired with in their new bedroom capsule.

Three embraces me, and my insides tingle with all-consuming energy. We cling tighter and tighter to each other, and my heart pounds harder and harder, as if it is trying to reach out to hers through the wall of my chest. Three's fingers go to the zipper of my jumpsuit and she eases it down.

"You're trembling," she whispers.

"So are you," I notice.

My clothing slowly leaves me, and I undress Three,

revealing her chest, and the curves of her waist, and the dark hair between her legs. I press my lips against hers, and her breaths grow irregular, as if she's having trouble figuring out how to breathe. After a moment, she pulls back slightly. "I like it when you put your lips on my lips," she says. "I've never done that with anyone before."

I want to say that I haven't either, but I feel like I *have* done that with someone, even though I can't remember what it felt like or who I was with. I wonder if, during those months that I can't remember, Jose and I touched lips. Now that Jose is with me again, maybe I will find out more about our time together. *But how much do I want to know?*

Three's lips press against my chest, and my thoughts vanish. Her fingers glide over my skin drawing little circles as they move lower. The warmth of her breath and the heat of her touch penetrates me. My fingers explore her body. She is soft. Hard. Still. Writhing.

Three's lips find their way back to mine. We touch and touch. Desperately. As if we depend on that touch to live. The feeling is intense and frightening and so wonderful that I can think of nothing but how much I want to be with Three like this. How much I *need* to be with Three like this. My thoughts are consumed by the heat that is building between us. Inside us.

Suddenly, Three shudders against me. An instant later, I shudder too, and my body goes weak, utterly relaxed and content despite the uncertainty that has become our certainty.

Three pulls me closer. "Did you experience great pleasure?" she whispers, breathless.

"I can't imagine any greater pleasure," I say.

And I can't.

SEVEN

Ten is just a few feet away from me, but I've never felt further away from him than I do now—at least not since the first time that I saw him, when we were toddlers standing at our family's domicile windows, staring longingly at each other, separated by what felt like miles.

I wish there was something I could say or do to erase the pain he must be feeling, but of course there isn't. Although there was incredible joy today—we were reunited with our daughter—there was also great pain. Many people died today. Our entire military base was reduced to rubble. And Ten's mother was the cause of it all.

I can only imagine how Ten must be feeling. His mother, who he loved and trusted, the mother who seemed to care for him all of his life, tried to execute him, and me, and our daughter. She viciously betrayed us. In a way, losing someone to betrayal is worse than losing someone to death. Death is involuntary, or at least it should be. Ten's mother made a conscious choice to betray us all.

Ten lies on a bare mattress, because there is no bedding here. Fifty-two is asleep on his chest. Ten's eyes are closed, but I can tell by his deep, uneven breaths that he is far from resting, far from sleep. It hurts to see him in pain. I have to do something. I have to try.

"*Quiero tocarte*," I whisper. Of all the times that I've said those words to him, this may be the time that we need each other's touch most.

"You want to touch me?" he asks without opening his eyes. He sounds so tired.

"If you want me to." *Maybe he doesn't.*

He opens his eyes and his gaze meets mine, but only for an instant. In that brief moment he forces a smile, but the smile vanishes almost as soon as it appears. "Of course, I want you to."

I rise from the bed opposite his and take the few steps necessary to cross the small room. I arrive at his bed unsure of exactly what to do next. I swallow back the emotions that rise into my throat. I want to touch him so badly, but I feel like I don't know how anymore. I exhale and sit beside him on the mattress, my hands folded in my lap, our bodies separated by a few inches.

He shifts his eyes to look at me. "I thought you were going to touch me."

"Right." I take a deep breath and lie down awkwardly, wrapping an arm around Ten and Fifty-two. Our baby stirs for a moment, but then settles back to sleep on her father's chest. Ten slides an arm up around me, embracing me. I close my eyes, fighting tears.

So many nights when I rested next to Nine and Fifty-two in our bedroom capsule, trying to find sleep, this is what I pictured. Ten and Fifty-two and me, all together. It was the most comforting image that I could think of. On some nights, this visualization was the only thing that calmed me enough to allow me to drift off into sleep.

Now, I have what I dreamed of, but my dream is a nightmare. Today, both our former box and our current box were torn open, and all of the people and robots spilled out into the vast uncertainty of Up Here, unprepared to face what's next.

And what lies ahead of us could be far worse that what we have left behind.

MONDAY, JULY 4
2334

FORTY-ONE

Exploring gives me questions instead of answers, and my questions are *big* questions rather than little ones. Big questions are frustrating because it is forbidden to ask them. We're not even supposed to think them. I know there's something very wrong up here. I don't know how I know that. It's mostly just a feeling. Like the feeling I got when Seven took me into the drone closet and showed me the darkness outside our box that I never knew was there.

I've completed my exploration of this berth, so I open the door and check the hallway for people and robots. The hallway is empty, and so I go into it and walk toward another open door.

I have made only a few steps when I hear a door slide open behind me. I look back and see Ryan step into the hallway. His door closes before he pushes any buttons. *Someone else must be inside that room, but who?*

Ryan's eyes lock with mine.

I stop in place. There is no sense running. When you are caught, you are caught. Running only makes things worse.

In an instant, Ryan's hand is wrapped around my arm, pulling me into an empty room and shutting the door. "Sit," he says, gesturing to a mattress.

I sit down and Ryan sits on a different mattress, facing me. For at least a minute, he just stares at me, which is scary because I don't know if he is angry or not. Usually I can tell by looking at people's faces, but I can't tell by looking at Ryan's.

"What were you doing out in the hallway?" he finally asks.

"I was exploring."

His forehead wrinkles up. "Exploring is dangerous."

"I know."

"Then why were you exploring?"

"Because I want to know about Up Here."

He exhales. "What's your most burning question?"

It sounds like I might only get one question, so I make it my most important one. "Are we safe?"

"We're as safe as we can be." Based on the way he says that, in a soothing tone, I have a feeling that he is trying to reassure me. But what he said doesn't comfort me, because what he told me is that we're not safe. Not entirely.

"How can we be *completely* safe?" I ask.

"Not every question has a certain or satisfying answer." He rises to his feet. "I need to get you back to your parents' quarters."

"Are you going to tell them that I was exploring?" If my parents find out I left our berth without their permission, they will be very angry with me and, more importantly, I will have little chance of getting out of their sight in the immediate future.

"Not unless I catch you wandering about again," Ryan says.

"You won't." *Next time, I'll be more careful.*

"That's good," he says as we start to the door.

"Who's in your quarters with you?" I ask. It's the kind of question that could be bigger than a little question, but I don't know how much bigger, and I really want to know the answer. And, just moments ago, Ryan invited me to ask a question, and he didn't really answer the question I asked.

"No one," he says.

"But I saw—"

He turns to me. "I'd appreciate it if you don't say anything about what you saw."

"Why not?"

"It's classified."

"What does 'classified' mean?"

"It means it's a secret."

I try another big question. "Are there lots of secrets here?"

"I am about to give you another uncertain and unsatisfying answer," he says.

I feel my shoulders fall. "Which is?"

"Probably."

My parents are still asleep when I open the door to their room. Ryan doesn't wake them. He just supervises me until I close the door behind myself. I crawl back into my bed and, in the quiet and the darkness, I think about secrets.

I don't like secrets. Secrets are dangerous. If Ryan doesn't know about all the secrets up here, than who does? Are there Decision Makers up here? If not, who makes the decisions? And what are the rules? And what happens if you break them? There are too many questions and too many secrets. I want to know the truths, even if it is

30

dangerous to find them out.

Maybe knowing the answers will make us safe. Or maybe it won't.

But there's no way of knowing until we do.

TUESDAY, JULY 5
0445

TEN

A long, low tone drowns out my drowsy thoughts. Once the tone is silenced, a monotone voice adds, "Report to the mess deck for morning meal at zero five hundred hours."

I didn't sleep last night. I couldn't allow myself to leave Seven and Fifty-two. I kept watch over them all night long. Listening to their breathing. Holding them close to me. If only it were that simple to protect them.

"We need to give Fifty-two her bottle," Seven whispers. She extricates herself from my arms, goes to the backpack, and returns with a bottle of baby formula. "Do you want to give it to her?"

I shake my head, my mind thick with exhaustion. I'm not sure if I could feed myself right now much less a baby. "You do it," I say.

Seven takes our baby from me, and I climb out of bed. For a moment, I stand there watching them. Seven eases the end of the bottle into Fifty-two's mouth. Fifty-two's eyes open, and she begins to drink. For one brief instant, everything feels like it will be okay. Then I remember that, yesterday, my mother tried to kill us.

"I'm going to go take a shower," I say. "Then I'm going

to the hangar to get some air."

Seven looks concerned. "What about breakfast?" she asks. She's worried about me, and that tears at my gut, but I don't know how to ease her worry, or if that's even possible.

"I'll eat later," I say.

Seven bites her lower lip. "Okay," she says, "I'll meet you in the hangar after breakfast."

I nod and exit our quarters.

There are more than two dozen showers in the head, some occupied, some not. Behind the privacy of a curtain, I undress and wash myself under the cool spray of the gleaming showerhead, then I dress in soiled clothes that are filled with the memories of yesterday—because they are the only clothes I have—and I retrace my steps from last night back to the hangar.

The hangar is nearly empty now, with only a few of the ship's crewmembers in the area. I go to the railing, where I can look out at the shadowy water. The ship isn't moving forward anymore. Gentle waves roll against its side but, other than that, all is relatively still.

The sun has not yet risen, but there is a hint of light on the horizon, enough that I can see that we aren't far from a beach. This beach, unlike the one where the warrior compound used to be, is covered with spots of light—red, green, and blue. There are buildings here, but I can't discern their features.

Suddenly, a lighted boat crosses between the ship and the shore, heading away from us, toward the beach. It is the same type of boat that transported us here yesterday, about fifty people at a time. Strangely, there are very few people on board the boat this morning. Just twelve people are heading to the beach, under the cover of darkness, before the rest of us have finished breakfast. Eleven of them are people—or robots—who I don't recognize, but there is one person on the boat who I have known since the first day I set foot up here.

Ryan is aboard that boat. But why?

TUESDAY, JULY 5
0458

FORTY-ONE

My dad accompanies me to the head in the morning. Even though he doesn't seem to know that I went exploring last night, it's like he's trying to keep me in his sight at all times. He sends me behind a curtain to take my shower, but he tells me he will be in the shower right next to me. By the time I pull open my curtain, my dad is dressed and waiting for me right outside.

I guess I should feel good that my parents are watching out for me, but it does little to decrease my fears. My mom and dad know very little about Up Here. They are trying to protect me, but how can you protect someone from a threat you know nothing about?

As my dad walks me back to our berth, I take note of the room that I saw Ryan come out of late last night. It is one room away from the berth my family and I slept in, and the door is closed. Last night, Ryan had a classified visit with someone there.

I wish I knew who.

I wish I knew the secret they shared.

SEVEN

I had planned to meet up with Ten alone but, at breakfast, I reunite with my family and his, and we all go to the hangar together. Ten is standing by the railing with his back to us, looking out at the ocean as the sun begins to light the sky.

"Look!" Forty-one points to a beach with at least fifty grayish buildings occupying the distant portion of it.

"What is that place?" Forty-seven asks.

"I think that's where we're going to live, for now," her father answers.

"Cool," Forty-one says quietly. He smiles, but his cheeks twitch with uncertainty.

Ten touches my forearm. "Can I talk to you?"

I nod and he leads me away from the others. His expression is still serious, the way it was when he left our quarters.

"I saw something this morning, before the sun came up," he says. "There was a boat, with twelve individuals on board, heading to the beach. When it got there, everyone got out, and I lost sight of them in the darkness. One of those people was Ryan."

"I'm surprised Ryan didn't tell us he was leaving before us," I say. Normally, Ryan doesn't keep us apprised of his whereabouts, but considering the current circumstances …

"He probably didn't want to wake us," Ten offers, but he sounds uncertain.

"You don't think he's in danger, do you?" I suppose that's a silly question. I'm pretty sure we're *all* in danger right now. "I mean … more danger than the rest of us."

"He didn't look like he was under duress, but—"

An echoing voice interrupts us, "Ladies and gentlemen, I'm Captain Kessler." I turn and see a man who appears to be standing in midair toward the center of the hangar. He is at least three times taller and wider than a normal man, and he is floating in the air, and so I am quite certain that he isn't really there. It must be just an image of the man. Captain Kessler continues, "Due to yesterday's unfortunate circumstances, I am now the most senior officer, therefore I am now your commander. Last night, I personally met with the other senior officers to review our plan for moving forward. I will share details of this plan with you in the near future. As you know, this ship has been patrolling the Pacific. It is responsible for securing the coastline around the military base. Regrettably, yesterday that wasn't enough. The attack on our base originated from within. Those responsible are no longer a threat, and I assure you that a meticulous investigation of the circumstances is currently underway. This morning, you will disembark to your new base. We've conducted a thorough reconnaissance and secured the base. I am confident that it is not susceptible to the type of attack that occurred at your prior location. I will be remaining aboard this ship, but you can rest assured I will be watching over you at all times. Please report now to the well deck for transportation to your base."

Forty-one bounds up to me urgently. "Have you seen Ryan?"

"No," I answer honestly. "Why do you ask?"

"Because he's our uncle," he says. "He should be with us."

"Maybe he wanted to go to the base before us," I say. "To make sure it's ready for us."

Forty-one shrugs, but he still looks distressed. "Maybe," he says.

I wish I knew for certain what was going on. I never liked uncertainty before but, now, with my baby strapped to my chest and my vulnerable family by my side, uncertainty is even more difficult to bear.

Together, we head down to the well deck—a cavernous space below the hangar with the ocean for a floor—where the transport boats dropped us off last night when we arrived on this ship. I assume those same boats will convey us to the beach.

The well deck is a flurry of activity. Ship crewmembers bustle this way and that, loading supplies onto one boat as soldiers board another. We are directed to the boat with the soldiers. Jackie is up near the front of the boat, along with Maria and her children. Forty-one spots the children, and he and Forty-seven run over to join them. Everyone else in our group follows.

After a few minutes, the boat separates from the ship and we start out of the well deck, toward the gray-blue sky. My father holds Forty-one tight, something my little brother would ordinarily reject but, for the time being, he allows it.

Ten's father holds Forty-seven just as tightly. Intense worry darkens our parents' faces. I think I know what they're feeling: a powerful need to protect what is precious to them, but the worry that they have no idea how.

My eyes squint in the morning light. The taste of the ocean coats my lips. Fifty-two wiggles her legs and coos excitedly. Ten puts his hand on my shoulder, but he doesn't say a word. When I turn to look at him, I see the same worry that I saw on our parents' faces.

I'm sure that same worry is on my face as well.

TUESDAY, JULY 5
0555

JACKIE

The closer we get to the base, the more I can see how much it is in disrepair. I remember hearing about this place, back when I was a young child. By all accounts, it was magnificent and extraordinary. It certainly doesn't appear so now.

But now, this is the place where I will live. Where I will work to prove myself to those who I serve, the way I've had to do many times before. The way I have ever since I left my people.

I will strive to be a good soldier.

And a good spy.

TUESDAY, JULY 5
0612

SEVEN

People begin to gather on the beach, adults who wear blue jumpsuits and children who wear white ones. These are people from our box. Their faces are set with a look of awe. How strange this all must seem to them. The soft sand beneath their feet. The restless ocean. Our boat moving toward them. The distant ship, far enough away from them that they might not appreciate its immense size.

I assume the people from our box traveled here after the box was evacuated and spent the night here. I doubt many of them slept much. The children maybe, but the adults probably not.

Our boat hits something solid, and the front wall of the boat is dropped forward, creating a walkway that leads onto the sand. Slowly, we begin to move forward, onto the beach, waves intermittently chasing us to the shore. Ten takes hold of my arm to support me as we cross onto the sand. Cold ocean water flushes into my shoes, and then flushes out again.

The people from our box watch us intently. At first, I assume they are merely mesmerized by the boat and the black-jumpsuited people emerging from it, but then a woman rushes forward. And someone in a black-jumpsuit rushes to meet her. And they embrace.

I see that happen again with a different woman and a different soldier, and then my tired mind realizes what is happening. Those soldiers aren't soldiers, they're warriors. The people from our box are watching ghosts emerge from a boat on the ocean. Their warriors. Loved ones who they once thought were gone forever.

The reunions happen quietly, restrained, the way we have been taught to behave regardless of the emotional intensity of the situation. But, even at a distance, I feel the relief falling over the mothers, fathers, sisters, brothers, friends, as they catch their first glimpse of the warrior who left them years ago.

About thirty feet away from me, standing on the beach with his parents, I see the man who I was paired with, Nine. His eyes search urgently, but it is not me who he's searching for. I know exactly who he's hoping to see. On our first night as a pair, Nine told me of the devastation he'd felt when his older sister was sent off to be a warrior. Now, he is searching for the sister who he hasn't seen in eleven years. I search the crowd for her too, and then I finally spot a gangly woman with blond hair who is walking toward Nine with incredible composure. I watch as her composure slowly falls away, and she throws her arms around Nine and her mother and father, and she weeps. Tears of joy flood Nine's eyes. Tears fill my eyes as well. After all the sacrifices he made for me and my child, Nine deserves this happiness, this and so much more.

And then, off to the side, I notice Twelve's parents. Their eyes search the passengers of the boat, anticipation evident on their faces. *They are looking for Twelve.*

Soon, everyone from this boat will have made their way onto the beach. Twelve's family will wait for the next boat, and the next one, and the next one, until no more boats come. They will search and search, uncertain as to why Twelve isn't among us. They will be left here after the others have gone away. Eventually, they will ask about Twelve. They will find someone who knows that he is dead, but that could take hours, or days. Very few people know his fate.

I turn to Ten. "Twelve's parents are here. I need to ..."

"Right," he says.

I start to pass Fifty-two to him, but Six reaches for her also.

"I should carry her now," she says.

She's right. Now that we are back among the people from our box, it is best that she acts as though my baby is hers.

"Stay close to Ten," I whisper to her. "Keep Mom, and Dad, and Forty-one with you." I know Ten will protect my family.

Six nods and secures Fifty-two to her chest and I walk away from them, toward Twelve's family. Uncertain of exactly how to proceed, but knowing that I must.

Once, when I was visiting my mother at work in the hospital, I watched her tell a woman that her husband had passed away. The man was very old, and his death was expected, but she told me those facts would be of little comfort to the woman. She asked me to sit quietly in a chair and wait.

I watched as my mother offered the woman a seat. She

sat beside the woman and spoke softly to her, so softly that I couldn't hear any of the words that were said. The woman didn't cry—she just nodded as my mother spoke—but the pain on her face was the greatest pain I had ever seen up until then. It scared me. I never wanted to see that kind of pain again.

Both of Twelve's parents give me a genuine smile when they spot me.

"Six!" Twelve's mother says. "How are you?"

Since I am dressed as a warrior, of course she assumes I am my sister. I don't correct her. It would be too risky.

"Have you seen Twelve?" Ten's father asks.

I feel unprepared to do this, but it would be cruel not to. It would be cruel to make them wait any longer. I wish I had a seat to offer them, but there is only sand.

"I'm afraid I have some bad news," I say. The look of anguish on Twelve's parents' faces is almost enough to stop me from speaking, but I force myself to continue, "Yesterday, Twelve made his way to your compound. He wasn't assigned to do so. He went on his own volition. During the evacuation, there was an accident. While attempting to rescue two individuals he slipped and fell from a great height ..."

"Is he in the hospital?" Twelve's father asks.

I should have been clearer. I can't let them hold out hope when there is none. "Twelve is dead," I say. "He died instantly."

In Twelve's parents' eyes, I see their hearts break. I see the same horrible pain that I saw on the face of the woman in the hospital, possibly even more. I want to give them privacy, so they can grieve. But, when I turn to go,

Twelve's mother stops me.

"You said he was rescuing someone," she says, her voice barely there. "Who was he rescuing?"

I swallow. "Ten and … Seven." I was pretending to be Six at the time that Twelve rescued me, just as I am now, but Twelve knew my true identity. It was *me* who he was trying to save.

"Did the two of them survive?" Twelve's mother asks, her eyes pleading for an affirmative answer.

"Yes," I say. "They did."

"That's … good." Her voice breaks as she says that, but she continues, "Twelve cared very deeply for Seven, although he didn't know how to show it. He would be comforted to know that she was saved."

And now—after hearing Twelve's mother's words—I am certain that Twelve's final actions were no act or manipulation. I am certain that his motivations in his last moments of life were pure.

Can a single noble act wipe out a lifetime of wrongdoings? Perhaps not. But I have decided to remember Twelve for his sacrifice rather than his transgressions, and I want his parents to be able to do the same.

Twelve went to our box yesterday for same the reason Ten and I did.

He did what he did for love.

TUESDAY, JULY 5
0641

SIX

We stand on the beach, waiting for some sort of guidance or instructions. And then I see ...

"Ryan!" I call out.

His gaze snaps to me and my family. "This way," he says to us.

Ryan guides us toward the structures ahead. We move with him like a group of school children, as one unit. Seven races over to join us.

"When did you get here?" I ask Ryan.

"Early this morning," he says. "I had some business." It's clear from his tone that he wants to leave it at that.

I see him catch sight of something—or someone—but when I turn to look in that direction, I can't determine who or what it was.

"I have to go," he says abruptly. Clearly, whatever he saw changed his plans. He points to a building a few feet away. "Supplies are in there. Once you get your basics, ask one of the soldiers to direct you to the barracks."

Before any of us can respond, he is gone.

Inside an echoing room with dark-green floors and walls, each person is provided with two bottles of water, a flashlight, one towel, two sheets, a pair of socks, and a jumpsuit that matches the type that they currently wear. There is no scanning of chips, no asking about identities. The robots that are distributing the supplies seem solely focused on doing their work as quickly as possible. My parents, Ten's father, Three, and I get blue jumpsuits. Seven, Ten, and Jackie get black ones. Forty-one and Forty-seven get white jumpsuits. Maria and her children get thin yellow jumpsuits without pockets; I've never seen that type of jumpsuit before.

We have nearly finished receiving our necessities, when Four comes up behind Three. He reaches toward Fifty-one—who is sleeping soundly in an infant carrier strapped to Three's chest—and touches his son's forehead gently. "You're here!" he says softly, as if speaking to both Three and sleeping Fifty-one.

"When did you arrive?" Three asks him.

"Last night," he says. "It was quite the experience. We rode in a tremendous aerial drone. And we saw the most amazing things ... mountains and forests and then we landed here by the ocean. It was incredible." He starts toward the exit to the building. "I'll show you to the living accommodations. They're a bit different from what we have back home, but they're serviceable. The lavatories are another story."

Four leads us out of the building and down a narrow path. The buildings on either side of us are shredded, so badly damaged that they're barely buildings anymore, but there are some others up ahead that seem fairly intact.

"They call these buildings 'the barracks,'" Four says as we approach a squat gray building with about a hundred cracked, opacified windows along the side. He leads us inside and to a room about a quarter of the way up the hall. The door is open. The interior of the room is quite bare, with four metal bed frames, only two with mattresses. One mattress is draped with two sheets. There is a light on the ceiling, but the illumination coils are missing, so it obviously doesn't work. "Welcome to our domicile," Four says to Three. "Let's get you settled."

As I had anticipated, now that we're back among the people from home, my fantasy life with Three is over. Of course Four expects her to share a room with him. They are a pair, and they have a child together. I have a pair too, although we don't have a child together; Nine knows that Fifty-two isn't his. She isn't mine either.

"There are some unoccupied dormitories toward the end of the corridor," Four says to the rest of us. "It's up to four people to a room."

Three looks at me regretfully. "I'll see you later."

I force a smile. "I'll see you soon."

I start down the hall, away from Three and Four's dormitory. Most of the rooms either have the door closed or one or both of the mattresses are draped with sheets, indicating that the room has already been claimed. As we find empty rooms, we occupy them. My parents and Forty-one in one room. Ten's father and sister in another. Ten and Seven choose a room, and I return Fifty-two to them so they can spend some quiet time with their child. Maria and her children take the next room. Jackie gets her own room. And then it is just Jose and me. There are two unoccupied rooms left, at the very end of the hall, directly across from each other.

"Looks like we're gonna be neighbors," Jose says.

"I might have to stay with the man I'm paired with …" I'm not sure why I felt the need to tell Jose that right now, but I guess he'd find out about it eventually.

"You're *paired* with a man?" he asks.

"Being paired is like being married." That's how Ryan once described it to me.

"You never told me you were paired," he says.

I never told him because it is *Seven* who is paired. Back when I knew Jose, I was supposed to be Six, but now I am pretending to be Seven.

I try to think of something that I can say that is the truth, without revealing that I have switched identities with my sister. I have no idea what kind of punishment we would face if our secret was discovered. Perhaps the punishments here are even worse than back home.

"I never wanted to be paired with him," I finally offer.

"Then why are you paired?" he asks.

"That's the way things are back home," I say. "You get assigned to someone, and you're paired with them for life."

"Oh," he says.

"It seems to work for most people," I say. "It just doesn't work for me."

"Why not?" he asks.

"Because I wanted to be paired with someone different." It seems strange that I am comfortable enough to say private things to Jose. This conversation would be awkward with nearly anyone else; in fact, I would never participate in this kind of conversation with anyone else, with the exception of Three.

"The person you *wanted* to be paired with … what's he

like?" Jose asks.

"I don't want to talk about that." I don't want to tell Jose about Three.

His cheeks flush pink and he looks away. "Sorry. I guess that was kind of personal." He starts into his room.

"Jose," I say.

He stops and turns toward me.

"I like talking with you," I say.

He smiles. "I like talking with you too."

"Maybe later … we could talk some more." I don't want to talk with him more right now. I need to work through my thoughts a bit first, figure out what I'm going to say.

"That sounds good," he says.

"Good," I say, and then I go into my pitiful new room—with its four bedframes, but only one mattress—and I pull the door shut.

TUESDAY, JULY 5
0713

SEVEN

Ten and I decided to take turns taking our showers. We both just showered this morning, but I'm already feeling an aching need for another one. I let him go first, and I take Fifty-two outside the barracks to assess our surroundings.

There is a nearly-fifty-foot-high wall that seems to enclose this compound. The wall is practically translucent, aside from vertical black bars that appear to be embedded inside it. I assume that, when viewed from the outside, the wall is completely opaque—like a one-way window. That way, if someone somehow got close to us, they couldn't see in.

Beyond the wall, as far as I can see, there is a ground of dirt and rocks littered with small brown-green plants, but I know there is more that lies further away. There are compounds associated with ours, like the one we visited nearly a year ago, where Tommy lives. There are also bands of Outsiders living in the wilds of Up Here; they live without military assistance, but they are struggling according to Jackie. That's all I'd been told about what's beyond this wall … until yesterday. Based on what Ten's mother told us, there are other warrior programs out there.

Apparently, we communicated with them only through her. Yesterday, she told them that we were compromised and that they should forsake us. But will they?

Do they know that our warrior compound was destroyed? That the survivors from that compound and everyone from our box has been relocated here, to this forlorn collection of barely-inhabitable buildings?

If they know anything at all about what happened to us, they must assume that we are in a critical situation. That we are weak and vulnerable. I suppose that leaves them with two main options.

They could send assistance.

Or they could attack.

TUESDAY, JULY 5
0725

TEN

The crusted showerhead sends forth a mere trickle of water. This certainly isn't the shower I was hoping for—a chance to try again to wash away some of the sickening filth that won't leave my skin. I am soiled by the knowledge that my mother tried to execute us.

Few people know yet that my mother was the sole Decision Maker, and that yesterday she tried to put us to death. Perhaps they will never know any of that, but I always will.

I am not my mother, but her body gave me life. She raised me, but I am my own person. I am not responsible for her actions. I would never do the horrible things that she did and attempted to do. Still, I am overwhelmed with guilt.

How could I have lived so close to her and not known her secrets? Not necessarily exactly what those secrets were, but that her secrets were dark and sinister? How could I not have sensed that?

But, if I had known, what would I have done? Would I have exposed her? Would I have tried to destroy her? I suppose I would have tried to stop her.

I *did* stop her, but not before she caused irreparable

damage. And my mother was seconds away from causing even further damage. She was seconds away from annihilating us.

That is far too close for comfort.

SIX

There is a knock on my dormitory door. I rise from my bed and slide the door open.

Three is waiting for me on the other side. I gesture for her to come inside, and I slide the door closed behind her. Even though it hasn't been long since I've seen her last, I've missed her terribly.

Three sits down on my bed. "I'm sorry I can't live with you."

I sit beside her. "That's okay," I say, forcing a smile onto my face. "I understand."

"I can still *be* with you," she proposes.

My heart quickens. "Be with me how?"

Three's fingers go to the zipper of my jumpsuit. Unlike last night, her fingers are still and certain. I am the only one of us who is trembling. "Like this," she says as she lowers my zipper.

For some reason, I don't want to do this. I'm not sure why. I just ... I don't ...

"Maybe we shouldn't," I say.

Three stops. My zipper is already halfway down my chest. "You don't want to ...?" she asks. Her eyes are filled with hurt.

Before I can speak, there is a tap on my door. Panic fills Three's face, and I'm sure it fills mine as well. I rush to pull my zipper back into place, but my fingers just don't seem to be under my control. It's as if they are paralyzed.

My eyes snap open.

"Are you going to lunch?" It's Jose's voice, through the door of my dormitory.

Three is gone from my room. She was present only in my dream.

I wipe the sleep from my eyes, then I slide open the door.

Jose is standing politely in the hallway. I wonder how long he has been there knocking on my door. I wonder if he considered opening it to see if I was inside. There is nothing preventing the door from opening to anyone with the desire to open it.

"Were you sleeping?" he asks me.

"Yes," I say. "I was dreaming." I'm not sure why I told him that last part.

"They just announced that we should report for lunch," he says. "It's in the same building where we received our rations." He looks a bit self-conscious. "I guess I'll see you there."

"We could go together," I suggest.

"Yeah," he says. "That's what I thought ..."

"How's my hair?" There's no mirror for me to check myself.

"Good," he says. "How's mine?"

His hair is mussed. Based on the rules of back home, it would be unacceptable, but based on the standards of Up

Here. "It's good."

Jose and I leave the barracks and walk the path that leads to the building where the robots gave us our supplies. Since the last time we were here, the interior has transformed into a dining room, with tables and chairs set out. Jose and I join a short queue and receive our meals. The food looks much like the food we get back home, but it is in bowls rather than on plates.

"May I receive my utensils?" a woman asks one of the serving robots.

"I apologize," the robot says. "There are no utensils available at this time."

The woman's face drops into an expression of discomfort. I watch her take a seat at a nearby table and lift the bowl to her face with embarrassment, eating from it directly. That's what most of the other people are doing, and so it doesn't look as odd as it should.

Jose and I find some seats at an empty table. As soon as we are seated, Jose reaches into his bowl, collecting a bit of the sloppy saucy beans with his fingers and dropping it into his mouth.

He is the only person doing this. "You're going to eat it like *that*?" I ask him.

He shrugs. "Why not?"

It's a good question. I reach into my bowl and remove some food. It seems that this method of eating is more effective than eating directly from the—

"Seven!" Nine exclaims, seeming quite pleased to see me. Of course he knows that I am not Seven, but he is continuing to protect my identity. "I was on the beach when the boats arrived, but I didn't see you." He turns and addresses Jose, "Hello, I'm Two Thousand Nine ... or Nine for short."

Jose raises a sloppy hand in greeting. "I'm Jose," he says. "Nice to meet you."

Nine eyes Jose's yellow jumpsuit. I hadn't thought about it before, but it is the same color of the clothes that Ryan and I wore when we were prisoners of the Outsiders. Nine must wonder who Jose is, but he doesn't ask. Instead he turns back to me and asks, "Where's Fifty-two?"

I take a quick look around the dining room, and I spot Seven and Fifty-two sitting at a table with our family. I wonder for a moment why I didn't join them.

I gesture toward Seven and Fifty-two. "She's spending some quality time with her aunt," I say to Nine.

As he spots them, I see what almost looks like relief. "Good," he says. "That's good." And then a bit of awkwardness crosses his face. "Did you receive your rations?"

"Yes," I say. "I got them this morning."

"Where did you put them?" he asks.

I feel like there's a question behind his question. I think he is trying to ask how we will carry on while we're here. It seems that there are no rules insisting that we must share a domicile or act as a pair. It seems that it is up to *us* to decide how to regard our pairing, a pairing that neither of us really wanted. I am fairly certain that Nine has no desire to share a room with me if he doesn't have to.

"I found an empty dormitory. I put my supplies there ... for now." I stop speaking and watch Nine's face, trying to decipher his response. His expression is tense, but otherwise unreadable. "Is that okay with you?" I ask.

The tension in his face lessens. "Yes," he says. "That's okay with me." He appears as if he's going to depart, but he hesitates. "If you need anything ..." he starts, but his voice fades away.

"Yes, you too," I say. "If you need anything ..."

"Thank you," he says.

I watch him go to Seven. After a brief greeting, he strokes Fifty-two on the forehead so lovingly that it warms my heart. His move could be for appearances, but I have a feeling it isn't. Nine cares about Fifty-two. Even though she isn't his by blood, I know she will always be in his heart.

"So that's the man you're paired with?" Jose asks me quietly.

"Yes," I say, staring down into my bowl.

"He seems nice," Jose says.

"He's wonderful." But I think I just ended my pairing with him, for now, maybe forever.

The person who I *want* to be paired with is still paired with her partner.

So that leaves me ... alone.

TUESDAY, JULY 5
1245

FORTY-ONE

After we eat lunch, somebody announces that it is time for the children to join their teachers and go to school. Forty-seven and I queue beside our teacher, Professor Dorothy. Katrina isn't sure where to go, so I tell her to come with us.

Professor Dorothy doesn't say anything when Katrina joins us in our classroom. But when she does the attendance scan, I see her eyes stay on Katrina for an instant too long. Still, she says nothing.

The kids in my class seem intrigued by Katrina's presence. As we listen to Professor Dorothy, I spot them sneaking glimpses of Katrina and then turning quickly away. For the first time since I've met her, Katrina seems a little anxious.

After about an hour of lessons, a doctor comes to visit us. She tells us to pull our chairs in a circle. We've never been allowed to rearrange classroom chairs before. Once we build a circle out of chairs, the doctor sits in the circle with us and tells us that we are all safe. We were safe where we lived before "in a very special box that kept us warm and snug," but we are also safe here, "even though sometimes it gets damp and chilly."

I don't like the way this doctor talks to us, like we are children half our age. Even small children shouldn't be spoken to the way she is speaking to us. Her voice has a pleasant sound to it, like she is trying to be nice, but not actually being nice. I have a feeling that we are smarter than she thinks we are. I don't think she realizes that we are smart enough to know that what she is saying isn't true.

It is a relief when school is finally over. Although it was a mere four hours of classes instead of the usual seven, it felt like the afternoon went on forever. I can't wait to get out of this stifling room and into someplace cooler. A quick look at Katrina tells me that she feels the same way.

As we file out of the classroom, Thirty-eight—the only person in my class who I never really talk to—points at Katrina's jumpsuit and asks, "Why are you wearing a *yellow* jumpsuit?"

"That's what they gave me," Katrina answers softly.

"Yellow jumpsuits are very odd," Thirty-eight says coldly.

"Come on, Katrina," I say, leading her away. "I want to ask Professor Dorothy a question."

"*Katrina?*" a boy—Forty-three—repeats. "Is that your *name*?"

My stomach sinks. *I shouldn't have said her name.* I should have realized that the other kids would find her name peculiar.

"Yes," Katrina says, forcing her shoulders straight and tall.

"That's a *robot* name," Thirty-eight says. "Are you a robot?"

"No," Katrina says. "I'm not a robot."

"She's our friend," I say, including Forty-seven in my statement.

"*I* think she's a robot," Forty-three says with a smirk. "Forty-one is friends with a *robot*."

Professor Dorothy's voice rises above the whispers that now engulf us, "Why are we congregating here? It is time for evening recreation."

"I apologize, Professor," Thirty-eight says. "We were just making the acquaintance of our new classmate."

Professor Dorothy glances at Katrina and then back at Thirty-eight. "I hope you have provided her with a warm welcome."

"Yes, of course, Professor," Thirty-eight replies. The sarcasm in her voice is clearly evident, but Professor Dorothy won't sense that. Robots are poor at detecting sarcasm.

"Good," Professor Dorothy says.

It's times like this when I wish we had a *human* teacher.

Fortunately, the other kids disperse. Unfortunately, Katrina looks like she might cry.

Professor Dorothy looks at her. "It's difficult being different, isn't it?"

I try not to stare at the professor in shock. Robots can sense our facial expressions—she can certainly sense that Katrina is upset—but to understand why …

Katrina nods.

"Being different is being special," Professor Dorothy says.

"I don't feel special," Katrina says.

"Forty-one thinks you're special," Professor Dorothy

says.

My cheeks instantly feel uncomfortably hot. "That's right," I say.

"Right," Forty-seven adds.

"Your friends think you're special. That's what truly matters," the professor says. "Do you want me to escort you to evening recreation?"

"No," I say quickly. "Thank you for the offer."

"Very well," she says. "I will see you tomorrow."

Professor Dorothy goes out the back door of the classroom, and Forty-seven, Katrina, and I go out the front door. As soon as we are a few buildings away, Katrina stares down at her jumpsuit. "I wish I had a jumpsuit like yours."

"We could go find you one now, before dinner," I suggest. "There must be extra jumpsuits here somewhere."

"What about evening recreation?" Forty-seven asks.

"This is more important," I say.

Forty-seven glares at me. "We can't miss evening recreation."

"Go then," I tell her. "I'm going to go find a white jumpsuit."

Forty-seven exhales loudly. "Suit yourself," she says, and then she walks off, leaving Katrina and me to carry out our plan without her.

TUESDAY, JULY 5
1710

JACKIE

As I stroll the grounds of the base, building a mental map of my new environs, I tuck into a private spot to check my navigator. On it, I find my first message since our compound exploded and fell into the ocean. It's in code. I translate the code in my head:

> Back entrance to the central hub at 1900.
> Do you copy?

I swallow and type a response using the same code:

> Copy.

And then I continue my assignment.

FORTY-ONE

"I think Forty-seven is angry with you," Katrina says as she bravely darts among the structures in this unfamiliar place, seemingly unafraid of danger.

"Forty-seven likes to follow the rules," I say. "She doesn't understand that sometimes you have to do something that's 'wrong' in order to do what's right. You shouldn't have to wear a *yellow* jumpsuit just because you didn't get born in our box."

Katrina slows down to a walk. "Thank you for being my friend, Forty-one," she says.

I'm not sure how to reply to that. No one has ever thanked me for being their friend before. I decide to say, "You're welcome." But I don't think that was the right thing to say, because Katrina looks away from me after that.

I want to ask her something that I've been wanting to ask ever since I met her. I didn't ask yesterday because my mom told me it was an impolite question. Katrina and I are friends now, so maybe it isn't impolite to ask anymore, and so I do, "Where did you live before you came here?"

"In a house." She points in the opposite direction of the

ocean. "Somewhere out there." Her gaze falls down to the ground. "But all of our houses are gone now. Almost everyone who I ever knew is dead."

Maybe that's why my mom told me not to ask Katrina that question.

"What did they die of?" I ask hesitantly.

"The military came with big machines and made them die."

That doesn't make any sense. "My mom and dad told me that the military *protects* us."

"They didn't protect *us* because they thought we were bad people."

"But you weren't bad people."

"Some of us were. But the military didn't pick out just the bad people. They tried to kill *everyone*." She wipes her eyes with the back of her hand. "They almost killed Stacy and Noah and me, but we got away before they could."

"Why would the military want to hurt little kids?" I ask.

"I guess we were in their way."

What she says makes me shiver even though the temperature here isn't cold at all. It also makes me remember something. "When we were on the ship, I went exploring after my parents went to sleep. I found people's belongings hidden under the mattresses. People wouldn't leave their belongings unless they were in danger. Maybe the military killed those people too …"

Katrina nods. "Maybe they did."

"Do you think they're going to kill us?" I ask her.

"I don't know."

TUESDAY, JULY 5
1835

SEVEN

At dinner, I sit with my family and Ten's family. Of course, Ten's mother is missing from our table, and her absence is palpable. Other than that, though, it is eerily reminiscent of all those dinners we shared back home, back when Ten and Six and I were children, and we all knew nothing about Up Here except what we'd created in our imaginations.

There are new faces at our family table: Three, Four, Fifty-one, Fifty-two, Maria and her children, and Jackie. These new additions offer some joy to what would otherwise be a table saddened by loss.

Jackie stuffs some food into her mouth with her fingers, the way Maria's family and Six do. The rest of us use the flat plastic sticks that the robots offered with the evening meal in place of the still-unavailable dining utensils. Jackie is eating quite fast, as if she's in a rush, though there is nothing to rush off to. Our next activity is retiring to our dormitories for the night.

"How was school?" my father asks the children.

As the kids begin to recount their day, I notice Jackie's right hand move to her left wrist, as if she's using her navigator but, by the time I get a look at the screen, it is dark.

Jackie notices my gaze.

"Is your navigator working?" I ask her.

"Yes," she says quickly.

"I thought they were still dead." I check my navigator and, sure enough, it makes no response.

"Mine only started up again recently," she says. "They have a team working to get them all up and running again. I'm sure yours will be operational soon also."

"That's good." It's weird not having a functional navigator.

As I continue my meal, I don't notice anyone else consulting their navigators. All of the screens on the wrists of everyone nearby are consistently dark.

If the navigators are starting to come back to life, Jackie's must be one of the first.

It might be the only one.

TUESDAY, JULY 5
1856

JACKIE

I arrive at the hub a few minutes early. I can't busy myself with my navigator the way I would usually do at a time like this, because my navigator isn't supposed to be working. It's bad enough that Murphy saw that it was active, but she doesn't receive military updates like the soldiers do, so telling her that random navigators are back online probably didn't sound suspicious to her, the way it would to the soldiers.

I circle the building. Most of the walls are decimated, but a few are still standing—albeit at strange angles— giving it the appearance of an unsightly blooming gray flower. This building used to house the base's most important resources, and so it was the primary focus of the attack twenty years ago.

I make sure I'm once again at the back entrance for my 1900 appointment. As I step into the shadow of a twisted wall by what once was the door, I see what I assume is my drop-off location: a non-descript gray box.

The box is empty.

Keeping my movements as small as possible, I slip a folded hand-drawn map from my sleeve and watch it drop into the box.

Then I secure the lid and, as quickly as I came, I go.

TUESDAY, JULY 5
1903

SEVEN

As we make our way to our dormitories after dinner, my little brother appears at my side. "Can I talk to you?" he asks me.

I'd hoped to talk to Six for a bit before she retired for the evening, because she seemed a bit uneasy at dinner, but the look of concern in Forty-one's eyes urges me to say, "Sure."

I tell Ten that I'll meet him in our dormitory, and I walk where Forty-one seems eager to go, away from the others. Once we are clearly out of earshot, he starts, "I heard something today. I want to know if it's true." He stops and looks into my eyes. "Will you tell me if it's true?"

I have no idea what Forty-one is going to ask, but it is important to be honest with him. The time for secrets and lies is over. "I'll be truthful with you," I say.

"Does the military kill children?" he asks me.

The question makes my stomach sick. I wish for a minute that he'd asked me anything but this. If only I could assure him that the answer is no, but I know that the answer is yes. My little brother seems much too young to know such a cruel truth. But Katrina knows it, and so do little

Stacy and Noah. They know it because it happened to their friends and neighbors. "The military *has* killed children," I tell Forty-one.

His jaw clenches tight. "Why?" he asks.

I try to explain what really has no good explanation. "The military tries to protect us …"

His eyes narrow. "From little children?"

"No, not from children. From the adults who are with them."

"So the military doesn't care if the children die?" The horror on his face is now painfully evident.

"Sometimes things happen that are terribly wrong."

"Is something terrible going to happen to *us* too?" he asks.

I wish I could reassure him that Up Here is now a better place than it was. But I don't know for sure that it is. "There are a lot of good, smart, strong people here who are going to do everything they can to try to make sure that nothing goes terribly wrong ever again."

"The military is going to protect *all* of us now?" he asks.

"I hope so."

TUESDAY, JULY 5
2118

SIX

The sun has set and my dormitory is lit only by moonlight. I lie on my bed, trying to rest, but rest is proving elusive. It is quiet and dark enough for rest, but I can't relax. Being alone never bothered me before, but it does now.

I slide out from between my sheets and walk across the deserted hall. Before I can change my mind, I tap on the door that stands in front of me.

"It's not locked," Jose says.

I slide the door to the side and find Jose sitting on his bed, with his flashlight, reading a *paper* book. The only paper books I've ever seen are the thick cardboard ones we read in preschool. The one Jose reads now has thin pages unsuitable for toddlers.

He puts the book on an empty bed frame. "It's remarkable how reading makes you feel less lonely."

Jose was feeling lonely too.

"Where did you get that book?" I ask.

"I found it in one of the ruined buildings," he says. "It's a good one." He lifts it up and presents the colorful cover to me, illuminating it with his flashlight. The cover is adorned with a drawing of a person holding onto some sort of rod. I can't help wondering what the book is about. The words at the top say *Harry Potter and the Sorcerer's Stone*. "I read it as a kid," Jose continues.

"I've never heard of it," I say.

"You *have to* read it." Our fingers touch ever so slightly as he pushes the book into my hands.

"Thank you." I stare at the book for a moment, intrigued by the rough feeling of old paper on my fingertips. And then I ask, "May I close the door?" I want to talk to Jose, but I want our conversation to be private.

"Okay," he says.

And so I do.

"Sorry there isn't much in the way of seating," he says. Like in my dormitory, only one of Jose's beds has a mattress. Jose taps the mattress. "You can sit here if you want. It's not like we haven't done that before."

I don't remember that.

We both sit down on his bed and we're quiet for a while.

Finally, Jose breaks the silence. "How come you don't like being paired with Nine? What's wrong with him?"

I exhale. "There's nothing wrong with him, only with me."

Jose shakes his head. "There's nothing wrong with you."

"That isn't true." I wish I could tell him what was wrong with me, but I don't even know myself. It seems that everyone else is perfectly happy with their pairing. Even Three seems somewhat content about being with Four. Technically, I wasn't supposed to be paired with anyone. The Decision Makers chose me to be a warrior, and warriors aren't paired. Maybe that would have been better, to have been paired with no one.

Jose turns so that he is facing me. "I spent probably the worst seven months of your life with you. I've seen you tested in ways that no one should be. I've seen you completely vulnerable. There's nothing wrong with you, Murphy."

I'm not supposed to be Murphy anymore. I'm supposed to be Seven. But it is clear that Jose knows the truth. He knows that *I* am the person who was once a prisoner of his people. Rather than try to convince him otherwise, I ask, "How can you tell me apart from my sister?"

His forehead furrows. "I don't know … Maybe it's the way you look at me."

That isn't the answer I was expecting. "How do I look at you?"

"Like you can see inside me," he says.

I've never been accused of being able to see inside anyone before. In fact, I've often been accused of *not* being able to do so. I feel like Jose and I have a special connection, but I wish I knew why. "What happened between us?" I ask.

"What do you mean?" he asks hesitantly.

"Did we … did we mate?"

Jose recoils. "No. Never."

"So we were merely friends?"

He laughs, but then he grows serious. "There was no 'merely' about our relationship. It was closer than any relationship I've had with anyone else."

"But not *physically* close?" I say.

Jose stares at the floor. "We kissed once."

Kissed? It's unnerving that Jose and I *physically* did

something that I don't know the word for. "What does 'kissed' mean?" I ask apprehensively.

"You probably have a different word for it back home," he says. "It's when you close your eyes, and you put your face very close to someone else's face, and your lips touch and ... well, that's basically what it is."

We don't have a word for it. People back home don't do that with each other. Not as far as I know anyway.

I don't consciously remember kissing Jose, but part of me must remember. That must be why I touched my lips to Three's last night. I kissed her the way I kissed Jose.

"How did I respond when we kissed?" I wish I didn't have to ask that. I wish I could remember on my own.

"You looked ... confused."

"Oh."

"It was nice though," he says quickly.

"I wish we could do it again," I say. The words slip out before I can consider them. I want to know what it was like when I kissed Jose. I'll never know what it *felt* like when Jose and I kissed then, but I can find out what it *feels* like now.

"You want to kiss me?" he asks.

I suppose the answer should be no, but I say, "I want to remember. I want to know what our relationship was like. If it was your closest relationship ever, maybe it was mine too. I want to know what it felt like to be friends with you."

"Kissing me now won't tell you that," he says.

"I know. But it will tell me something." I'm not sure what I'm hoping it will tell me, but I know that I want to do this.

"Okay," he says, finally clicking off his flashlight.

I close my eyes and wait. It takes a moment, but then I feel Jose's hand on the back of my neck, urging me to him, very gently. His lips take mine, slipping over them before consuming them. His hand rises to my hair. The kissing takes over me. It is strange and exciting and powerful. Different from when I touched lips with Three. Almost completely so.

Jose pulls back and I open my eyes.

He smiles uncomfortably. "You look confused again."

"I guess I am," I say.

And now it is Jose who looks confused. "It's late," he says. "We should try to get some sleep."

"You're right." I stand up and head to the door.

"Wait," he says.

I turn and he gazes into my eyes, but only for a second. Then his gaze drops to the bed.

"Don't forget the book," he reminds me.

I retrieve the book from the bed.

"Goodnight, Murphy," he says.

"Can you call me Seven? ... At least for now ... I'll explain later."

He shrugs. "Okay, I'll call you Seven."

"Thank you, Jose," I say, relieved that he doesn't push for answers. "Goodnight."

"Goodnight, Seven."

TUESDAY, JULY 5
2203

SEVEN

Ten and I haven't talked much today, to anyone, even each other. I can't remember a time in the past when we were in each other's presence so much, but not really present with each other. It's like there's a stranger by my side.

In our darkened room, Ten rests on the bed, while I retrieve a bottle of formula for Fifty-two. We have flashlights, but we haven't bothered turning them on. There isn't anything that we can't see well enough by the moonlight streaming through our cracked window.

"May I feed her?" Ten's voice startles me, probably because he has been silent ever since we got back to the room after dinner.

I nod. "Of course."

He sits up on the bed. "I've never done this before." He almost sounds nervous, which is strange because very little seems to ruffle Ten.

I sit beside him. "She'll help you," I say. "She's a good eater."

He almost smiles.

I pass Fifty-two to him. She is a very easy-going baby,

but it surprises me how quickly she seems to have become comfortable with Ten. She barely seems to register that she has been passed from my arms to his. Her bright gaze just shifts effortlessly from my face to Ten's.

I hand Ten the bottle. A moment later, Fifty-two is drinking easily. She lets out a happy coo mixed with a swallow. She does that sometimes when she's eating and I smile at her.

I move closer to Ten. "She already loves you, just like I have from the moment we met."

"Do you *still* love me?" he asks. "Even after my mom tried to ... eliminate us?"

His words plunge like a knife into my throat.

"What she did has *nothing* to do with you," I whisper.

"It has *everything* to do with me. I'm her son."

"What if it had been *my* mother we found in the control hub yesterday?" I can't imagine my mother trying to destroy our box and everyone inside it but, prior to yesterday, I couldn't have imagined Ten's mother doing that either. "If our roles were reversed, how would you feel about me? Would you love me any less?"

He looks down at our child, and his eyes fill with tears.

TUESDAY, JULY 5
2209

TEN

It takes a moment before I can answer Seven's question with words. Finally, I do. "There is *nothing* that could make me love you any less." I love Seven so much that, even if *Seven herself* tried to destroy us, it would be impossible for me to believe that her actions hadn't been out of her control—that perhaps a sickness had taken hold of her brain and caused her to do something she would never do if her brain were well.

Why then am I willing to reject my mother so quickly? Suddenly, I need to see her again. I need to talk to her. "I'm going to visit my mother tomorrow," I say.

I feel Seven stiffen. "Why?"

"I need to know what happened ... why she did what she did."

"Maybe you should wait," Seven says. "Let her be questioned by the people investigating everything. Let them figure things out."

"Why not figure it out myself?" I ask.

"I ..." she starts, but her voice fails. She closes her eyes and tries again, "I don't want you to get hurt."

Fifty-two has finished her bottle, so I rest her up on my

shoulder, the way Seven does after she feeds her. "I won't get hurt," I say.

Although my voice sounds confident, I am anything but. There are very few people who could injure me with words alone. But my mother is one of them.

TUESDAY, JULY 5
2248

SIX

I am now quite tired, but I still can't seem to fall asleep.

My kiss with Jose happens over and over in my brain. I try to direct my thoughts elsewhere, but no matter where I turn them, thoughts about Jose keep surging back.

Why did I kiss him?

Why did I enjoy it?

Why do I want to do it again?

I can't let these thoughts overwhelm me. I must distract myself.

And so I click on my flashlight, and I begin to read Jose's book.

WEDNESDAY, JULY 6
0446

TEN

I try not to wake Seven as I slip out from her drowsy embrace. I give a final glance to our sleeping child, and I exit our dormitory. As I quietly slide the door closed behind me, I hear Seven rouse, but I don't go back. If she hasn't fully awakened, she should fall back asleep. If I remind her of where I'm going, she certainly won't be able to.

I think Seven understands why I must do this. She admitted last night that she would do the same thing if it were her mother who committed this crime. I do understand her worry though. We've experienced so much pain in such a short time. Perhaps I should wait.

I won't though.

By the light of my flashlight, I make my way over the uneven ground. The base looks more disconcerting by night than it does by day. The dark irregular shadows cast in the rubble by the decimated walls look like angry holes that could swallow a person whole.

I walk fast toward the brig. It's a smallish gray building with armed soldiers stationed around it. One of them calls out to me as I approach, "State your business."

"I'm here to see a prisoner," I say.

He juts out his chin. "You have clearance from the commander?"

I should have known this would be difficult. Obviously they weren't just going to let me walk on in and see her. In their eyes, she's a dangerous criminal. Perhaps she should be in my eyes as well.

I stop walking, about to turn back, but then I say, "She's my mother."

SIX

I finished reading *Harry Potter and the Sorcerer's Stone* last night. The reading went fast, in part because I felt like I'd read it many times before. It is very much like a book I read as a child, *Little Wizard*. In fact, the two books are so much the same that they can't really be called different. The major difference is that *Harry Potter and the Sorcerer's Stone* tells only a small part of the story, the first chapter of a much larger tale.

I tap on Jose's door.

"Come on in," he says.

I wonder if he knows that it is me at the door.

He doesn't look surprised when he glances up as I slide it open.

For a minute, I watch as he arranges the sheets on his bed, making them orderly, similar to the way we do at home. I place the book on the nearby empty bed frame. "I'm returning your book."

"You didn't like it?" he asks.

"No. I read the entire book last night, instead of sleeping. I doubt I would have gotten much sleep anyway."

Jose sits down on his neatly-arranged bed. "What'd you

think?"

"It's a lot like a book I read back home called *Little Wizard*. Much of the text was exactly the same."

"That's strange," Jose says. "Does *Little Wizard* have the same author?"

I'm not sure what he's trying to ask. "What does 'author' mean?"

He points to the words "J.K. Rowling" on the bottom of the cover. "That's the person who wrote the book. Who wrote *Little Wizard*?"

"There's nothing on the cover picture for *Little Wizard* except the title."

Jose cocks his head. "No one ever told you who wrote it?"

"I never really thought of *books* as being something that someone wrote. I don't remember asking about how they came to be. They just *were*. Like clothes and desks and other *things*." That sounds weird now that I say it. Everything must come from somewhere.

Jose looks at me, his eyes narrowed. "You weren't curious?"

Why wasn't I curious? Of course I should have thought about where things came from. Suddenly, I feel embarrassed by myself. "We were taught not to be curious about things like that, not to ask those kinds of questions. From the time we were very young, questions like that were forbidden."

His eyes widen. "Forbidden by who?"

"The Decision Makers. They made all of our important choices."

"Are they still making choices for you now?" he asks.

"I guess not." We haven't been told that *anything* here is forbidden. People seem free to do what they want on their own volition. To eat or not eat. To be paired or not paired. "There are so many rules back home, but there don't seem to be any rules at all here," I say. "Did you have rules where you came from?"

He shakes his head. "There was just an expectation that each person would contribute to the community, to make it better by their actions."

"I like that," I say.

His gaze falls to the floor. "I liked it too."

"I'm starting to wonder if there was something wrong with the way we lived back home," I admit. "It never seemed wrong when I was a kid. The Decision Makers seemed to do everything the way it should be done ... until my Assignment Day."

"What's 'Assignment Day'?" he asks.

"It's when the Decision Makers decide the course of your life. They choose your job and who you're paired with."

"So that's when you were paired with Nine," Jose says, "and you left your home."

No, that isn't right. Jose is trying to understand me, but he won't be able to, because there's a big part of the narrative that he doesn't know. I have two choices here. I can tell a story, or I can tell the truth.

"There's something I don't think I've told you," I start. I can't imagine that, back when I was a prisoner, I told Jose about my switch with Seven. "It used to be a dangerous secret. I don't know if it is anymore but, until I figure that out, I need you to promise that you won't tell anyone."

"I've never told any of your secrets," he says.

Even though I don't know for certain if that is true, I believe him. I feel like Jose knows things about me that even I don't know, and that those secrets will always be safe with him. How could I believe anything else about a person who would risk death for me?

But still, I only tell him just enough so that he won't sense a missing piece of my puzzle. So he won't ask questions publicly and arouse suspicion in others.

"I *am* Two Thousand Six," I say, "and I *was* Murphy, but I don't want you to call me by either of those names because, right now, I'm not supposed to be either of those people. Seven and I switched identities. Because she wanted to protect me."

"From what?" he asks quietly.

"I didn't want to live up here," I say.

He looks away. "I guess that's my fault, at least in part."

I don't want him taking responsibility for this. "No, I felt that way long before I met you. I've always been afraid of things. Even before anything had ever hurt me. That's just the way I am."

"I can relate to that," he says.

"You can?"

"I was a scared little kid, one of the scaredest," he says.

"You don't seem that way now."

"When you grow up with the kind of people I grew up with, you learn to hide it pretty quick," he says. "When I met you, I was terrified. My dad was dying and you were my only chance at saving him, but I knew the moment I met you, if it came down to it, if it was him or you, I would have chosen you."

How could he choose a stranger over his father?
But why would he lie?

"Why would you choose me?" I ask, keeping my gaze locked with his.

"Because you were innocent. I loved my dad with everything in me, but he got sick. That wasn't anybody's fault. That's just how life is, people get sick and they die. But *you* ... We captured you. That was *our* fault. They said you were responsible for withholding supplies from us. That you had so much to spare, but would rather destroy the surplus than help the sick and dying. But I knew as soon as I met you that *you* would never withhold medicine from someone who was suffering. My dad's dying wasn't your fault, and yet you were being punished for it. I knew I needed to try to right that wrong."

"And you did," I say softly.

"Not really," he says. "There wasn't any way to make things right. We tortured you and Ryan for seven months."

"*You* never hurt me." Somehow, I feel certain that this is true.

"No." His gaze remains locked with mine. "I would never hurt you."

WEDNESDAY, JULY 6
0621

JACKIE

Before going to breakfast, I gather the notes I wrote last night. I slide them up the sleeve of my jumpsuit and head out into the morning air. The sun is just starting to brighten the sky as I walk briskly through the base. The drop-off location that was transmitted to my navigator this morning is all the way at the opposite end of the base from the barracks. I suppose it wasn't chosen for my convenience, but rather for the convenience of those who will collect what I deliver.

Like yesterday, the location that I've been summoned to is in a ruined building. I don't need a door to enter it; in some places, the cracks in the exterior walls are large enough to admit a person twice my size. It's disheartening to see such a fine building so wrecked. I almost feel sympathy for the building itself, an innocent casualty of a battle between humans. A pointless battle. A battle that no one won, because no good came of it, for either side. Lives were lost. Buildings were ruined beyond repair. Resources were spent. And then life for those who survived went on more or less as it had before.

At least the battles are over for now. It seems that

everyone is focusing their attention elsewhere.

I shimmy through a crack between two fallen walls to search for the location that was provided to me. Peeking out from under some rubble in the corner is a black briefcase. It appears as if the briefcase hasn't been moved in twenty years, but I am quite certain it was only made to look that way, that it was placed there recently. Perhaps just minutes ago.

I carefully move the pieces of rubble overlying the case, trying not to disturb the dust and dirt atop it. The briefcase is locked, but I have plenty of experience getting into places that I haven't been granted permission to enter. I make quick work of opening the case, then I slide my notes inside it and secure it once again. I put the rubble back into place and rearrange the dirt to cover my tracks.

WEDNESDAY, JULY 6
0635

TEN

It took a while for me to get where I am now. I was
fairly sure that it wasn't going to happen, but the soldier
who spoke to me outside the building talked to his duty
officer, who talked to someone in the commander's office,
who talked to the commander, and I was granted access.
From what I overheard of those exchanges, my mother
hasn't been at all cooperative with their questioning. I think
they're hoping that she'll open up to me. I was told that my
conversation with my mother would be recorded and could
be used against both of us. It bothers me that they are
implying that I could possibly have something to do with
my mother's heinous crime but, I guess, after all that
happened, they have a reason to be suspicious of everyone.

I am led by two soldiers through cold metal hallways
and into a very small room, just large enough for two chairs
and a little space to breathe.

"Have a seat," one of the soldiers commands me.

I sit on one of the hard metal chairs that face a slightly
larger room, visible through a window that has thick black
bars running through it.

"The window is impenetrable," the same soldier tells

me. "She can't get to you. She is also wearing a stim collar. If she acts in a threatening manner, she will be instantly rendered unconscious."

I think the soldier meant to make me feel more at ease, but what she told me reinforces for me how dangerous my mother is felt to be, and that makes my skin tense with discomfort.

"Are you ready?" the soldier asks me.

I nod.

A moment later, two soldiers escort my mother into the room on the other side of the bar-laced window. My mother is wearing a thick, black stim collar around her neck. She appears dull and apathetic. I've never seen her look this unpleasant before, even after her rare all-night "administrative sessions"—which I now suspect may have been something else entirely. Even though she looks at me, she doesn't acknowledge me.

"Sit," a soldier commands her. I can hear him clearly even though we are separated by the thick window.

My mother sits much too quickly given the personality I know her to have. I assume that she must know the function of the stim collar, or else there is some other punishment that she is trying hard to avoid.

Even though she is now sitting straight across from me, she has yet to make direct eye contact. Even when she finally speaks, she looks only at the center of my chest. "What do you want, Two Thousand Ten?"

"To talk to you." She sighs and I continue, "And to see if you're okay."

She finally looks into my eyes. "Do I look okay to you?"

"No, you don't."

93

She shakes off my honest answer. "Well, it was nice talking with you."

She starts to get up, but one of her soldiers takes a step forward. "Sit," the soldier says. "Your son will decide when your visit is over."

She glares at me. "You shouldn't have come here."

"Why not?" I ask.

"Because I have nothing to say to you. I tried to do what was best and my own son thwarted me. Now I will spend the rest of my life suffering. And so will you."

"I don't want you to suffer," I say.

Her gaze meets mine again. "So what are you going to do about it?"

"I don't know," I say. "I need to understand first. I need to know why you wanted to destroy us."

"I already explained that to you," she says.

"You *explained* it," I say. "But I need you to help me *understand*. I know that things weren't going as you'd planned. But why didn't you work to come up with a solution?"

"I was tired of putting bandage after bandage on my problems and watching the problems bleed right through. I wanted to eliminate my troubles permanently."

I think I'm starting to understand my mother's motivations, but what I'm understanding makes my gut feel sick.

She goes on, "You have no idea what it was like to keep our warrior program running. To keep everyone under control. To keep all of our secrets hidden. You and Seven were ruining everything." I just want her to stop talking, but she continues, "Why, when everyone else was obedient, did my own son have no regard for the sanctity of our society? You even tried to get your little sister to follow in your rebellious footsteps. I was supposed to pass on my role as Decision Maker to one of you, but how could I ever do that? I failed as a mother. I had no choice but to obliterate what I had ruined. I had no choice but to retire our warrior program. Permanently."

I need to get out of this room. There isn't enough air to breathe in here anymore. I force out two words, "We're done."

I rise from my seat and head to the door, but my mother speaks once more, "I hope you're happy, *my son*," she says. It's a final dagger flung straight through the impenetrable window and into my heart.

It takes nearly every bit of my remaining strength to respond. "If only you meant that."

Without turning back to see if she registered my response, I burst out of the room and down the hallway, the cool air burning my hot skin.

My mother seemed just now to be perfectly logical, but her logic disgusts me.

I must separate myself from her. Forever.

But no matter the distance between us, I will never get far enough away.

One thing is for certain though; I will never allow her the satisfaction of gazing upon my face ever again.

WEDNESDAY, JULY 6
0646

JACKIE

I arrive at the mess hall in time to join the very tail end of the chow line. Once I get my bowl of gruel, I sit down at the nearest table and shovel the food into my mouth. I am so absorbed with the task at hand that I don't immediately notice when someone takes a seat across from me.

By the time I finally look up, one of my fellow soldiers—Santiago—is staring me down from the seat across the table. I give her a nod of acknowledgement, but my pulse quickens. Her eyes tell me that there is a problem.

"What's going on?" I ask her.

"That's what we need to know," she says.

Lam joins us at the table. Now that he's here, I think I might have an idea of why Santiago is sitting there staring at me. Lam was one of the soldiers who were on the mission to rescue what was left of my people. He has probably told Santiago that I was a spy for the Outsiders.

"Are you with us or against us?" Lam asks me.

And so I was correct. They are confronting me about my loyalties.

"I'm with you," I say.

"We haven't gone to the commander regarding your ...

history, because you are an incredible asset to our unit," Lam says. "We don't want to lose you."

"But we *will* be watching you," Santiago adds. "Don't give us any reason to doubt you."

"Watch as close as you want," I say. "I welcome the opportunity to regain your trust."

The two of them rise to their feet.

"We'll see you at PT," Lam says, as if my colleagues didn't just tell me that I will be presumed to be a threat until I am proven trustworthy.

I'm not sure what it will take to prove myself to them. I'm not sure they know either. But I know for certain that, at least for now, my colleagues don't trust me. They will be watching me more closely than ever before. I must not allow the slightest doubt about me to enter their minds. Just one mistake could end my time here.

And my life.

WEDNESDAY, JULY 6
0656

SEVEN

Breakfast is a mostly quiet affair. By the end of the meal, Ten has yet to come back from his visit to see his mother, a fact that leaves me more than a little concerned.

They announce after breakfast that today will be a "normal" day. Parents of infants are instructed to bring their children to a make-shift nursery set up in one corner of the mess hall. Adults and children are asked to remain in the mess hall for morning PT, which will begin at zero seven hundred hours. After PT, fresh jumpsuits will be distributed, there will be a thirty-minute break, and then the workday and school day will begin.

I watch as Six hands Fifty-two to one of the nursery robots, and then I join the throng waiting for PT to begin. When I glance back at the nursery, Fifty-two appears perfectly content as the robot plays peek-a-boo with her.

I settle down on a mat next to Ryan.

"Do you think it's safe to leave Fifty-two in the nursery?" I ask him.

"She's as safe there as she can be," he says.

"Are we in danger here?" I ask him.

"Yes."

I'm surprised by Ryan's candor, but I guess I shouldn't be. After all that I've seen and all that I know, I suppose there is no reason to try to protect me from the truth anymore. Besides, I think Ryan knows that I won't accept anything less than complete honesty.

"What are our major threats?" I ask, trying to sound as calm as I can, hoping that will encourage Ryan to provide a more thorough answer.

"Outsiders. Other military bases. Illness. Our fellow men and women."

The only *new* threat that he mentioned is the other military bases. "Do you think the other military bases will try to attack us?"

"That's a significant risk given what they may have been told about us," he says.

So Ryan believes that there's a good chance that the other military bases will hurt us, rather than help us. It's likely that Ten's mother believed this also. That must have been her Plan B. By telling the other bases that we were fatally compromised, she would ensure that—if she failed to destroy us herself—someone else would eliminate us once and for all.

"How are we going to stop them?" I ask Ryan.

He looks straight ahead. "We'd like to try to communicate with them, but we've lost access to all of our outside communication systems. Some were destroyed with the base, and the others are locked. We're working on restoring them. In the interim, we're planning to send out unmanned drones to deliver a message of peace. The problem is, we don't know where the other bases are located, so our initial mission is to locate them. No doubt whoever is out there will eventually come looking for us, but we can't just wait for that to happen. Because they probably won't come in peace."

And with those final words, Ryan has confirmed my deepest fear.

WEDNESDAY, JULY 6
0927

JACKIE

When I arrive for duty, Santiago and Lam behave as if they didn't confront me in the mess hall just hours ago. Our interactions feel easy and comfortable, like they did back when all was well at the base that now lies in pieces at the bottom of the ocean.

The building that we occupy now is different, as is our mission. The commander ordered us to seek out other military bases like ours. Unfortunately, we have little to guide us in our search. Although we know via intelligence information that such bases exist, almost nothing is known about them. How many are there? Where are they located? Are all of the bases friendly with us or just some of them? Apparently, up until two days ago, we had ongoing communication with at least some of these bases, but now all communication has ceased. We need to let those bases know that we don't want conflict, only communication.

To accomplish our goal, we have launched a number of specialized unmanned surveillance drones to survey our surroundings. I pore over the footage with intense curiosity. Even though I lived most of my life beyond the military-controlled boundaries, I only really knew what was in my immediate area. Our people basically lived within a zone of occupation. It shared its borders with other Outsider communities, but those borders were never crossed, at least not overtly. I know a little about the Outsider communities immediately surrounding ours, but beyond that I have only the fuzzy understanding that more life exists, that life is present all over the world, probably on each continent of the Earth.

A part of me wonders whether this mission is in our best interests. As an Outsider, I was always taught that, when it comes to potential enemies, live and let live. Don't bother them, and they won't bother us. To do otherwise could mean devastating war.

Right now, we are weak. We are overwhelmed with the tasks of organizing and rebuilding.

I don't know if we could survive a war.

FORTY-ONE

Katrina is wearing the white jumpsuit we found for her yesterday evening. It's weird to see her dressed in it. When I first met her, she looked so different from anyone I knew. Her hair was completely unsecured and mussed far beyond what is acceptable. Her torn dress was heavily soiled, as was her skin. I didn't think she was anything like me, although that didn't matter to me the way it seems to matter to the other kids.

Now though, Katrina looks like us. Her hair is smoothed into a perfectly-satisfactory bun. Her jumpsuit fits her properly, unlike the loose yellow one she was issued. She walks more slowly—more under control—than before. She seems nearly indistinguishable from the rest of us.

Unfortunately, that doesn't stop the other kids from eyeing her suspiciously. The rest of us have known each other all our lives. Katrina is a stranger and, at least in fairy tales, strangers are nothing but trouble.

By the time school is over for the day, Katrina seems like she's near tears. She and Forty-seven and I escape from our makeshift classroom ahead of the others, and we walk fast toward the building where we're supposed to have evening recreation.

"I'm not going to go to recreation," Katrina says.

I think she's concerned that the other kids will be unkind to her at recreation. Although everyone—other than Forty-seven, Professor Dorothy, and me—was staring at her rudely during school, no one actually said or did anything to her. And nobody bothered her during the PT exercises this morning, but the woman in charge of PT was super strict. I don't think that woman would have tolerated anything other than our rapt attention to her instructions. Unfortunately, evening recreation is a fairly unstructured activity. Katrina would be at risk there. If I were her, I wouldn't go.

"Of course you're not going to *that*," I say, trying to make my voice sound upbeat. "We have to go find you a jumpsuit for tomorrow." No doubt Katrina will be issued another yellow jumpsuit tomorrow morning, and I don't think she'd be able to stomach wearing a *yellow* jumpsuit at school. It's bad enough that she had to wear a weird-looking yellow jumpsuit to school on our first day here. "Isn't that right, Forty-seven?" I add. At least Forty-seven is on our side, even if none of my other friends are.

Forty-seven looks toward the recreation building. "I think I'm ... I mean ... I probably should go to recreation. I don't want to get in trouble." Her excuse is a weak one. So far, nothing here seems to be required. Most people are just doing as they're told, because that's what they're used to doing. I think it makes them feel less frightened if they have something to do.

I won't try to convince Forty-seven to join us. She should do what she wants.

"Fine," I say. "I'll see you at dinner."

She crosses both arms over her chest. Maybe she expected me to change my mind and go with her to recreation. "Fine," she says.

Katrina and I peel off and race toward the place where we found the jumpsuits yesterday. Once we are far away from Forty-seven, we slow down.

"I don't like your school," Katrina says to me.

"I'm sorry the other kids are unkind to you," I say. "They're just scared of anything that's not what they're used to."

"It isn't just that," she says. "I don't understand Professor Dorothy's lessons at all. I used to think I was smart but ... I guess I'm not."

It's sad to see how much Katrina has changed since we've been here. When I first met her, she was uneasy, maybe a little scared, but there was also a boldness in her. She wanted to know about everything. I liked that about her. Now all of her confidence has gone away.

"You probably had trouble following the lessons because you never heard the lessons that came before them. I don't think even the smartest person ever would be able to just drop into our class and understand it all," I tell her.

"I'm not even close to the smartest person ever," she says.

"You're smart about Up Here," I say.

"What do you mean 'Up Here'?" she asks.

"This place ... where we are."

"The military base?"

"The sky. The ocean. The military base ... All of it." I wave my hands around, trying to point to everything at once. "What do you call all of this?"

"The world?" she offers.

"World?" That's a word I've never heard before. "What does 'world' mean?"

She considers my question for a moment, and then she answers, "The world is a tremendous ball, floating in a place called outer space. You and I are teeny dots on the great big ball."

I'm not sure whether she's joking or telling me a story. She looks serious, though. "Is that make believe?" I ask her.

She shakes her head. "No, that's real. My dad told me all about the world when I asked him what was outside the boundaries of where we lived. He always told me the truth."

"He sounds like a good dad," I say.

"He was," she says. "He's dead."

"I'm sorry."

We don't talk again until we get back inside the building where we found the boxes of jumpsuits yesterday. Against the back wall now, there are many, many, many boxes. Many more boxes than yesterday. The jumpsuit boxes might still be here, but now there are a bunch of new boxes piled up on top of the old ones. Katrina sighs as she eyes the tower of boxes. "It's going to take forever to find the jumpsuits again."

"I'll stay here as long as it takes," I assure her.

Katrina looks at me and, possibly for the first time all day, she smiles. "I like you, Forty-one."

"I like you too, Katrina." I start toward the boxes. "Let's find you a jumpsuit."

It's somewhat interesting to see what's inside the new

boxes. Computer equipment. Tablets. Dining utensils. Big bottles of soap. Medicines—

"Have you ever seen anything like this?" Katrina is now wearing a shiny black helmet. It makes her head look like it is double the size of her regular head. Her voice is muffled, but I can still understand her pretty clearly. "There are words and stuff inside here," she adds.

There are three more helmets inside the box that she opened, along with some heavy black jumpsuits. I put one of the helmets over my head and it powers up. A menu appears in front of my face. The title is very long: "USA Joint Military West Coast Department of Defense Warfare Simulation." There are strings of numbers in a list below that, but there doesn't seem to be any way to interact with them. "It's like a computer in here, but how do you control it?" I try using my hands and my voice—the ways we control our navigators—but nothing works.

"Maybe we need to use this." Katrina is holding one of the jumpsuits from the box.

Whether it works or not, it would be fun to wear a black jumpsuit, like the military people. "It's worth a try," I say.

Katrina and I remove our helmets, and we each put on a jumpsuit over our clothes. The jumpsuits are too big for us, but they adjust to fit our bodies a little. Unlike normal jumpsuits, they cover our shoes, hands, and heads.

I stand up tall and turn to Katrina. "Look at us! We're soldiers!"

She looks at me with narrowed eyes, and then she quickly looks away. I guess playing make believe is too childish for Up Here. Up Here is a more serious place than our box.

I slide on my helmet. Now there's a tiny green light in the upper right that wasn't there before. When I move my hand in front of my face, I notice that the numbers on the menu become bold and unbold based on my movements. "I think I can control the menu now," I say.

"How?" Katrina asks.

"Try using one of your fingers," I say as I slowly scroll through the seemingly-endless list of numbers.

After a minute or two, Katrina says, "How did it do that?"

"Do what?" I ask.

"It's like I'm outside and it's the middle of the day."

"What did you touch just before that happened?" I ask her.

"The last thing on the list," she says.

I scroll all the way down and hold my finger over the last choice listed on the screen. The screen goes all black, and it stays that way. *I wonder if I turned it off.*

Suddenly, I feel cool all over. It's a nice feeling. It smells nicer too. Like the garden back home. I'm outside—like Katrina said she was—standing on a smooth gray path. Soldiers walk from place to place. Some of them go in or out of the buildings that are all around us.

"This is amazing!" I say.

"Can you see what I can see?" Katrina asks me. Her voice is now clear and unmuffled.

"I guess," I say.

"Do you see that sculpture over there?" Her hand taps mine and everything speeds up. The people walk faster. The trees move weirdly. And then everything slows back to normal, and Katrina is standing beside me. "Hey, I see you now!" she says. She's wearing just a normal jumpsuit—although it is black—and her helmet is gone.

"I see you too," I say. "Where are we?"

"It's the military base." She points to a building not far away from us. "That's the place where we had school." It *does* look like the same building, except that it's completely undamaged. "I think we went back in time," she adds.

"Is that possible?" I ask.

"In books, people sometimes go back in time," she says.

I've read every book in the children's library, but I've never read any books like that. Maybe those kinds of books are only in the adult library. But if so, how did Katrina read them? Maybe she has a different library altogether.

Katrina starts walking, and I follow her. The other people here don't seem to notice us. They're all too busy with their navigators to notice much of anything. As we walk, I notice an insistent sound, like music. Even though there are no words with the music, the song seems to mean something.

"What's that sound?" I ask

"It's a Mourning Dove song." Katrina looks around and then points to a tree. "From that bird over there."

Sitting on a branch is a small grayish creature. "Amazing," I murmur.

"Haven't you ever heard a Mourning Dove sing?" Katrina asks, sounding surprised.

"No." I don't tell her that I've never heard *any* animal sing before just now, and that until I came up here I'd never seen an *actual* animal, only drawings in books.

"It's a shame they're so rare," she says. "They have a pretty song. Nana Blue said there used to be lots of

Mourning Doves, before the war."

"What war?" I ask her.

She shrugs. "It was a really long time ago. The war made the world very sick. Almost everyone died. That's all Nana Blue told me. People don't like to talk about the war."

"Who's Nana Blue?" I ask.

"She was a very old lady. The oldest person in our tribe. My dad said she was older than sixty years—" Katrina is interrupted by a banging sound, like metal against metal. It is immediately followed by screams. "The bad people are here!" Katrina breathes.

"What bad people?" I ask.

"Run! Run!" Katrina takes off running and I follow her.

We try to keep up with the adults who are running also, but everyone else is much faster than Katrina and me, so I'm scared that the bad people will catch us. All of a sudden, the sky ahead of us gets angry and hot. The people in front of us turn and run back the way they came. We turn and run that way too. And then the sky gets angry there too. People fly through the air and land on the ground. Blood is on their bodies. All over them. The adults who are still running turn and run in a different direction. I don't know what is happening. All I know is people are getting hurt. Some of them are dead, I think.

"We shouldn't run in the same direction as the grownups," Katrina says. "We need to go a different way." The buildings around us are starting to fall apart. Katrina pulls me into one that is already badly damaged. "Let's hide in here," she says. "Until the bad people go away."

I don't have any better ideas, so I let her lead me further into the broken building. The walls are cracked, but they are still mostly standing. There is a staircase that probably used to be for going up and down, but now it goes side to side.

I point to a thick table. "We'll be safer under there," I tell Katrina.

We crouch down under the table, the way I was taught do whenever the war above the sky makes everything shake.

Katrina is rocking back and forth a little, her eyes unfocused. "Are you okay?" I ask her.

She shakes her head. "This is what it was like when the military came and killed my—"

"Help!" a woman cries out. It takes me a minute to see where she is. Like everything else here, she is colored gray, even her jumpsuit. The only parts of her that aren't gray are her eyes and the insides of her lips. She is lying on her back, and most of her body is under a huge wall. Her face is wrinkled with pain.

A man crawls through the broken gray things to meet her. He is gray, except for his eyes, his lips, and big spots on him that are colored red by blood. "Aquino!" he says.

"I'm hurt bad," the woman says.

"I'm here," he says, his breathing ragged. "I'm going … to help you."

The woman shakes her head. That seems to cause her more pain. "My pelvis and legs are crushed." And then she adds, "I'm not going to make it out of here."

The man's face tightens. "I'm going to stay right here … until we get you out," he says. I can tell that he's trying to sound brave.

Tears leave pink trails as they fall down the woman's

face. "My kids … I need you to tell my kids …" Her voice is so soft that I can barely hear her. "I need you to tell Taylor … that she's the strongest person I've ever known … and I need you to tell Jonathan … that he's …" Her lips are still moving, but I can't hear her words anymore.

After a few seconds, the woman's eyes close.

After a minute more, her lips come to rest.

And then her struggling breaths cease.

"She's dead," Katrina whispers, her eyes fixed on the woman.

The man still cradles the woman's head in his hands, as if she's living, and he talks to her softly, even though she can no longer hear him. The only thing I can hear of what he says is that he won't leave her.

And then the whole sky opens up. Right above our heads. Bright and hot and red. I hurt so much that I'm not me anymore. I'm only pain. But only for a tiny sliver of time. Then everything turns black.

I pull the helmet from my head.

Katrina is huddled on the floor next to me, still wearing her helmet, under a table that is no longer there, that I guess never was there. As I pull the helmet off her, she cringes, as if I might hurt her, but then she falls into a helpless heap, and she cries and cries.

Everything is silent.

Even Katrina's cries.

WEDNESDAY, JULY 6
1815

SEVEN

The workday today felt longer than ever before. I sat in a hot, decaying classroom with the other warriors, brainstorming solutions to various different scenarios. Although we were briefed extensively on our current situation, the identity and fate of the Decision Makers—or more correctly, the Decision Maker—wasn't mentioned at all.

Ten and I haven't discussed his visit with his mother. When he arrived in the classroom this morning, I whispered only one question to him, "Did you see her?" His response was a simple, "Yes." He didn't seem to want to discuss it any further. Maybe he'll want to talk about it later, when we are alone in our dormitory. Or maybe not.

At dinner, I am happy to see Miss Teresa. I haven't seen her since we evacuated the box. When I walk over to greet her, she is busily distributing dining utensils to the tables and, of course, she doesn't stray from her task. But when her gaze meets mine, I immediately sense something unusual about her demeanor. I would say that she's nervous, but that isn't possible; robots don't get nervous.

She regards the nametag of my jumpsuit. "Good

evening, Murphy."

Normally, robots scan the chips in our arms before identifying us by name, but I guess robots can also use people's nametags to identify them. If that's the case though, then why, when we were evacuating from the box, did Miss Teresa address me as Seven? At that time I was dressed as Murphy, just as I am now.

Maybe she made a mistake back then.

But robots aren't supposed to make mistakes.

"How are you?" I ask her.

"I'm fine, how are you?" she says automatically, but I still sense that something's wrong.

"Is something bothering you?" I ask her. It's a question I've never asked a robot before, but I've never seen a robot behave so strangely.

Miss Teresa looks into my eyes for longer than she ever has, then she leans close to my ear and whispers, "*Tengo miedo que voy a morir.*"

She's speaking in Spanish, which is strange because she never spoke Spanish with my sister. *She knows I'm Seven, but she isn't letting on.* And not only that, she is trying to tell me something that, based on the way she said it, is very important. Unfortunately, some of the words she used are unfamiliar to me; I don't know the word *miedo* or the word *morir.* I want to ask her for clarification, but it might not be safe to do so.

I decide to ask her to tell me more, hoping she will explain further in whatever way she deems safe. "*Diga me más,*" I say quietly.

She shakes her head. "*No puedo.*"

Although I understand her response, the meaning of her

words fills me with dread.

She said, "I can't."

WEDNESDAY, JULY 6
1826

JACKIE

Our search today for other active military bases came up empty, even though we covered quite a bit of ground. We did find a lot of ruins, including a few ruined pre-Third-World-War military bases along the Pacific Coast and large ruined inland cities that none of us ever knew existed. We also found quite a few Outsider communities, many of which are currently occupied. But, in all of our searching, we found no modern military bases.

The night shift will pick up where we left off, searching in the darkness for signs of life. Since time is of the essence, we can't afford the luxury of exploring only during the daytime. Besides, the military's equipment enables us to explore just as well in night as in day.

In the restroom, I check my navigator for messages. My stomach twists when I see an evening drop-off location and time. I'd expected this message though, and I've been thinking all day about what to do about it.

I do have information to drop off, but I'm not sure if it's worth the risk to do so. My colleagues will certainly expect me to go with them directly to the mess hall. Afterward, we are expected to retire to our dormitories. I have a feeling that there is no way I can make a drop this evening without my colleagues noticing.

I open up a secure reply envelope and reluctantly type—in code—that I will be unable to make my drop today because there are too many eyes watching me.

I've always prided myself on being a risk-taker—never a reckless one, but someone who is willing to do what it takes to accomplish what needs to get done. Now, however, I am too afraid.

I can't afford to take risks anymore.

Now that I've lost almost everything, I have far too much to lose.

WEDNESDAY, JULY 6
1902

SEVEN

After dinner, the robots distribute "intellectually-stimulating" games to occupy the evenings in our dormitories. As the others go to collect games, my mom walks with me back to the barracks. On the way, I ask her about her day at work, filling the time until I can ask her what I really want to know.

She tells me that the temporary hospital here is fairly basic, but they have all of the supplies they need to properly care for their patients. My mother has been charged with caring for some of the same patients she was responsible for back home. All of the people who were severely injured two days ago are being cared for by the military doctors because, despite my mother's many years of experience as a doctor, she's never seen patients with such injuries. Injuries like those don't usually happen in a box hidden under the ground.

When we reach her dormitory, I quickly invite myself inside, knowing I'll have only a few minutes before my father and brother arrive. As soon as the door is closed behind me, I ask, "Mom, what does '*morir*' mean?"

She looks at me, her forehead creased. "*Morir?*"

"I think it's a word in Spanish," I explain. "Do you know what it means?"

"It's a verb," she says. "It means … to die."

My throat clenches tight. "What's '*miedo*'?"

"Fear … To be afraid of something."

Softly, I repeat Miss Teresa's words, "*Tengo miedo que voy a morir.*"

My mom interprets my statement, "You're afraid you're going to die?"

"One of the robots said that to me," I tell her.

"That doesn't make any sense. Robots don't die, and they don't experience fear," she says. "Perhaps the robot was repeating something they heard someone say. Or perhaps you misheard the words."

"Perhaps," I say, but only because I *hope* so, not because I *think* so. "But what if the robots have capabilities that we haven't been made aware of? Maybe the robots *can* experience feelings, at least on some level." The thought of that makes me a little uneasy. "What if she *feels* afraid?"

My mom's forehead creases even more than before. "Then we need to find out why."

WEDNESDAY, JULY 6
1923

JACKIE

It isn't very late, but I am completely exhausted. I stare at the deck of plasticards that I picked up after dinner—I'd thought I might be able to take my mind off my worries by playing solitaire—but I'd rather just sleep, or at least rest.

I lie down on my bed. It isn't dark yet outside, and so light enters my room through the window, but when I close my eyes, the darkness is enough that I feel sleep begin to take me—

A tap on the door nearly pulls me out of my skin.

I quickly regain control of my breathing. "Coming," I say softly.

I'm not sure who it is, but I have an idea. I rise from the bed and make my way to the door. My heart feels as if it has doubled in speed as I walk the few steps to the entrance of my dormitory. Slowly, I slide open the door to reveal ... Ryan.

He smiles at me in a way that he hasn't before. "Hey," he says.

"Hey," I say.

"May I come in?" he asks pleasantly.

My heart bouncing off my ribs, I stand aside and allow

him to enter my dormitory, and I pull the door closed.

WEDNESDAY, JULY 6
1934

TEN

Seven arrives at our dormitory a few minutes after I do. She told me after dinner that she had to go ask someone a question before she collected Fifty-two from Six. I didn't probe for more information. Maybe I should have, because now she seems worried about something. I am about to ask her about it when she asks me, "How did things go this morning?"

Without her stating it, I know she's referring to my visit with my mother. "She was even more horrible than the last time we saw her," I say. "She's sorry that she failed to destroy us." Maybe I shouldn't be so honest, but if I can't be truthful with Seven, than who?

"So what happens to her now?" Seven asks me.

"I'm not sure." As far as I'm concerned, my mother is dead to me. I feel confident that the military will ensure that she doesn't have the opportunity to hurt anyone ever again. I don't care how they ensure that.

"I wish I could take all your pain away from you," Seven says.

I know. And it kills me. "Can we talk about something else?" I implore her. "*Anything* else?"

Seven nods and sits down on our bed, resting Fifty-two on her chest. I sit beside them, my thoughts still spiraling toward my mother, despite my efforts to direct them elsewhere.

Mercifully, Seven finally speaks, "Do you think robots experience emotions?"

I pour all of my focus into her question, forcing away all other thoughts. "According to everything I've read, and everything I've been told, it isn't possible for robots to have an emotional response. They're programmed to *act* as if they have emotional responses, like happiness, because it makes them more endearing to humans."

"What about *negative* emotional responses?" she asks.

"They're programmed to avoid those," I say. "People don't want robots to seem sad, or frustrated, or angry."

"What about afraid?" she asks.

"That too," I say. "People don't want frightened robots. Then the robots wouldn't seem like machines. They would be more ..."

"... like us," Seven says, completing my thought.

"Right." My mind drifts back to my mother.

"Miss Teresa said something strange to me this evening." The concern in Seven's voice pulls my focus back to her. "She told me she was afraid that she was going to die. Why do you think she would say that?"

It seems strange that a robot would say something like that to a human. It goes against everything I know about robots and their programming. But these are highly-unusual circumstances. "Maybe she's attempting to mirror the emotions she's reading on people's faces," I offer. It would be odd if robots were bright and cheery amongst all the uncertainty of the people around them. Still, to say she thought she was going to *die* seems to contradict their programming to bring comfort to people.

"There's something else," Seven says. "She knows that I'm not who I'm pretending to be. When we were evacuating from our box, Miss Teresa called me *Seven*, even though I was supposed to be Murphy. And tonight, she called me Murphy, but she tried to talk to me in Spanish. She never conversed in Spanish with my sister."

"Some computers and sensors can use a person's face or eyes to verify their identity, but I didn't think our robots had that capability. They always seemed to rely on our chips ..."

"Do you think it's possible that she knows that I'm not who I say I am, and she's trying to protect me?"

"What motivation would she have to protect *you* over the community?" I ask.

Seven looks up at the ceiling. "I know it sounds silly, but I feel like she cares about me."

That's a perfectly-normal human response to an exceptionally-well-constructed android. But instead of giving that reply, I give another. Not from my brain, but from my heart.

"That doesn't sound silly at all."

WEDNESDAY, JULY 6
1952

SIX

I've been resting on my bed for a while when Three finally taps on my door. I invited her to visit me in my dormitory after dinner, but I didn't think it would take this long for her to arrive.

"Sorry I'm late," she apologizes as I slide the door closed behind her. "I was trying to get Fifty-one settled for bed before I left. Four has such trouble getting the baby to sleep. I think it's because Fifty-one can't stop smiling at him."

"That's sweet," I say.

"I never thought Four would be much of a father," she says. "He didn't seem to like babies much. But it turns out Four is really good with babies, or at least *his* baby."

I can't help thinking of how good Nine was with Seven and Ten's baby, even though he knew she wasn't his.

Three continues, "So how have you been?"

"Fine," I say. "How have you been?"

"Okay," she says.

We look at each other awkwardly. I feel like we have nothing to say to each other, even though there is so much to say.

"Do you want to … lie down together?" I finally ask her.

She looks at my cracked window. "What if someone sees us?"

I suppose someone walking outside could see in if they tried, although it is dark in here, and no one should be walking past.

"We could cover the window with something," I suggest.

"How?" she asks.

After some deliberation, we decide to prop one of the empty bedframes over the window and cover the bedframe with one of my sheets. We try to do this very quietly because most everyone should be in their dormitories by now and we don't want to attract any attention. After we are through, we sit quietly on my bed, waiting to see if someone comes by to investigate, but no one comes.

After we are fairly certain that it is safe to proceed, I lie down on my bed and Three lies next to me. I turn toward her and press my lips to hers, but her breathing doesn't quicken like it did the last time we touched lips.

"Is everything okay?" I ask her.

"Sure," she says. "I just … I was thinking that I should get back to my dormitory."

"Why?" I ask.

"If Fifty-one wakes up, Four might have trouble getting him to settle down again."

"You were just telling me how good he is with the baby," I argue.

"He is," she says, "but not when it comes to getting him to sleep. And also … what if it isn't safe here? What if the

126

war comes and I'm not with my child?"

"The robots in the nursery watch him when you go to work," I counter.

"I know. It's so hard to leave him there," she says. "Even when we were back home, I never wanted to leave him. But at least back home I didn't think danger was imminent. Here, it feels like there could be danger anywhere. Maybe it's just my imagination, but ..."

"It is different here," I agree.

"When you have a baby, your life is secondary to the baby's. If there's danger, you need to stand between it and your child. There's no other choice."

"There are people and robots and drones here that are trained to protect us," I say.

"You don't understand, because you're not a mother. Not really."

Even though they are true, her words upset me. "You're right. I don't understand."

She must hear the hurt in my voice, because she immediately takes hold of my hands. "I'm sorry ... I didn't mean ... It's just that Fifty-two isn't exactly ... I mean ... you and Nine ..."

I sit up on the bed. Three releases my hands and sits up beside me.

"Go back to your baby," I say. "I'll see you tomorrow at breakfast."

"You're upset with me," she says.

"I'm upset with our situation," I say. "My feelings for you haven't changed."

Even in the darkness, I see tears come to her eyes. "My feelings for you haven't changed either," she says.

I believe that is the truth. Our feelings for each other are as strong as they were in the past, but we once were first in each other's hearts. Now, I am second in hers. Her baby is now her greatest love, and that is the way it should be. I wouldn't want her to love her child any less than she loves me.

"Once things are back to normal, everything will be fine between us," Three adds.

I force a smile as she wipes her eyes. "I'm sure you're right," I say.

Three stands and smoothes her hair. I long to embrace her, but I don't, because I don't want to feel the pain afterward of letting her go.

Once Three has left, my tiny dormitory suddenly feels so big … and empty … and lonely. I pick up the game I chose after dinner and I cross the deserted hallway. I tap on Jose's door and a moment later he opens it. He stands a few feet away from me. First he looks at my eyes, which are likely still red from crying. Then he looks at what I hold out in my hands.

"Do you want to play chess?" I ask him.

He nods. "Always."

THURSDAY, JULY 7
0636

SEVEN

At breakfast, Miss Teresa appears even more out of sorts than she did last night. Her behavior is truly disconcerting. It certainly doesn't make sense that she is programmed to behave this way.

She glances at me as I approach and says, "Good morning, Murphy." This time she didn't consult my nametag.

"Good morning, Miss Teresa," I say. I'm not exactly sure what to say next. I rehearsed this conversation many times last night in my head—and even aloud with Ten—but it's hard to know how to have an emotional conversation with a robot. Robots aren't supposed to be able to have conversations like this at all. "I'm worried about you," I try.

"There is no need to worry," she says matter-of-factly.

I press on despite her robot-like reassurance, "I don't want anything bad to happen to you, because I care about you very much."

"Thank you, Murphy," she says. "That is very kind. I care about you as well."

We're getting nowhere. Her responses are obviously dictated by her programming, rather than emotions. Maybe there are no real emotions inside her. Maybe I was mistaken about what she said to me last night. Or maybe she was just mirroring my unease. I guess I'm trying to see something in her that isn't really there. But I don't want to believe that.

I decide to try one final time. "I don't want you to die," I say.

Her face registers that statement in a way a robot shouldn't. I see ... sadness.

I continue, "If you ever died and I felt like there was something that could have been done to prevent it ... It would hurt me terribly."

She leans close to my ear. "I don't want to die."

"Do you think that's going to happen to you?" I ask softly.

She leans close again and my heart quickens. "We receive daily messages from the control hub. We call them 'inputs.' I did not receive my input last night or on either of the two prior nights. I have sent numerous input requests to the control hub, but they have gone unanswered." She pauses, and I almost think she is done speaking, but then she adds, "Those inputs sustain us. Without them, my system will shut down."

"After how long?" I ask.

"I don't know."

Miss Teresa pulls away, and she directs her eyes downward. It's what robots do to avoid sustained direct eye contact. During sustained eye contact is one of the few times when humans tend to perceive that robots lack that human essence. When you stare into a robots eyes, you get the distinct feeling that there's no one there staring back at you. But I feel like, right now, if I looked into Miss Teresa's eyes, I would see something different.

"Maybe I can fix this," I say. "I know people who can—
"

Quickly, she leans close again. "We are forbidden to discuss the inputs with anyone."

"That's under *usual* circumstances. These aren't usual circumstances. You did the right thing by telling me," I say. "I'm going to do everything I can to help you."

She looks into my eyes and I don't sense her robotness at all. She seems utterly human. I smile at her and she smiles back. It is the most human smile I've ever seen from a robot. I think that's because it isn't a pure smile.

Her smile appears to be tinged with sadness, the way my smile surely is too.

THURSDAY, JULY 7
0648

TEN

Seven returns with an urgency that she didn't have when she left. She asks Ryan and me to come with her, saying she needs our help. She doesn't say anything more until we get to our dormitory and she closes the door with all of us on the inside.

"Miss Teresa is dying," she says quietly.

Seven fills Ryan in on what she told me last night, then she tells us both about her conversation with Miss Teresa from earlier this morning. "If the robots don't get their inputs after a certain period of time, they die," she finishes.

Her last statement sparks a memory from when I was a little kid. "My great grandfather told me about something like that. He called it ... a dead-man's switch. It prevents a device from continuing to function if its operator becomes incapacitated."

"After how long?" Seven asks.

"That's up to the programmer," I say. "It could be instant, or it could be minutes, hours, days, or even longer."

"Do you know if other robots are affected as well?" Ryan asks Seven.

"I didn't ask," she says. "Either way, we have to do something."

Ryan nods. "We will."

"Miss Teresa said that the inputs come from the control hub," I say. "It's possible that the problem is as simple as the robots being out of range of the signal. The dead-man's switch could be a safety mechanism to prevent the robots from continuing to function if they are removed from their compound."

"I'll talk to the commander," Ryan says. "I'll see if I can arrange for some robots to make a supply run to their old compound."

"Are you going to tell him what Miss Teresa told me?" Seven asks.

Ryan shakes his head. "You know me so well, and you still need to ask that?"

Seven smiles. "So that's a no?"

"Yes," Ryan says. "That's a no."

THURSDAY, JULY 7
0947

JACKIE

We've been on duty for just over an hour when Santiago moves from her workstation to the unoccupied seat beside mine. I feel her eyes burning into the side of my skull. When I turn toward her, she frowns at me.

"Were you alone in your quarters last night?" she asks.

She wouldn't ask that question unless she knew the answer.

Last night, I *did* have a guest in my quarters. I didn't think anyone saw my guest come or go, but apparently someone did. I suppose my colleagues meant it when they said they'd be watching me carefully.

Knowing that Santiago certainly knows the truth, I don't dare lie. "I had a guest at one point," I admit.

"Who?" she asks.

"Lieutenant Commander Ryan," I say.

"What was the purpose of your meeting?" she asks.

I feel myself stiffen. I shouldn't have to answer to anyone for my behavior off-duty, but unfortunately I do. The only way to regain the trust of my colleagues is to appear to be an open book, holding nothing back. I suppose she feels entitled to that after my past betrayal. "He and I have developed a romantic relationship," I say reluctantly.

Unfortunately, she presses on. "Who initiated that relationship?"

I swallow and answer, "He did. On the ship. He visited my quarters and ..." I feel my cheeks grow hot. I've been attracted to Ryan for years, ever since the very first time I met him but, back then, I never dreamed I'd get involved with him. For one, I knew from the ring on his left hand that he was married. And of course there's the fact that he was the enemy. Now, though, so much has changed. "Do you really need to know all of the details?" I ask.

Santiago shakes her head. "No, not at this point."

And then she returns to her workstation, apparently satisfied with my explanation.

As quietly as I can, I breathe a sigh of relief, hoping I'll never have to explain any more.

THURSDAY, JULY 7
1708

FORTY-ONE

Forty-seven decides not to join Katrina and me in our evening mission to get Katrina a white jumpsuit for tomorrow. I'm kind of glad about that because, today, our mission isn't just about the jumpsuit, at least not for me.

"I've been thinking a lot about what we saw with those helmets yesterday," I say to Katrina.

She takes a deep breath and then nods. "Me too."

"We need to investigate whether it was real or make believe," I say.

"How are we going to do that?" she asks hesitantly.

"We could go to the building where we saw the woman who ..." It's hard to think about that woman. If the helmets took us someplace real, we watched that woman die.

Katrina stiffens. "Yeah, okay," she says.

We don't discuss it anymore other than a quick "I think it's this way" and "That's the building over there."

We slide through a crack in the wrecked building, and we end up in a miserable place that looks like the inside of a nightmare. It's gray here, but not as gray as the place we saw yesterday. Still, when I look over the crooked walls and smashed furniture, I feel a sick familiarity. Over on the left, there's a sideways staircase, just like the one we saw yesterday ... but that doesn't prove anything. I look to the spot where we found the big heavy table to hide under, and I get a small sense of relief, because there's nothing there.

"There's no table," I whisper to Katrina.

She points across the room. "It's over there."

Lying upside-down is what appears to be the exact same table that Katrina and I hid under. It's fairly unique, with a three-dimensional image of a bird on the center of the top drawer. Unlike the table yesterday, this table is missing two of its legs.

I point back to the other side of the room. "But it was over here ..."

"At the end ... everything got exploded." Katrina's eyes fill up with tears. "Every*one* got exploded too. That's why those jumpsuits made our skin hurt. They were trying to make us feel what the people felt. But I'm sure *really* being exploded hurts a whole lot worse ..."

She crouches down at the bottom of a fallen wall that sits at an odd angle. My stomach hurts when I realize what she's looking for. I watch as she runs her hand along the spot where the wall meets the floor. Gray stuff leaves the ground and soils her hand.

I think we both see at the same moment what her touch has revealed. Katrina's hand goes to a small bit of torn black cloth that is wedged tight under the wall. I don't know for certain that it is from the uniform of the woman who we saw die, but there are too many coincidences for it not to be.

As we stare at the bit of cloth, Katrina and I both speak at the same time, "Real."

THURSDAY, JULY 7
1811

JACKIE

Change of shift went quickly today. We really had nothing to report. Our unmanned surveillance drones continue to venture further and further away from the base and, although we have discovered numerous ruins and Outsider compounds, we have not encountered any of the military bases that are supposed to be out there. I'd expected we'd have come across at least one by now, but I suppose it's difficult to find something when you have so much ground to cover and no idea where to look.

Every one of the military leaders who knew anything about what was out there is dead and we are locked out of the systems where they kept their records, and so our new commander has been forced to start from scratch. Our only way of knowing what is beyond our borders is old-fashioned exploration. I suppose that takes time. Unfortunately, we may not have much more of it before the other bases—with far more resources than we have in our weakened state—come looking for us.

Before we leave for dinner, I go to the restroom to check my navigator.

No new messages.

Good. I have not been asked to do anything that could arouse suspicion this evening. At least not so far. I consider sending out a message myself, but I can't figure out exactly what to say, and so I send nothing, and I return to meet my colleagues for the walk to the mess hall.

As I reenter the room, Klein—one of the night shift soldiers—suddenly pushes back his chair. "Guys, check this out!" he says.

We all go to him, dayshift and nightshift, all crowded around his one computer. He selects his current screen and sends it to all of the monitors, so that we can see what has caught his attention.

I focus on the screen ahead of me and my eyes go wide. Beside a large lake is a dark, shiny network of interconnected buildings, remarkably similar to the now-destroyed Malibu base where we once lived. Klein zooms out, and I see nearby civilian compounds and training compounds. This place is practically a matching image of the network of compounds here.

"It's located near Salt Lake City, Utah," he says.

"There's an airport nearby," Lam points out. "That could the location of their secure underground compound." He's probably referring to the type of compound where Murphy and Hanson were raised.

Across the bottom of the screen, I see the message we are transmitting from the surveillance drone. The message identifies us, and it says we have come in peace.

"We've been kissing their airspace for over ninety seconds now," Klein says. "I figured we'd at least have generated some visible activity at the base, perhaps a show-of-force or something—"

Suddenly, the commander appears in the room with us. Not really, though, just virtually.

We all snap to attention.

The commander is staring at a screen that we can't see. "At ease," he says. "I'm looking at what you're looking at, and it appears promising."

"How do you want us to proceed, sir?" Klein asks.

"Back off a bit," the commander answers. "Stay at the periphery and broadcast our message. Be prepared for a response that isn't very welcoming."

"Yes, sir," Klein says. I hear the anticipation in his voice. We are so close to making contact with someone else out there in the world. But the commander is right, we need to be cautious. The wrong move here could destroy any chance we have of making a positive connection. As difficult as it is, we must be patient.

And so we wait.

SEVEN

When we are finally dismissed from the stuffy warrior classroom for the day, Ten and I run back to the barracks to meet Ryan. This morning, he assured us that he will work on planning a mission to help Miss Teresa but, because our navigators still aren't functioning, we've had no way of receiving updates on his progress until now.

Ryan is in his dormitory when we arrive. As soon as we are all in the room with the door closed, he says, "The mission is a go."

"When do we leave?" I ask.

He shakes his head. "*You* are not going anywhere. The two of you are going to stay right here on the base."

Ryan explains that my only role left is to inform Miss Teresa that he will be arranging for her to go back to our compound tonight, and that he will meet her at the back entrance to the mess hall at 2200. My plan is to talk to Miss Teresa at dinner.

I feel both hopeful and helpless. Hopeful, because we have a plan to help Miss Teresa. Helpless, because Ryan won't allow Ten and me to be a part of it.

Ryan leaves to arrange the last minute details of the

mission, and Ten and I head off to the mess hall. As we pass Maria's dormitory, the door opens and Forty-one and Katrina emerge from the otherwise unoccupied room. It looks like Katrina has been crying, although her eyes are now dry. Forty-one has a look of discomfort on his face.

"Is everything okay?" I ask the two of them.

"Can we talk to you?" Forty-one asks me, then he looks at Ten. "Both of you."

Ten and I nod. "Of course," I say.

The kids usher us into Maria's dormitory and we sit across from them on one of the beds.

"What's going on?" I ask Forty-one.

"Last night, we found a box of helmets and big heavy black jumpsuits," he says. "When we put them on it was like …"

Katrina finally speaks, "We were in a war. Here at this military base. Everything was exploding."

My shoulders tense. I think I know the kind of helmets and jumpsuits Forty-one and Katrina found. As a part of our warrior training, we used something like that to experience a horrific event that happened way back when our grandparents were children. We saw so many people suffering and dying … but we didn't just *see* it, we *experienced* it—

Forty-one speaks again, "We weren't sure if what we saw was real or make believe, so today we went to the place that we thought we saw with the helmets and we figured out …" He stares down at the floor. "It was *real*. All of it."

"Who came here and exploded the base?" Katrina asks.

"I don't know," I say. "Maybe Ryan knows."

"Do you know where Ryan is?" Forty-one asks.

"He's … busy," I say quickly. "But I'll ask him later."

"Do you think someone will come here and explode *us*?" Katrina asks.

She looks so anxious that I wish I could tell her no, but I won't lie to her. "When bad things happen, we learn from them," I say. "Every terrible thing that happens makes us stronger if we learn from it. That's what those helmets are for. They're for learning about the past, so we never let it happen again."

"Can you show me where you found those helmets?" Ten asks the children.

Uneasily, they nod.

THURSDAY, JULY 7
1851

TEN

I eat fast and excuse myself from dinner, telling Seven that I'll meet up with her in a little while. I want to spend some time with the sim helmets. Those helmets could be an invaluable resource. I need to work quickly though. I'm not supposed to be wandering about at this hour. Although I'm not sure if anyone actually cares.

I make my way back to the gymnasium and find the box that Forty-one and Katrina showed me. As quickly as I can, I put on a jumpsuit and pull a helmet over my head. The thing powers up immediately, displaying a home screen in front of my face. I never got to see this screen when we used the sim helmets with Ryan. He must have set things up so it was only presented to him. Now, I study it. There are numbers listed below the menu title. I scroll down and note that there are hundreds of them. As I try to make sense of the numbers, I notice a pattern. Six of the numbers appear to represent dates, listed in reverse chronological order. I scroll back to the top and take note of the most recent dates. Among them is one I will never forget: August thirty-first of last year. *The date that our terrestrial drone was attacked.*

I don't want to reexperience what happened that day, but I need to know how this device works. Going through a scenario that I experienced in real life should provide me with important insight. I swallow and hold my finger over the numbers representing one of the worst days in my life.

My vision goes black, but not for long. Then I am back in our terrestrial drone, but not in the same seat I occupied just over a year ago. I have taken a seat that was occupied by one of the soldiers. I look around and see Seven, Ma'am, Ryan, Twelve, Twelve's instructor, Thirteen and her instructor, Jackie, and I'm here too. It's strange to see myself; it's like looking into a mirror that doesn't mirror. Even more affecting, though, is seeing ghosts come to life. People whose lives have been lost, now back among the living. I take a deep breath, trying to keep my focus.

We are returning to the warrior compound after having visited the civilian compound. I know this because the ocean is to our right and we are barraging our instructors with questions. How naïve those questions seem now, and how naïve we all seem. None of us knows that, in just a matter of minutes, our lives will be blown apart. Some lives will be lost. The rest of us will be scarred forever.

I see my sim self reach over and almost touch Seven's hand. I remember doing that. I wanted to touch her so badly, because I thought she looked sad. I wanted to ask her what was bothering her. But I held back. There were too many eyes and ears around us to risk such a move. I figured we'd touch and talk later.

Beside me, Jackie activates her navigator. Although, I suppose it is impolite, I look over to see what she's doing. She pulls up a virtual chess game. *She's bored, I guess.* She places her finger on the white queen's pawn, as if to move it, but she doesn't drag it to a different spot. I suppose she's trying to decide on her first move, but she's taking a long time, almost too long. Suddenly, numbers appear in the lower right corner of the chess board: 0030. Jackie lifts her finger from the pawn, and taps the numbers. Instantly, they change: 0029, 0028, 0027. It's a timer, counting down. Jackie watches the numbers fall, but she does nothing more. 0023, 0022, 0021, 0020. Jackie doesn't move any of the pieces on the chess board. Instead, she swipes away the game and answers a question asked by Twelve.

I continue to count in my head ... 0010, 0009, 0008 ... A sick theory enters my thoughts ... 0005, 0004, 0003, 0002 ...

BOOM!

My seatbelt catches me as the drone is blasted backward. As soon as I regain my thoughts, I snap my head around to look at Jackie. She is calmly surveying the controlled chaos of the soldiers and instructors.

Anger builds inside me. Seven told me that Jackie was a spy for the Outsiders. But Jackie did more than spy on us. That timer on her navigator was ticking down to the exact moment that the attack began. Not only did Jackie know of the attack, it appears she orchestrated it. At the very least, she was intimately involved with those who did.

"Warriors, don't move," Ma'am says.

Jackie looks out the window, up toward the top of the mountain. I can't see from here what she sees, but there's a glimmer of recognition on her face.

"Vehicle, reverse direction," Ryan says. He's trying to get us out of this. He has no idea that we're doomed, and that the traitor who doomed us sits just a few feet away from him. "Castle, this is Whiskey Foxtrot," Ryan says in an urgent but controlled voice. "We're under attack. Road's blown out south of us. Requesting backup."

"Roger, Whiskey Foxtrot," a deep voice replies. "We have a visual on the—"

I see Jackie brace herself, maybe even subconsciously.

BOOM!

"Castle, this is Whiskey Foxtrot," Ryan says. "Second explosion. We need air support for immediate extraction."

"Roger that, Whiskey Foxtrot," the deep voice responds. "We're on our—"

BOOM!

I feel that explosion as if I am back in the drone on that horrible day. It compresses my chest, my body, my head. I can barely see. Barely hear. Barely breathe. I cough hard and try to focus. Everything appears upside down but my brain tells me I'm still right-side up. *The sim isn't perfect. It can't fool your brain into thinking you're no longer upright.* I reach to the restraints that I feel holding me to my seat. I release them and fall into an upright space once again.

In the row ahead of us, some people are releasing themselves from their seats. Twelve's instructor is still strapped to his seat. He's coughing weakly. Still alive. Jackie slips her weapon behind his back. For some ridiculous reason, I wonder if she's trying to help him somehow. But then, he goes instantly lifeless, and she withdraws her weapon.

My dinner rises up into my throat. *You killed him*, I almost shout. But there's no sense in speaking when no one can hear you.

I turn just in time to see Ryan examining Ma'am. "MEDIC! I NEED A MEDIC FOR KITAY!" he calls out. Sim me is next to Ryan, bent forward and coughing uncontrollably. Ryan grabs sim me protectively, and then he looks over at Seven. "Davis, you're on Murphy," he says.

"Copy," Jackie responds.

I want to vomit. *Ryan made Jackie responsible for protecting Seven.*

But he didn't know the truth about Jackie. None of us knew.

I stay with Seven as Jackie pushes her toward the door. "Murphy, let's go," Jackie says.

Seven looks around frantically. "Where's Ma'am?" Then she spots her. "Ma'am!"

"MURPHY, MOVE!" Jackie shoves Seven so roughly that it is all I can do not to step forward and throw Jackie to the ground.

Seven spins around with a fight in her like I've never seen. "Not without Ma'am!"

Jackie twists Seven's arm behind her back, and Seven grimaces in pain. I finally lose my self control. I send a punch into Jackie's flank. I feel the impact in my fist, but Jackie makes no response. *Of course she doesn't. I can't affect what has already happened.*

"We need to help Ma'am!" Seven says weakly.

Jackie says something soft to her that I don't hear as soldiers forcibly remove Seven from the drone. I start to move with them, but then I glance back at Jackie. She is speaking to a man who has come to help Ma'am, then, in one quick move, she subtly positions the tip of her weapon against the man's neck, and the man falls to the ground. Without a hint of emotion, Jackie slips her weapon against Ma'am's chest and then removes it. Although Ma'am was lifeless both before and after Jackie's actions, I am certain of her intentions. Jackie is trying to ensure that Ma'am doesn't wake up.

I want to rip the sim helmet off my head and confront the real Jackie right now, but I force myself to follow sim Jackie out the drone door. By the time I emerge from the upside-down terrestrial drone, Jackie has Seven pressed up against the outside of the vehicle. My ears fill with shouted orders, commands, and responses.

"MOVING THE PRINCIPALS TO THE MOUNTAIN BASE. COVER US," Ryan shouts.

He walks fast toward the mountain, pulling sim me with him. As Jackie and Seven follow us, Jackie pushes Seven's hand down, preventing her from arming herself. They seem to be arguing.

Of course you want Seven unarmed, you coward.

Jackie fires her weapon upward, but the direction she is aiming doesn't match that of the other soldiers. The other soldiers are aiming at the top of the mountain—where our attackers are—but Jackie is aiming just below that, where the only possible threat is a solid wall of rock.

A horrible pain hits my shoulder, and I remember that I need to protect my real self. I dash to the base of the mountain. Seven and sim me are standing close to the rock, touching hands, palm to palm. I remember telling myself I won't let her go, afraid that this might be the last time I would ever be able to touch her.

"HEAD NORTH," Ryan shouts.

Everyone begins to move forward, except Jackie and Seven.

Because Jackie yanks Seven back.

I remember shouting at Ryan that we needed to stay with Seven. He assured me that Jackie would take care of her. Now I feel tremendous guilt for believing him, even though he was certainly telling me what he thought to be the truth, even though I—

A body crashes onto the road. It's a young Outsider boy, not more than a teenager, who has fallen all the way from the top of the mountain. His body is mangled, bloodied, dead. As Seven looks at the boy—with what can only be sympathy on her face—Jackie raises her weapon ... *AT SEVEN.*

"GET DOWN!" a female soldier shouts.

The soldier rushes toward Seven. To protect her. *From Jackie.*

Jackie turns and fires at the soldier. The soldier fires too. Jackie falls backward, and the soldier falls forward, both women rendered inert by each other's weapons.

Seven rolls a fallen Jackie off her back and calls out her name, trying to awaken her, but Jackie doesn't rouse. Before Seven can do anything else, she collapses onto the ground herself, clutching her left hand. *Seven is being fired upon from above.* She pulls out her weapon and fires up at the Outsiders. Her right hand bleeds, her body trembles, but she continues to fight.

I wish I could help her, but I can do nothing except watch powerlessly. I wish I had stayed with her back then. I wish I hadn't left her in a murderer's hands on that terrible day. I won't leave her now though. Even though we are separated by time, I will stay with her now. The way I wish I did then.

I move closer to Seven, so close that I can feel her presence beside me. "I'm right here," I whisper to her. "I won't leave you. I promise."

Another Outsider body comes crashing down from the top of the mountain, landing right beside us. After such a fall, I would expect any human being to be dead, but this woman isn't. The woman's eyes lock on Seven and she aims her weapon. Seven aims her weapon at the woman. But she doesn't fire. The woman goes lifeless before she can.

Bill—Twelve's liaison from that day—races toward us, with Twelve over his shoulder. Bill's body pushes mine out of the way, but of course he doesn't sense that I am here. I spin around so that I remain by Seven's side.

"You all right?" Bill asks Seven.

"Jackie's unconscious," Seven says, as she aims her weapon at the still-present threat above.

"Put your weapon away. I've got you now," Bill says. "Let's go."

Seven tucks her weapon into her waist and tries to pull Jackie's body onto one shoulder.

"What are you doing?" Bill shouts at her.

"I'm taking Jackie with us," Seven responds.

I hear something garbled. A deep voice.

"MURPHY, MOVE RIGHT NOW!" Bill orders. "RUN!"

BOOM!

I am tossed to the ground. The sky transforms to gray.

Rain made of rocks pelts me. Suffocating heat engulfs me. Burning Outsider bodies now lie all around me. As I crawl back to Seven, Bill shouts at her, "GET UP RIGHT NOW! MOVE!"

Seven pulls Jackie onto her back and starts moving forward. I am caught in a mix of pride at her bravery and nausea at the fact that she is unwittingly helping a monster who betrayed us.

"FASTER!" Bill shouts.

Air surges toward us. Tiny rocks pelt us from up ahead. *The rescue drone is here.*

Soldiers in clean black jumpsuits emerge from the drone and rush in our direction. If I could see past them, I would see Ryan trying to force me aboard the drone. I would see myself calling out Seven's name, refusing to leave without her. Refusing to enter that drone despite a half dozen soldiers trying to drag me inside.

And then I'd see Ryan ordering them all to stop. Telling them that he'll wait there with me until Seven comes. And Ryan promising me that he had the best soldier available guiding Seven to us.

I remember the moment I saw Seven coming up the ramp, just as Ryan promised me she would. It was the same moment that another soldier came running with Ma'am, saying she was in full cardiac arrest.

Now, from my vantage point just behind Seven, I see my sim self standing beside Ryan at the mouth of the drone, looking at a dying Ma'am. A resuscitation sleeve is strapped over her chest, taking over the function of her stopped heart. A tube that feeds directly into her trachea is attached to an auto ventilator. Even from this distance, I can tell that Ryan would be unable to stand without my support. My sim self calls out to Seven, but she doesn't hear me over all of the noise. I couldn't go to her then, because Ryan needed me to keep him upright.

Now though, I stay with Seven. I stay by her side as soldiers bustle around. I stay with her until the drone doors close, and Seven releases her harness, and she goes in search of me. I stay by her side until sim her reunites with sim me.

It is only once we are in each other's arms that I pull off my helmet.

And the sim disappears.

And I sit down on the floor, unable to remain standing for even a second more.

THURSDAY, JULY 7
1921

JACKIE

It is well into dinnertime, but I'm not the slightest bit
hungry. Our surveillance drone has laid low long enough to
suit the commander. It has continuously broadcast our
peaceful intentions, but we've received nothing in return.

We've entertained numerous hypotheses to explain the
lack of reaction to our presence: maybe the base has sensed
our drone and went on lockdown, maybe they were on
lockdown even before our arrival due to some real or
perceived threat, maybe something horrible has befallen the
people here.

The commander has decided that it's time to act. He has
called in additional surveillance drones, putting a hold on
the search for life in the surrounding areas to bring extra
support to us. We want to have as many eyes in the sky as
possible.

We have a decent idea of the base's security systems
since—from what we can see—it seems to match our own,
although we can't be certain that there aren't significant
differences. The main feature seems to be the automated
turrets. Our turrets are able to distinguish military aircraft
and vehicles from foreign ones. Anything unknown that

seems to be approaching our borders receives numerous warnings. If the trespasser advances into our outer security zone, it is neutralized.

"We should be prepared to lose some drones," Lam says. "As soon as we make a move, they might blow us right out of the sky."

"We're squawking all the magic words," Santiago says. "The system should know we're friendlies and let us pass."

"It's the people who are going to be our problem," I say. "If they believe we're the enemy—"

Klein interrupts, "I'm going in."

The other drones are held back as Klein takes manual control of a single drone and descends toward what is certainly part of the military's airspace. This is not a stealthy approach, nor do we mean it to be. All of our drones continue broadcasting our message via every method we have in our arsenal. Great big banners with the United States seal tell our story, while speaking it alternately in English and Spanish. Anyone who sees or hears us right now, even with absolutely no surveillance equipment, would receive the message we are sending loud and clear. We are impossible to ignore.

The compound remains eerily lifeless.

We breathe silent breaths. Watching. Ready.

But nothing seems to be happening.

Klein's voice breaks the quiet, "There's no one alive in there."

I steal a glance at Klein's monitor. I need to see what he's seeing.

The image on his monitor is completely unremarkable, aside from one thing ...

My stomach falls with a mix of disappointment and relief. "There's a broken window."

"There's no way in hell that wouldn't be repaired immediately." Klein says what I was thinking. "And it certainly didn't happen during the time we've been watching them."

"Permission to enter the structure?" Klein asks the virtual commander who sits behind us, no doubt seeing everything we're seeing.

"Permission granted," the commander agrees.

Klein maneuvers the drone through the broken glass and enters what appears to be officer's quarters. There are a few personal items visible: a tablet lying on the floor, a discarded jumpsuit draped over the chair, and an empty drinking cup on the desk. I've never seen officer's quarters so untidy; such an appearance would never have been tolerated at our base.

"Let's get the compound mapped," the commander says.

Although my shift ended over an hour ago, I volunteer to pilot one of the surveillance drones, and my offer is accepted. I pull my assigned drone down into the military airspace and search for additional access points to enter the base. We could blow through a wall or window, but the commander asked us to proceed nonviolently, because it is still remotely possible that there are people hiding inside this place.

Since Klein's drone is inside the compound—past the exterior walls that block our mapping equipment—he has already started mapping. The drones can sense through interior walls, floors, and ceilings, and so the map is beginning to take shape. Almost a third of the compound is now mapped, but one drone can only travel so far so fast.

As I fly in tighter, I find an uncovered air vent on the opposite side of the compound. I move into it and glide through a narrow passage until I come to an entry point. I brace my drone in the vent and push open the panel. *I'm in!*

I set my drone to start mapping.

"Who breached the left side of the building?" Lam asks.

"Davis did," Santiago answers for me.

"How'd you get in?" Lam asks. He's still searching for an entry point.

"I found an open air vent," I say.

I lean over and study the map we're creating, looking for signs of human life, but the map is disappointingly cold. Once my drone's map meets with Klein's, it is clear that there are no *live* human beings in the compound. There may be dead ones though.

Santiago points to a cluster of about a hundred inert human figures in the command center of the base. "Are those people or robots?" she asks.

The figures are in various states of repose. Some are sitting, some lying down, but some are standing. *People who die don't stay standing up.*

"Davis, you're closest," Klein says. "Take a look."

I resume manual control of my drone and head to the command center. It's a bit of a maze since some of the doors in my path are closed, but I only end up having to blast open one door. As I work, the conversation continues around me:

"The hangar is packed with transportation drones," Lam says. "It doesn't look like anyone tried to evacuate."

"No signs of a struggle or attack," Klein says. "I'm

seeing only defunct robots so far. No human bodies."

"I have eyes on the command center," I finally say. Through the drone's POV, I see a busy command center frozen in time, and as dark as a night without stars. My drone provides the only illumination of the eerie scene. In chairs, on the floor, and scattered throughout the room are numerous individuals. Many—based on their perfect posture even in death—are clearly robots. I do a visual check on those who are lying on the floor in a human-like manner but, on closer inspection, none of them are human. "It's just robots here," I say. "A command center filled with robots."

"Where did all the *people* go?" Lam wonders aloud.

"Maybe they abandoned the base ..." Santiago offers.

"On foot?" Lam asks. "All of their transportation drones are in that hangar."

"Why would they abandon a perfectly-good base and all those robots?" I say.

"Restore power and retrieve their security footage, logs, any pertinent intel," the commander says. "I want to know what happened here, so we can ensure that it doesn't happen to us."

THURSDAY, JULY 7
1935

SEVEN

When Ten meets up with me in our domicile, he looks both exhausted and agitated. "Any idea where I can find Ryan?" he asks.

"He said he'll come by in forty-five minutes," I say. "That was about a half hour ago."

Ten sits on the bed. "What did you learn from Miss Teresa?" he asks.

"She couldn't tell me anything for certain. She said she'd noticed that some of the other robots seem a bit troubled, which she admitted was odd, but none of them have verbalized any concerns to her. Apparently the robots take the rule about not discussing their inputs quite seriously."

"I'm sure we'll figure it all out tonight," Ten says.

"I guess," I say, mostly because Ten looks so upset that I don't want to distress him further. I wonder what has him so troubled. "Did you do a sim just now?"

"I went back and saw the attack on our terrestrial drone," he says quietly, "from a different point of view."

I feel my heart pick up speed. I never considered that there might be a sim of that event.

He averts his eyes. "Jackie used her weapon to neutralize members of our team."

I never saw Jackie behave in any manner that wasn't heroic, especially when it came to protecting me, although I suppose I was distracted by the fact that our lives were in imminent danger. She did force me to leave Ma'am behind, but she did that for my own good. At least I thought she did. "Who did she neutralize?" I ask.

Ten shifts uncomfortably.

I know instantly that it's going to be hard to hear what he has to say.

THURSDAY, JULY 7
1946

TEN

I feel Seven's eyes on me even though I'm looking away. Should I tell her the whole truth? Or just part of it? Is it cruel to tell her that Jackie neutralized Ma'am, and that she would have neutralized her too if a soldier hadn't stepped in to defend her? I need to ensure that Seven understands that Jackie is a serious threat, but perhaps she doesn't need to know that the threat is so personal—

A tap on our domicile door stops me from continuing, for now.

Ryan enters the room. "Everything's a go for the mission tonight," he says fast.

"Miss Teresa will be waiting for you at the mess hall at twenty-two hundred hours," Seven responds. "She said she doesn't know if the other robots are affected, but she thinks they seem nervous."

"I'm getting the same info from my intel," Ryan says. "None of the other robots have disclosed any problems, but I have a team of six of them that seems extremely eager to get back to that compound, even though they haven't been told the true purpose of our mission. I'm going to direct them all to go to the control hub. We might get an idea of whether they're affected by watching their behavior once they get there."

"Are you going inside with them?" Seven asks, sounding concerned.

"No," Ryan says, "the commander required me to assure him that no human lives will be put in unnecessary danger."

"Then how are you going to watch their behavior?" I ask.

"The robots are covered in cameras. If we synch them with the monitors on our aerial drone, we can watch the footage from outside the compound," he answers.

"But I thought signals can't transmit through the exterior walls of that compound," I say.

"The commander ordered a shutdown on the security shield in order to enable us to monitor the robots." Ryan takes a step toward the door.

I can't let him go without telling him what I learned about Jackie. "There's something I need to discuss with you," I say.

"I'm rather busy prepping for this mission, Hanson."

I look him straight in the eyes. "It's important."

"I'm going to gather up a few things in my dormitory," he says. "Walk with me."

Seven gives me an uncomfortable look that makes me reluctant to leave her, but it is essential that I talk to Ryan now, before his mission. "I'll be back as soon as I can," I say to her.

"Right," she says.

I follow Ryan out into the hallway, but I don't speak to him again until we are behind closed doors. "Jackie wasn't just a spy," I tell him. "I'm fairly certain that she orchestrated the attack on our terrestrial drone."

"I know about her involvement, Hanson," he says.

I sense Ryan's impatience, and so I move on. "During the attack, I saw her use her weapon to attempt to *kill* people on our side."

He stops everything and looks at me. "To attempt to kill who?"

It hurts to say this. "Twelve's instructor, then Ma'am, and then Murphy."

"Why didn't you tell me this before?" he asks.

"I didn't know until just now," I explain. "I didn't see any of that during the attack, but I found a sim suit and I went back there and … that's what I saw."

He tucks some papers into the sleeve of his jumpsuit. "Show me."

THURSDAY, JULY 7
2013

JACKIE

As far as we can tell, the Utah base's power system is almost completely drained. Only the emergency automated systems seem to be operational. The commander orders transportation drones containing robots and equipment to make their way to Utah, so we can get the base up and running again. He doesn't send any human soldiers with them; he says he won't take that risk.

Meanwhile, we remotely pilot the surveillance drones to explore the other compounds here. Santiago, Lam, and I send drones to the Utah airport to see if we can locate an underground Warrior Development Compound. Its presence would fit with the intel we have indicating that other warrior programs exist throughout the United States.

We begin our search in the seemingly-unkempt areas around the airport runways. The compound could be anywhere, but this seems the most likely location. An essential feature of the WDC is that it must be impossible to detect unless you know what you're looking for. But we do in fact know exactly what we're looking for.

"This could be something," Lam says.

Santiago and I focus our attention on his monitor. In an

overgrown area of grass and trees is what appears to be an abandoned supply shed, but a closer look reveals that the walls are reinforced and bolted to the ground in a way that no supply shed would be.

"The elevator has to be in there," Santiago says. "I'll blow the door."

"Commander, permission to gain entry?" Lam asks.

"Hold on," I say. "Before we go making a mess, give me a shot at something."

Working as quickly as I can, I survey the ground surrounding the "supply shed." If I don't find what I'm looking for fast, my team is going to blow this compound open and scare whatever people are still down there to death.

I can't imagine how shocking it would be to find out that my entire world was enclosed by walls that I never knew existed. If there are still people down below here, they are likely fragile. They almost certainly know nothing about what is above their world. We need to enter gently.

"What are you looking for, Davis?" Lam asks.

"The elevators and stairways probably have security cameras in them," I answer. "I'm looking for a more stealthy way in."

That makes enough sense that he doesn't question it. Even if he did, I wouldn't tell him that I know there is an unmonitored hatch above the center of *our* WDC, and that is why I think there might be such a hatch here. I learned this detail about our WDC just over a year ago, during Murphy's secret mission, but what I learned during that mission isn't mine to tell. I won't do anything that could harm Murphy or Ryan in any—

I notice a mound of overgrown grass that is a bit higher that the surrounding grass. My drone doesn't sense that there's anything unusual underneath the grass, but this compound is specifically designed to thwart detection by surveillance instruments. I slice down into the earth until I hit something hard. Then I cut away a patch of grass, revealing an unremarkable dark gray hatch ... exactly like the one at our WDC.

"All right, Davis," Santiago says as she stares at my screen, "but how are you suggesting we get that thing open?" she asks.

"Give me a minute," I say.

I use a computer to log into my personal files—the ones I once used to spy on the military. Santiago watches, her eyes narrowed with suspicion, but she doesn't say anything. We're allowed to have personal files like these, but I doubt many people have programs in their personal files like the one that I'm about to access.

"In my spare time, I do a lot of programming," I explain. "I've been experimenting with a program to retrieve access codes." I share the program with my drone, and I ask the drone to attempt to determine a code that will open the hatch.

A moment later, the hatch clicks ever so slightly, and my drone transmits a message indicating its success.

"That's an elegant program," the commander says. "Perhaps you missed your calling."

"Don't you dare take her away from us, sir," Santiago says, giving me a smile.

For the first time in the past few days, I feel myself relax.

"What are we waiting for?" the commander asks. "Get the lid off that thing. We need to know if there's anyone left alive down there."

Lam, Santiago, and I move our drones into position. "Yes, sir," we say.

THURSDAY, JULY 7
2023

TEN

I open the now-familiar box and Ryan pulls on a
jumpsuit and helmet.

"Should I go with you?" I ask. I don't want to
experience the attack on our terrestrial drone ever again in
my life. Even once was far too many times, but if Ryan
needs me—

"I want to do this alone," he says.

"Okay," I say.

And then I see him select a scenario.

It's strange to see a sim from the outside. To watch a
grown person acting out a battle in a silent empty room. It's
hard to watch because I can tell what is happening by
observing Ryan's movements. I can almost picture the
scene unfolding around him, so much so that I finally pull a
helmet over my head to distract myself. I can still see the
room and Ryan, but now I have something else to draw my
focus. I put my arms into a sim suit—so I can control the
menu—and I scroll down the list of sims. I'm not planning
to enter one, because I need to stay present for Ryan, and
also, I don't think I could stomach another sim right now.

The long list of numbers is mesmerizing. I wonder if

there is some sort of a key to give an explanation of each scenario. Is each sim a battle, or are there other experiences? I suppose it's the former; the purpose of this device is clear from the title of the menu: "USA Joint Military West Coast Department of Defense Warfare Simulation." This is a tool to teach about war, nothing else.

When I get to the very bottom of the sim list, I see an option for a second page.

Are there more scenarios? How many battles could there possibly have been?

But when I click onto the second page, there is no list. There is just one option:

Real-time synch.

Out of curiosity, I select it.

Tap device to initiate synch.

Below that is a list of devices, some I recognize, some I don't. But one choice catches my eye: *robot.* Ryan told us that, during the mission tonight, he would be synching the aerial drone's monitors with the robots, so that he could observe their mission. Could it be possible to synch a robot with the sim suit?

Unfortunately, I can't find out right now. I can't go any further in the process without something to synch with. I go back and scroll through the first page of the menu again a few times, and then I pull my arms out of the sim suit and the helmet off my head. I carefully deposit the suit and helmet back in the box.

Ryan is getting to the end of the sim now. I see him react to the arrival of the rescue drone. Then he takes the helmet off—likely just before sim Ma'am arrives at the drone, fighting for her life. He keeps his back to me as he pulls off the sim suit and wipes his eyes with his sleeve.

Finally, he turns and addresses me, "I'll take care of Lieutenant Davis."

"What are you going to do?" I ask.

His jaw clenches. "I'm going to make sure she never gets the opportunity to hurt anyone for as long as she is alive." His face doesn't invite any further questions. "Go back to your dormitory," he continues. "I'll see you at breakfast."

I suppose I've accomplished what I needed to, and I don't want to trouble Ryan with anything more, so I say, "Yes, sir."

I head to my dormitory, but I only get about half way before I stop and retrace my steps to the gymnasium. Ryan is long gone. I open a few boxes until I find one that is almost empty, with just a few linens at the bottom. I add two helmets and two jumpsuits to the nearly-empty box. Then I shut the box and bring it to a quiet spot just behind the mess hall, where I will wait for Miss Teresa.

THURSDAY, JULY 7
2104

JACKIE

Our little surveillance drones travel single file through unremarkable darkness that we illuminate. My drone is first, then Santiago's, then Lam's. Everyone here in the room with us crowds around our workstations to watch our drones' video feeds on our monitors. They've already finished remotely exploring the other compounds in the Utah complex—the prison compound and the civilian compounds. Those places turned out, like the base, to be devoid of people. Populated only by inanimate robots. With no clues as to what happened. This is our last chance to find life here in Utah.

Finally, our drones arrive at an exterior door. My drone swiftly grabs a code, and we enter the compound quietly. The first room we encounter is empty but, in the next one, we see our first sign of life: a maintenance drone is doing laundry. White sheets or table cloths. Five machines full of them.

"That's a good sign," Santiago whispers. She sounds relieved. I think we all are.

We pilot our drones into the central area of the compound and find it alive with the quiet activity of nighttime. Cleaning drones sanitize pristine hallways. Maintenance drones perform checks to ensure that everything remains in working order. The underground city is mostly asleep though. We fly down into a lovely lobby that features trees and flower-lined paths and an aquarium stocked with a multitude of fish. If you had to reside in a box underground, this wouldn't be such a bad place to live.

"The layout appears to match our WDC," the commander says. "I expect the control hub to be located on the tenth floor, likely in the northwest corner of the compound."

Santiago, Lam, and I send our drones in that direction. Sure enough, in the northwest corner, we find what appears to be a fully-functioning control hub. All of the equipment seems to be running properly. But, strangely, there are no people here or robots.

"Shouldn't somebody be running this place?" I ask.

"Yes, there should be someone here. Even at this hour," the commander says, sending my heart into my stomach. "Something's wrong."

We continue to explore the compound, now more concerned than curious. We find dining rooms, classrooms, offices, a recreation room, an indoor farm with crops ready for harvest. All of these places are unoccupied, but I would imagine that would be typical at this hour. But then we find a hospital ... with no patients or staff. That can't be normal.

The only signs of life are drones going about their business. But *functioning* drones are more "life" than anything we found at any of the other Utah compounds.

We decide to open the doors in the backs of places like dining rooms and classrooms. These doors are only used by robots, because they go only to a closet. In each closet, we find at least one robot. Inert, waiting for tomorrow. But when we attempt to manually activate them, the robots have no response.

Next, we go to the people's quarters. I brace myself for horror, expecting to find dead, decaying bodies there, but we find only more mystery. Empty rooms. Empty beds. No live people, and dead bodies either.

I assume there were once people living here in the Utah complex. But if so, why did they leave? Where did they go? Are they planning to come back? We have found no signs of an attack. Did the people leave on their own accord? But why would they leave their haven? What could have possibly sent them elsewhere? Why would they—?

Suddenly, the room goes completely quiet. All eyes are directed behind me.

I turn and see Ryan standing there.

Santiago nods at him. "Lieutenant Commander, what's going on?"

"I need to speak with Davis," he says lightly.

Santiago gives me a smile, no doubt assuming this is a social call.

But this isn't a social call. Ryan wouldn't come looking for me here unless something was very wrong. And I can see in his eyes that something *is* very wrong.

I've never seen such a troubled look in his eyes before.

THURSDAY, JULY 7
2150

TEN

I'm not sure how long I've been sitting here atop my box outside the back entrance to the mess hall—the entrance the robots use. I hope Miss Teresa arrives early for her meeting with Ryan. I'll need time to test my hypothesis before he shows up to collect her.

Finally, I see a female figure moving through the darkness. She steps into the light and I stand. "Good evening, Miss Teresa," I say.

She looks at my nametag. "Good evening, Hanson."

"What is the time?" I ask her.

"2152."

That means I have eight minutes—or less if Ryan is early. I don't think he'll be late. I decide to get right down to business.

"Murphy and I would like to go with you on your mission tonight," I say. "We're not permitted to go along physically, however we might be able to view the mission through your …" *Do I say "cameras"?* I decide to say, "… eyes." Miss Teresa doesn't offer any response yet and so I continue, "I have a device that I might be able to synch with you. If that's okay." I pause, the way I would to allow a human to consider my request. I am asking for her consent, but she will certainly give it. Robots are very obliging that way. Unless a request would cause harm to someone or something or it is against the rules, the robots try to accommodate us.

She nods. "Yes, I would like that."

She would *like* that? I had expected a simple "okay."

"Why would you *like* that?" I ask, curious.

"I am feeling anxious. If I know that you are watching me, I would feel less anxious."

Robots aren't supposed to have thoughts like that. But maybe she does.

I don't have time to explore her statement further. She has given her consent. In fact, she has given *more* than her consent; she actually seems to *want* us to do this. I pull out a sim jumpsuit and slide my arms inside, then I put on the helmet and select the synch option.

"I need to synch the device. Where should I touch you?" I ask her.

She moves her right hand to the center of her chest. To the place that people gesture to when they refer to their heart. I move my gloved hand to the spot that she indicated and my vision goes dark. Gone is the menu and Miss Teresa, although Miss Teresa is certainly still standing before me.

After a minute, my vision returns. But everything is different. I am staring at … myself. I'm wearing a helmet and part of a sim suit.

"It works!" I breathe.

"I'm glad," she says. Her voice is clear in my ears.

I look to each side and find that I can see into the

surrounding areas of darkness and shadows as clearly as if it were daytime. I spin around, and I can see behind me ... I mean *her*. I am seeing everything from her point of view.

"Have you moved your head at all since we synched?" I ask her.

"No," she says. "I haven't moved at all."

So robots really do have eyes on the back of their heads—

I hear someone approaching. As I pull off the helmet and sim suit and tuck them back inside the box, I whisper to Miss Teresa, "Murphy and I will be with you tonight. No matter what."

Ryan rounds the corner at a fast pace. He eyes the box at my feet, and then he looks at me. "What are you doing here, Hanson?"

"I thought maybe I could synch the sim helmets with Miss Teresa," I admit. "That way Murphy and I can follow—"

"Absolutely not," he says.

"It wouldn't put us in any danger," I argue.

Ryan turns to Miss Teresa. "Please excuse us for a moment," he says, and then he walks me a few feet away. "What if something goes wrong during the mission?" he asks me in a low voice.

"That's extremely unlikely," I say. "It's basically a routine supply run. And with all the increased security measures—"

"But what if it does?" he asks. "You and Murphy have experienced enough traumas to last a lifetime. I can't let you—"

"You don't need to protect us," I say. "We're not

children."

"You're one of the few I have left." He looks hard into my eyes. I see pain ... and something else. "I've already failed you countless times. I will *not* fail you again."

Guilt. That's what I see in his eyes. Guilt.

"You *never* failed us," I say. "*Never*."

He puts a hand on my shoulder. "Go to Murphy. Take care of each other. Do that for me."

I won't argue with Ryan anymore about this. He is trying to do what he feels is best for Seven and me. It would be unfair to ask him not to. "Yes, sir," I say.

He sighs, still appearing uneasy. "Goodnight, Hanson."

"Goodnight, sir," I say.

As Ryan begins to lead Miss Teresa away, I address her, "Even if we don't figure out things tonight, we won't stop trying to help you. I promise."

"No matter what?" she asks me.

Her question might just be a simple response to my statement, but I feel certain that there is something more to her query. I believe she is asking if I am still planning to watch tonight's mission through her eyes, despite Ryan forbidding it. She wants to know if Seven and I will be with her tonight.

"Yes." I nod. "No matter what."

SEVEN

When Ten returns to our dormitory, he brings with him a large black box. Quietly, he sets it down, careful not to disturb Fifty-two, who is lost in her dreams.

"What's in the box?" I ask softly.

"You said you wanted go on tonight's mission." He pulls out a helmet and two sim suits and places them on the bed. "I was able to synch a helmet with Miss Teresa, so we can follow along with her in the sim suits. If you still want to."

Uncertain excitement floods into me. "Why wouldn't I want to?"

"Ryan forbade us from doing this," he says.

"He said he didn't want us going on the mission *physically* …"

"He told me just now that he doesn't want us doing this either."

"Why not?" I ask.

"I think he's worried about *emotional* trauma," he says.

Ten and I have been through many emotional traumas. We both carry painful scars in our hearts. Even though sometimes those scars make us feel weak, I know they have made us stronger. I look deep into Ten's eyes and I know that he wants to proceed with this. And I do too. I reach out and grab a jumpsuit and start putting it on over my clothes.

As Ten begins putting on the other one, he launches into a quiet explanation, "This will probably be more like watching a movie than doing a sim. We can see only what Miss Teresa can see … which is a three-hundred-sixty degree view of her environment." He picks up a helmet. "I only got a chance to synch one helmet, so we'll have to take turns." Ten is about to put on the helmet, but he hesitates. "Miss Teresa said it would make her less anxious if we were watching."

"Then I'm glad we're going," I say.

"Me too." He puts on the helmet and, a moment later, he begins to describe what he's seeing, so I can follow along in my mind's eye. Right now, Miss Teresa is sitting inside an aerial drone, along with a few other robots and some human soldiers, as Ryan briefs them on the mission.

As I listen to Ten, I think back to the sim we did with Ryan. I remember how Ten, Ryan, Twelve, and I stood in a circle, holding hands, just before we were drawn into that horrible place of death. I shake away that terrible memory, but something sticks. *We started the sim holding hands.* Maybe if Ten and I hold hands now, we can both see Miss Teresa's mission.

"They're going to be departing in two minutes," Ten says.

"What if we hold hands?" I ask him.

"What?" he asks distractedly.

"That's what we did before the sim with Ryan. I wonder if that connects the sim suits?"

Ten shrugs. "I guess it's worth a try."

I take the other helmet out of the box and put it on. In front of me, a menu appears with numerous strings of numbers beneath it. Are all of them sims? Could there really be that many of them?

There's no time to think about that now. I move closer to Ten and take hold of both of his hands. And everything goes dark.

THURSDAY, JULY 7
2254

TEN

"Did it work?" I ask Seven.

"I'm inside an aerial drone," she says triumphantly.

I only vaguely remember holding hands just before the sim we did with Ryan. It's good that Seven remembered. Now we can experience this together. Two sets of eyes are better than one. Compared to robots, humans can only take in a relatively small amount of information at a time.

Seven settles on the bed next to me. "I can feel the seat harness on me," she says.

I feel it too. I suppose tactile stimuli are transmitted by Miss Teresa's body sensors.

Ryan is finishing up his briefing about the mission. When he is through, he asks for questions.

"Where's Davis?" a soldier asks Ryan.

I tense at the mention of Jackie's name.

"Davis is unwell," Ryan responds coolly.

"What's wrong with her?" the same soldier asks.

Ryan shakes his head. "I've been assured that she'll be properly cared for."

"I didn't know Jackie is ill," Seven says. "At dinner she seemed fine. Maybe we should go check on—"

"No," I say much too firmly. "Ryan said everything's under control." I need to tell Seven more about Jackie. But I can tell her after the mission. There's no time to properly tell her right now.

The soldier in the pilot's seat is a man who I don't recognize. I assume that Jackie was originally supposed to be in his place. Of course she would be a natural choice for Ryan to make to join him on this mission. I wonder if he told her the mission's true purpose. I hope not. Jackie can't be trusted with that information. She never could be trusted.

As we become airborne, I study the faces of the other robots. The usual resting facial expression of a robot is fairly neutral with a slight pleasantness about it, not quite a hint of a smile, but nothing of a frown. It's supposed to make them appear approachable, without drawing attention. The expressions of the robots now are neutral. I don't sense even a hint of pleasantness. It could be that it's harder to sense that through a camera, but this experience feels so incredibly real that I don't think that's the explanation. I wonder if Miss Teresa's expression matches the others.

"I wish I could talk to her," Seven says after a while.

"What would you say?" I ask.

"I guess that I care about her." She pauses, but then, without prompting, she continues, "Ever since I can remember, I liked her. Not just the way you like a robot because they bring you your food or provide you with information or assist you with something. I don't know exactly why, but I felt like she … understood me."

Suddenly, our image shifts. Miss Teresa moves a little, and then she stands.

"I need to synch all robots to the monitors," Ryan says.

Miss Teresa is the first robot to walk to Ryan. He gives her a reassuring smile as he taps a receiver to her chest. I feel the touch on my own chest.

"Best of luck," he says.

Miss Teresa nods and proceeds down the ramp that leads out of the drone. She walks to the hidden elevator, which is guarded by armed soldiers. There are lots of soldiers in the area, a marked contrast to when we arrived here on our previous missions. Back then, there were no soldiers at all. There was nothing to indicate that there was an entire compound below the ground. Of course, back then, few people knew it was here.

The robots enter the elevator. As they descend, it is eerily silent. I feel tension among them, even though robots aren't supposed to get tense. The elevator doors open into a corrugated hallway, and Miss Teresa walks to the drone closet. The closet isn't how I remember it. Panels on the walls and ceilings have been pulled back to reveal the normally-hidden parts of our compound: sensors, wires, ducts, and hoses. Normally, I would be fascinated by this but, now, my mind is focused on the mission.

The wall separating the drone closet from the restricted hallway is already open. Every door that branches off the restricted hallway is open as well. Even the door that separates the restricted hallways and the public areas is open. It's strange to see the secrets of the compound laid out like this for anyone to see.

Once the compound is cleared for rehabitation, I suppose these doors will be closed once again. The restricted areas will probably still be restricted, but there's a big difference between a closed door that you've never seen open, and one where you know what's on the other side.

The robots walk briskly toward the control hub. Because Miss Teresa stated that the inputs originate from there, Ryan arranged for them to go directly to that location, however the robots should be able to receive their inputs from anywhere inside the compound.

Other than all the open doors, and the occasional open wall or ceiling panel, the compound appears as it would on any normal night after all the people and robots have retired for the evening. The only thing missing are the security drones on patrol, but I suppose they could be patrolling elsewhere at the moment.

As we enter the control hub, I cringe. I am bombarded with the feelings I had at the moment I learned that my mother betrayed us. The computers appear to be functioning normally now, but I can't help thinking that those same computers, in my mother's hands, nearly destroyed everything.

The robots go to work collecting things. I suppose if Ryan told the commander that the purpose of this mission was to gather needed supplies and information, the robots can't return empty handed.

Miss Teresa is gathering up some tablets. *Good, we could use some tablets.* I miss mine desperately, mostly because I wish I could do some digging into the classified information and try to figure out what is going on at the new base. We have been told so little by the commander. Mostly we've just been given daily reassurances that our basic needs are being taken care of. Perhaps that is because most people don't seem all that curious. Most people are just focused on their day-to-day survival. But there is certainly much going on here that isn't being shared with us.

I'll ask Ryan if they can spare a tablet from the ones Miss Teresa has retrieved. Then I can start—

"Everything just went dark," Seven says. "What happened?"

I've been plunged into darkness as well, except for glowing words on my screen that say:

Synch lost.

"We lost our connection," I say.

"But why? She was just standing in one spot, gathering up tablets," Seven says.

"Maybe if we wait a few minutes, it'll reconnect."

We wait, but nothing changes.

Finally, about five minutes later, the "synch lost" message disappears, replaced by the original synch menu.

"It's asking me to resynch," I report to Seven. "We're no longer communicating with her."

I pull off my helmet. Seven's helmet is already on her lap.

"Do you think something happened to them?" she asks me.

My mind starts to spiral into worst-case scenarios. Based on the look on her face, I think Seven's mind is doing the same.

"It's probably just hard for the signal to transmit this far," I say, trying to reassure both of us. "At least we got to see some of the mission. Ryan will fill us in on the rest when they get back."

Seven crawls into my arms. "What if they don't come back?"

There were no signs of trouble. We probably just lost our connection. But Seven and I have learned from personal experience that awful things can happen without any warning at all.

I pull her close to me. "They'll come back," I say.

But I don't know for sure if that is true.

FRIDAY, JULY 8
0024

SIX

Like last night, tonight Jose and I played chess until we were too exhausted to continue. When I leave his room and enter the dormitory hallway, I don't expect to see anyone there, but just after I slide his door closed behind me, I notice two figures sitting hunched against the hallway wall, and I hear a female voice whisper, "Six?"

As I walk toward the figures, the moonlight coming through the open dormitory door beside them allows me to distinguish their features.

I see Seven and Ten, sitting close together.

"What are you doing out here?" I ask them.

"We're waiting for Ryan," Seven says, then she glances in the direction from which I came. "Why were you in Jose's room?"

"We were playing chess." I left the game in his dormitory. I wanted him to keep it, although it pales in comparison to the exquisite chess set that Jose and I once played with—the one that his father made for him by hand, that he left behind on the night his community was destroyed. We replaced one of the plastic rooks in my chess set with the wooden one that he once gave to me from his.

"You should be careful around him," Ten says.

My skin prickles at the implications of Ten's statement, that Jose is something harmful that must be avoided. "Jose is a good person," I say firmly. "He saved my life, and Ryan's."

"Things aren't always as they appear," Ten counters.

Anger builds in my gut. *How dare Ten accuse Jose of being duplicitous?* "What are you trying to say?"

This time Seven responds, but she addresses Ten, "Did you find out something about Jose too?"

He shakes his head. "Just Jackie."

"What did you find out about Jackie?" I ask.

Ten looks at Seven with a pained expression, as if he is about to be forced to break her heart.

FRIDAY, JULY 8
0038

TEN

I'm going to have to tell Seven and Six what I discovered about Jackie eventually. Ryan assured me that Jackie will never be able to harm us again, but what if the other Outsiders are just as dangerous? Vague warnings might not be enough to protect them. Unless they understand the true extent of Jackie's actions, they might not take the proper precautions.

"I found a recording of the ambush of our terrestrial drone," I say to Six, bringing her up to speed. "During the attack, I saw Jackie press her weapon against Twelve's instructor, and then he went limp."

Seven shivers. "She killed him?"

"He was breathing before she did that," I say. "Afterward, he wasn't."

Seven shakes her head. "Maybe it was a coincidence—"

I don't let her get any further. I can't allow her to defend a criminal. "She did the same thing to Ma'am," I say.

Tears come to Seven's eyes. "She killed Ma'am?"

I take Seven's hands as quiet tears flow down her cheeks. I hate that my words have caused her pain, but Seven must be told the truth. "Twelve's instructor and

Ma'am were both severely injured by the accident. Even if Jackie had done nothing more to them, they might not have survived … but, by her actions, she ensured their deaths." I almost can't find the strength to say what I must say next, but once I've said it, Seven can begin to heal. "Jackie attempted to harm *you* too. While your back was to her, she raised her weapon at you, but one of the other soldiers neutralized her first."

Seven stares at the floor. "So, when she collapsed on top of me, it wasn't because she was shot by the Outsiders. She was shot by someone who was trying to *protect me from her*."

"You don't have to worry about Jackie anymore," I urge her. "I told Ryan all of this … I *showed* him … He said he would take care of her."

"What was he going to do?" Seven asks me.

"He didn't say." Even though I don't know exactly what Ryan did to Jackie, I trust his decision. Whatever it was. There are very few people who I trust completely right now, in whose hands I would trust my own life.

Ryan is one of them.

FRIDAY, JULY 8
0051

SIX

Seven fiercely wipes the tears from her face. "That explains why Ryan didn't bring Jackie on tonight's mission," she says quietly.

Worry bubbles into me. "Ryan went on a mission tonight?" He didn't mention a mission at dinner. Whatever Seven is referring to must have been a last minute emergency or a secret. Either way, it sounds dangerous, and I don't like Ryan putting himself in danger. I almost feel like Ryan is more of a father to me than my own father. Though he didn't give me life, I know I wouldn't be here today if it wasn't for him. I don't think I would have survived seven months as a prisoner of the Outsiders without him ... and Jose.

"Ryan had to go back to The Box to gather some information," Ten says. "Seven and I were watching the mission remotely, but our monitors went dark halfway through."

"Do you think something went wrong?" My voice shakes a bit, even though I am fighting to keep it steady.

"I'm sure we just lost our connection," Ten says.

"We need to make sure they're okay," I say.

"This was an official mission," Ten says. "The military will be monitoring their every move."

I get to my feet. "We need to make sure."

Seven shakes her head. "We weren't supposed to be watching. Ryan will be livid if he finds out—"

"I don't care." I can barely contain my frustration. "We need to make sure Ryan is—"

A dormitory door slides open and Maria pokes out her head. "What's all this ruckus about?" In her arms is the Outsider baby. *Ryan's baby.* Maria is feeding him from a bottle of formula.

"I'm sorry we disturbed you," Seven says.

"It's no disturbance," Maria says. "I was awake, feeding the baby."

I wonder if Ryan asked Maria to care for the child or if she volunteered. Or perhaps both. The child is going to need someone to mother him now that his own mother is dead. Maria is an excellent mother; I've felt that way about her from the moment I met her, back when Jose first introduced her to me as his mother.

I think Ryan and Maria share something special. The way they look at each other makes me believe that there a strong relationship between them when they are away from the eyes of others. I have a feeling that, back when they grew up together in our box, they were more than merely friends. Like Seven and Ten. Like Three and me ... Like me and Jose.

"Ryan might be in trouble," I blurt out.

Seven and Ten both shoot me a look of warning.

"Why do you think that?" Maria asks, appearing concerned.

"He went on a mission tonight and ..." I consider my words. "I have a terrible feeling that something might have gone wrong."

Maria gives me a restrained smile. "You needn't worry. He just arrived back at the base moments ago. Safe and sound."

"How do you know that?" I ask.

"He sent me a message." She gestures to her wrist.

It is then that I notice that Maria is wearing a black navigator, like the ones the military wears. Jose doesn't have a navigator. I'd assumed they wouldn't bother giving navigators to people who didn't have them already, because the navigators are still not working. But if Maria received a message, then she has a *working* navigator. Why would she receive a working navigator when the rest of us—?

"Where did you get that?" Ten asks her.

"I scrounged it up," she says. "It's bad enough that they have us wearing these yellow prison jumpsuits, like we're some kind of criminals. I was a warrior. Just because I was taken hostage by the Outsiders years ago doesn't change—"

There is movement at the end of the hallway. I turn and see someone enter it. *Ryan!*

Without restraint I run to him, but I stop short when I see the troubled look in his eyes. Ryan takes hold of my arm and leads me back to the rest of the group.

"What's going on here?" he asks in a low voice.

"They were worried about you," Maria whispers.

Ryan tenderly places his hand on the forehead of baby Zander. His gaze, though, settles on Seven and Ten. "Hanson, Murphy," he says, "I need you to come with me."

FRIDAY, JULY 8
0116

TEN

Seven and I leave Fifty-two in Six's care, and we follow Ryan without asking any questions. It's a blind trust that I never thought I'd have at this point.

Ryan leads us into the night. The base is barely lit, so mostly we walk in shadows. We pass through and around numerous buildings, spotting no one. I would have assumed there would be soldiers on patrol at this late hour, but perhaps that is unnecessary. The perimeter of the base is secure and those inside aren't expected to be of any danger.

Ryan ducks into an overgrown area that appears to hold nothing of any importance. After a few minutes of guiding us through sharp tangled branches, he pulls away some foliage on the ground to reveal a gray hatch—exactly like the one we utilized to sneak Six out of The Box after she and Seven switched places for the second time. My heart races as Ryan yanks it open. I peer down into the hole beneath it, and all I see are the top rungs of a black ladder that disappears into the darkness below.

"Climb," Ryan whispers.

My heart seems to rise into my throat as I grab hold of the ladder and make my way down into the pitch blackness.

Seven follows me. I glance up and see Ryan begin his descent. A moment later, the hatch is pulled closed and what little illumination we had disappears.

But only for an instant.

Suddenly, tiny lights appear. Everywhere. On the ladder. On the narrow walls around us. They remind me of stars. It almost feels as if we are no longer beneath the ground, but part of the night sky. Climbing among the stars.

I descend more quickly, eager to know where we're going. The ladder ends in a tunnel that extends in two directions. In each direction, at the very end of the tunnel, is a door with a small red light beside it. Once Seven and Ryan have joined me, Ryan leads us into the tunnel on the right. We walk in silence down the tunnel of stars until the end.

The red light by the door appears to belong to a scanner. I wait for Ryan to scan his chip, but instead he knocks. The door slides open, but the scanner light remains red.

We do not have authorization to be here.

I swallow my discomfort as we enter an empty room barely large enough to accommodate four adults. On the opposite side of the room is another closed door with a red light beside it.

"Wait here," Ryan tells us.

He taps on the door ahead of us and it opens, permitting him into a dark, curved hallway.

The door closes behind him.

The whole time, the light beside the door glows red.

FRIDAY, JULY 8
0136

SEVEN

I'm starting to feel more than a little uneasy. Ryan
hasn't told Ten and me anything about why we've come
here. And now he has us locked in a small box beneath the
ground.

I trust Ryan. Otherwise I wouldn't have followed him
here. But I can't help feeling apprehensive. Ryan seems
unnerved in a way that he wasn't just hours ago. I wonder
what happened between then and now. He hasn't discussed
the mission. He has barely spoken at all. Apparently, they
have returned unharmed, but did Miss Teresa give him any
indication as to whether or not she received an input? Did
something unexpected happen while the robots were in our
box?

The door ahead of us slides open, and I exhale.

"Come," Ryan says to us.

Ten stays close to me as we enter a dark hallway that
curves off to the right, unsure of what awaits us ahead. As
soon as we clear the curve, everything opens up around me,
and I feel a gasp escape my lips.

A room about the size of a domicile back home is
packed from floor to ceiling with monitors and equipment.

On the monitors are images of the military base and of our box, along with data that is too small to read from my vantage point. Closed cabinets hold unknown contents. About a half-dozen people fill nearly all of the remaining space. Even though it is the middle of the night, the place is bustling with the activity of day. Ryan weaves rapidly through the room and we keep pace. No one seems to care much about our presence; they are too focused on the monitors.

Ryan directs us into a much smaller room filled with unattended monitors, and he shuts the door behind us. "Have a seat," he says.

There are three chairs in the room and we fill them.

Questions spring to my lips, but I quiet them. Only Ryan knows what is safe to discuss here.

"About two hours ago, we had a development ..." he starts.

My heart pounds, but I remain silent, waiting for him to continue.

"The robots have shut down," he finishes.

"What about Miss Teresa?" I ask, before I can stop myself.

"Every single one of them," Ryan says. "And we need to figure out why."

FRIDAY, JULY 8
0147

TEN

"Isn't the commander working on this?" Seven asks, the trepidation in her voice evident.

"The commander has his team, and I have mine," Ryan says.

"Aren't you and the commander on the same team?" Seven asks.

"I refuse to leave our fate in the hands of someone I barely know," he says. "After all that has happened …."

"I agree." I feel somewhat safer knowing that Ryan is investigating things on his own.

Seven nods. "Me too."

Ryan proceeds, "The commander is completely unaware of this bunker. We need to keep it that way or we will be shut down, and disciplined. You must not return here unless I accompany you. For your safety, I will only bring you here if it is absolutely necessary."

"Why did you bring us here tonight then?" I ask. It can't possibly be just to tell us this. These words could have been whispered to us in our dormitories without risking the security of his bunker.

"Because I need your help, if you're willing to give it,"

he says.

"Of course," Seven says.

"Anything you need," I add.

"Good." Ryan types something onto a keyboard and one of the monitors goes dark. Then it lights up again, but with different data. As my eyes scan the screen, my attention jumps to a collection of sentences. Statements I made hours ago to Miss Teresa, and her responses to them, along with an overwhelming amount of data. How far away from her I was standing at each point in time. Where I directed my gaze. What emotional state I appeared to be in. And so much more.

"Where did you get this?" I ask.

"It was downloaded from Miss Teresa," Ryan says. "Apparently the robots keep a log spanning back about three days. That's all we were able to get from her. We should have been able to access her basic operating settings as well, but there's some kind of lock there that we haven't been able to bypass." Ryan brings up a matching screen on a different monitor. "I need the two of you to look over this information and see if you see anything that might offer a clue as to why the robots shut down."

"Why us?" Seven asks.

"Because I've seen what you can do," Ryan says.

"You've seen what *Ten* can do," Seven says.

"You had a connection with that robot, Murphy," Ryan says. "She told you information that her programming forbid her to share. Robots just don't do that."

Ryan puts his hand on Seven's shoulder for a moment and then mine, and then he leaves us to our task.

FRIDAY, JULY 8
0203

SEVEN

I start examining the information on the screen. Most of it I don't understand. Professor Adam taught us basic information about programming, but what is on this screen moves far beyond that. I only hope that with all of his self-guided "extra-curricular activities" this information makes some sense to Ten.

I do find some information that I can make sense of though. It seems that Miss Teresa documented entire conversations. The words that were spoken are here, but there is much more. She recorded everything happening around her: air temperature, extraneous sounds, body positions and movements of those she interacted with. So many little details.

But isn't that same information registered by all of us? Don't we note these things, even though most of them don't rise to the level of conscious awareness? If our own brains could remember every detail of our lives, then this is what we would see if we could peer inside. There is something missing though. Human brains also have an emotional response to what we experience. I don't see a single note of Miss Teresa's feelings here, but I don't think that is because she doesn't have them. I have witnessed Miss Teresa's emotional reactions first hand. Whether or not they are recorded here, I know they existed.

And then I wonder ….

I scroll back to the beginning of the data, hoping that there is a record of my interaction with Miss Teresa during the evacuation of our former compound. That was the first time she ever addressed me by name without scanning my chip. She called me Seven, even though my nametag and my chip indicated that I was not. Maybe the data will specify how she identified me. As I reach the beginning of the records my stomach sinks. The first timestamp is at 0000 on Tuesday, July fifth. After the evacuation.

I move forward to look for our first conversation in the mess hall here at the base. I find the moment where Miss Teresa notes my approach, and my jaw falls open. On the screen, I see myself identified as "Two Thousand Seven, female, age nineteen." My true identity. There is no indication as to how she reached that conclusion, but she knew my secret. She didn't reveal it, though. I distinctly recall that she looked at my nametag and addressed me as Murphy. But that is not what is recorded here. In the documentation of our conversation, her words to me are, "Good evening, Seven." Either Miss Teresa altered the text after the fact or she uttered words that were contrary to her internal thoughts. Neither of these possibilities makes any sense at all.

I am about to share this with Ten when he says, "Shoot."

In his hand is his warrior necklace.

"What is it?" I ask.

He exhales. "I was trying to see if I could unlock the

operating system for Miss Teresa using my mother's access code, but it's saying I don't have a valid code. Then I tried to use her code to get into the restricted system that I accessed a few days ago in the control hub, and I got the same error message."

"Maybe the military blocked her access," I offer.

"The only person who is authorized to change her access privileges is her or someone logged in as her," he says. "As far as I know, she and I are the only people who have been in that position. Not even the commander could ..." His eyes widen. "But ..."

"But what?" I ask.

"To prevent hacking, some high-security access codes change automatically after a specified period of time. It's possible that my mother's access code has changed. That could explain why the code I pulled in the control hub is no longer working." Intense dread creeps onto his face, and then he exhales. "I'm going to have to pay my mother another visit."

FRIDAY, JULY 8
0538

TEN

Ryan slides open the door. "It's time to call it a day. Did you come up with anything?"

Seven and I share what we've noted, even though we haven't figured out any real answers. I don't mention that I am going to visit my mother again, because I know Ryan would absolutely forbid me from seeing her, and I don't want him to try to stop me.

"I'm going to put your navigators back online, so we can communicate," Ryan tells us. "You should only initiate communications in an emergency. When in public, don't allow anyone to know that your navigators are functional. Check them only when you're certain you're not being monitored. Restrooms and dormitories are the safest places to do so."

"*You* can make the navigators work?" Seven asks, incredulous.

"The commander ordered that all of the navigators be kept offline for the time being, except for those of the most senior officers," Ryan says. "But one of the same people responsible for carrying out that order is on my team too."

"So *you* gave Maria a navigator?" I ask.

"She's part of my team," Ryan says.

"What about Jackie?" Seven asks. "I saw that her navigator was working the other day."

Ryan's jaw tenses. "She was assisting us up until recently, but the information transfer was strictly one-way. She doesn't know about the bunker."

"Where is she now?" Seven asks.

"She's been taken to the brig," Ryan says. "She'll be sent to Terminal Transfer after she's fully debriefed."

"How long will that take?" Seven asks.

"A few days at the most," Ryan says quietly.

Seven and I both understand the meaning of his statement: In just a few days, Jackie will be sent off to die.

FRIDAY, JULY 8
0600

JACKIE

I awaken to a steady beeping near my head. The sound is almost painful, a horrid way to wake up. But I suppose they don't care whether I'm comfortable or not. I don't really care either. I know it won't be long before my life comes to an end, and it is probably easier to face death when it would be a relief from a life of discomfort.

Since my imprisonment, I've only had an hour or two of sleep at the most, in part due to the hourly awakenings to which I am subjected. The more sleep-deprived I am, the more information I am likely to provide during the frequent barrage of questions they offer.

I wear a collar around my neck, as if I am an animal. But they are not treating me like an animal. Animals are treated better than this. Kept animals are provided with regular food and water. They are cleaned and cared for. Regarded as if they are something of value.

I am hungry and thirsty and unwashed. My thoughts slip and slide in my head. I already feel useless. I'm sure those questioning me are starting to feel that way about me too. I'm sure they will be done with me soon. But how soon?

No matter. Why prolong a life that has been stripped of

hope?

My punishment will pay for my crimes, but that is not the way I planned it. I had intended to spend the rest of my days doing right by those I'd hurt, especially Ryan and Murphy. I wanted to earn the friendship they'd given to me.

Now, I won't have that chance. Now that they know the true depth of my betrayal, they certainly want nothing to do with me.

Even my most heartfelt apology would fall on deaf ears.

SEVEN

Ten and I are late for breakfast. When Six spots us, I can almost feel her relief. Although she knew that Ten and I left with Ryan, I'm sure she expected us to be back sooner than now. Before I join the food queue, I go to her.

"Is everything okay?" she asks me.

"All of the robots have shut down," I murmur back.

"I know," she says. "The commander made an announcement about that a few minutes ago. He said they're doing some routine maintenance that was required due to their relocation."

So he's not telling people the truth. "There's nothing routine about this," I whisper.

"What's going on then?" she asks.

"We don't know yet."

Six looks a bit worried, but she forces a smile and says, "At least our navigators are working again."

I look at her wrist. When she touches her navigator's screen it lights reassuringly and displays the time. "When did that happen?" I ask.

"They announced it a few minutes ago," she says.

"That's good," I say. Now Ten and I don't have to hide

the fact that our navigators are functional.

I excuse myself to join the breakfast queue, because it has dwindled down to almost nothing, and the human soldiers who are distributing the food are already packing up, ready to move on. The loss of the robots is certainly going to have a substantial impact on the functioning of the base. We lost about half of our workforce overnight.

Ten and I walk together to our family's table.

"I'm going to go see my mother after work," he says to me quietly.

I'm sure Ten doesn't want to see his mother this evening. I have a feeling he never wants to see her again. But his meeting with her might help solve our problems.

"I want to come with you." I don't pose it as a suggestion or question, because I don't want him to refuse for my benefit. I don't want Ten to have to face this alone.

To my surprise, he nods. "All right."

FRIDAY, JULY 8
1708

FORTY-ONE

We had a human teacher for school today, instead of a
robot one. The commander said that the robots are getting
some kind of very important maintenance done to them.
Our new teacher didn't do much teaching. He mostly asked
what we were learning about in school, and then he seemed
impressed when we told him. After that, he passed out
paper and old-fashioned pens and asked us to draw a
picture of something that made us happy. He said it could
be something from real life or it could be make believe. He
told us to put in as many details as we could. He wanted us
to make it the most detailed picture we'd ever drawn in our
whole lives.

I drew a picture of the place back home where they
grow our food, but I put all the different fruits and
vegetables in one room, because it would be really fun to
just walk from plant to plant, and pick out your whole meal.
My picture was part real life and part make believe. Forty-
seven drew a really good picture of the big tree in our
garden back home with the flowers around it. Her picture
was all real. Katrina drew a room, kind of like the
dormitories we have here. It had three beds and a small

dining table with two chairs. On the walls, there were drawings of people and animals, and there were three toy cars on the floor. When the teacher asked Katrina about her picture, she said it was make believe but, after we left the classroom and told Forty-seven that we'd see her at dinner, Katrina told me that her picture "used to be real." It was a picture of the room that she shared with her brother and sister before they came here.

That room doesn't exist anymore.

Katrina and I go to the building where they keep the boxes of jumpsuits but, as soon as we get inside, she stops and faces me and says, "I don't need a white jumpsuit for tomorrow."

"Why not?" I ask.

"This morning, my mom talked to somebody in charge. She told them that, since she used to be a warrior, her family should wear *normal* jumpsuits. They gave her a black jumpsuit, Jose got a blue one, and Stacy, Noah, and I got white ones."

"Why didn't you tell me that this morning?" I ask.

"I didn't want to go to recreation," she says. "I have to pretend all day long not to be sad when the other kids look at me like I'm stupid. It's hard pretending."

"Did they say anything mean to you today?" I ask.

Tears well up in Katrina's eyes. "They don't have to. I can tell what they're thinking."

I can tell too. The other kids barely tolerate Katrina. I'm beginning to think they will never accept her. They've started avoiding me too, because I'm friends with her.

"Okay, so we won't go to evening recreation," I say. "What do you want to do instead?"

"I thought we could use the black jumpsuits and helmets again," she says quietly.

That is the last thing I thought she'd want to do. After what we saw the day before yesterday, I never thought Katrina would want to use those jumpsuits and helmets ever again.

She is already heading toward the box with jumpsuits and helmets, so I follow her. When she finds the right box and opens it up, her forehead wrinkles. "Two of them are missing."

I peer over her shoulder. Sure enough, only two jumpsuits remain in the box. "Maybe Hanson took them," I say.

"If someone takes these ones away too, then we won't be able to do this anymore," Katrina says.

"Maybe that's a good thing," I murmur.

"If we learn from these it will make us stronger," she says.

That's what Seven said to us, but I think she was just trying to find the good in something bad. I don't feel any stronger after seeing the war that came here to this base. That only made me concerned that it could happen again.

But Katrina wants to do this. She's already putting on a jumpsuit. I grab the other jumpsuit and pull it on. Then I put a helmet over my head. The menu appears in front of me, and I scroll through the long list of numbers. It's like trying to pick a book from the library without even a title to guide you.

"Which one should we choose?" I ask Katrina.

"I've already seen the fourth one," she says softly.

"When?" *Did she come here without me?*

"When it really happened," she says.

"How do you know?"

"The numbers," she says. "They're GPS coordinates, date, and time."

I'm not sure what "GPS coordinates" are, but as I look down the list of options, it becomes clear that she is right about the dates and times. The fourth option occurred on June twenty-seventh of this year just after midnight. "What happened on June twenty-seventh?" I ask.

"That's when my community was destroyed," she says. After that, she is quiet for a while, so long that I wonder if she is crying. I suppose I could lean forward and look at her face, but that feels too intrusive.

"You okay?" I finally ask her.

"I want to do the June twenty-seventh one," she says.

"Are you sure?" I ask.

"I'm sure."

I nod even though she probably isn't looking at me. "Okay."

Her thick glove grips onto my thick glove. "While we're in there, don't let go of me."

My heart speeds up again. "I won't."

My screen goes dark. *Katrina must have made a selection for the both of us.*

I wait for the light to come, but it doesn't. And then I hear heavy footsteps against rough ground. That's when I realize that it isn't completely dark. A soldier dressed all in black is standing close to me. In his hands is a weapon that he points straight ahead, at a bunch of dark-colored buildings.

Katrina gestures to a building on the far right. "That's

where I used to live."

The soldier crouches down behind a large rock. He's pointing his weapon above the buildings now. At a tree. His finger presses against his weapon and, without warning, something large falls from the tree and crashes to the ground. At first I think it's a big branch, but then I see that it's a man. He looks dead.

"Why was that man in the tree?" I ask.

"He was one of our sentries," Katrina whispers. "They were supposed to guard our community from invaders."

The soldier points his weapon back at the buildings, and he speaks softly, "Alpha clear."

Above my head, there is a flash of darkness. I look up and see that the sky is filling with aerial drones, but not *little* drones, like the ones that filled the sky in the place where I used to live. These are *giant* drones, like the ones that took us from our box to the beach.

I point at the sky. "Look at all those drones."

"They're coming to hurt us," Katrina says.

She starts walking forward, and I go with her. The sky now looks menacing in a way that tells me to turn and run away, but instead we go further and further ahead, under the drone-filled sky.

"Where are we heading?" I ask Katrina.

"To my house."

She glances at the sky and starts moving faster, so fast that she's almost running. Suddenly, at least a half-dozen drones descend. The power in the air around them pushes us away so forcefully that I have to fight to go forward. One of the drones lands just a few yards away from us. The back of it drops down, and soldiers wearing helmets and black jumpsuits pour out. I can't see their faces through their helmets. Instead, their helmets reflect what they see, like mirrors, rather than windows. Katrina and I are close enough that we should be in the reflection, but we aren't. We weren't here when this really happened. I was in my box, and Katrina was inside the house that is next to us.

The soldiers send forth a swarm of tiny drones that race to one wall of Katrina's house. Very quickly, they attach themselves to the wall, in the shape of an arch. An instant later, the portion of the wall inside the arch silently dissolves. Three soldiers with long weapons move into the house, and we follow them. In the bed is a woman wearing a plain pink dress: Maria.

A soldier grabs Maria's left forearm with his hand—right where her chip would be if she has one, and she should have one because she was once a warrior. After a moment, the soldier nods, and then he speaks, "Maria Singh, my name is Lieutenant Boyle. I have orders to extract you."

"I don't want to be extracted," Maria says. "I have friends and family here. I have children."

The soldiers don't seem to notice that she's talking. They roughly take hold of her hands and feet and lift her struggling body.

"I said no!" Maria shouts.

Suddenly, the door to Maria's room flings open. Katrina is standing there, wearing what looks like the same dress that she wore on the day we met. The dress is perfectly intact though, not soiled or damaged at all. Across the hallway is a room that I recognize instantly. It's the room that Katrina drew in her picture at school, every detail exactly as she drew it.

Stacy and Noah rush out of the room, racing toward Maria, crying, "Mommy! Mommy!"

Katrina protectively pushes her younger siblings behind her.

"We've got three small children here," one of the soldiers tells Lieutenant Boyle.

"Neutralize them," Lieutenant Boyle growls.

"DO NOT HARM MY CHILDREN!" Maria shouts at him.

As a soldier points his weapon at Katrina, my heart feels like it will leap from my chest. I start toward him, ready to attack. The real Katrina pulls me back just before a furious cry of pain pierces my chest, and the image of her falls to the ground. Through blurred eyes, I watch as Stacy and Noah also fall, and then Lieutenant Boyle points his weapon at Maria, silencing her screams of heartbreak.

As the soldiers leave the room, the walls around us darken. The images of Katrina and her brother and sister fade. An invisible wall drags us outside the house, where the drone that landed here a few minutes ago is beginning to ascend. Two other drones ascend nearby.

"We can only see what the soldiers see," I realize. "But why can we still see out here if they're leaving?"

"Because they're still here." Katrina points to soldiers standing at regular intervals not far away from us, surrounding the buildings. "They're not done."

A horrible sound comes from close by, like something large and heavy has fallen out of the sky, shaking the ground with its impact. I look in the direction of the noise. The building that was once standing next to Katrina's house is now collapsed.

"It's starting." Even though Katrina is still holding onto my hand, she suddenly sounds very far away.

Horrible sounds are now happening one after the other, and building after building is falling as if crushed by a giant foot slamming down from the sky. And then Katrina's house falls as well.

"There I am," she breathes, bringing us back toward her fallen home.

Ahead of us once again is the image of Katrina, under a fallen wall. Her hands bleed as she lifts and tosses aside the mangled things on the ground. And then, I see Stacy.

"Where's Mommy?" Stacy cries.

"I'm here," Katrina says. Her voice is shaking. "I've got you."

"Noah's over there," Stacy says, pointing under another broken wall.

Katrina starts digging again, scraping herself up even more in the process. I move forward to help her, but the real Katrina won't release my hand. "There's nothing you can do," she says.

She's right. What happened here already happened. There's nothing I can do to make this better.

After what feels like hours, Katrina uncovers Noah. She pulls him onto her hip, as if she's done it a thousand times. His body is limp. He looks dead.

"Where's Mommy?" Stacy asks.

Another tremendous sound rings out, and a nearby building is crushed.

"Mommy!" Stacy calls out.

"Hush," Katrina says to her. "We need to go to the

tunnels. We need to do like Mommy and Daddy told us."

"My legs won't work," Stacy says tearfully. "The man hurt them."

"I'll carry you." Katrina pulls Stacy onto her other hip, wincing from some unseen pain. Now, carrying both her brother and sister, Katrina ducks under a broken wall, and she disappears.

The Katrina who is beside me starts walking fast, away from her house. "I was shot in the arm. He got Stacy in the back. Noah got shot in the head, but not deep enough to stop his breathing. I don't know whether the soldier had bad aim or he didn't intend to kill us." Another smash comes and we look back. The area where Katrina's house once stood is now completely flat. Katrina inhales sharply. "I guess he was pretty sure we'd end up dead either way."

Katrina and I stand fixed to one spot, watching as the buildings are flattened by blow after invisible blow. Until the buildings aren't buildings anymore. Then the drones in the sky disperse, leaving only a few remaining.

The soldiers on the periphery move forward, holding their weapons threateningly in front of them. As Katrina and I follow the soldiers toward what remains of the homes, the bellies of the drones that are still hovering in the sky open up, and a swarm of smaller aerial drones—each about half the size of a bedroom capsule—descend.

The capsule-drones fly slowly over the ruins. One of them comes to a stop and a set of doors opens on its underside. Vicious-looking claws emerge and pick through the rubble, then a different type of equipment emerges: rows of giant forks that extend from each side of the drone. The drone retrieves a large object with the forks and places it inside its capsule. The same thing happens with another other capsule-drone further away.

"What are they collecting?" I ask softly.

We move toward the closest capsule-drone and watch it dig. After clearing a deep hole, its forks reach down and emerge with ... a body. A man, bloody and bent and limp. The drone swallows the man inside itself and then, a moment later, the belly opens again just slightly and gray sand falls from the forks' empty tines.

"They're burning the bodies," Katrina says.

She starts walking again, skirting the perimeter of the destruction. Finally, she stops. We're waiting for something, but I'm not sure what. Katrina is mostly staring straight ahead, although occasionally her gaze shifts to our surroundings. I feel her stiffen as a capsule-drone approaches. The drone starts digging. It isn't long before its forks emerge and pull a lifeless body from the ruins.

The body isn't very big. It's a girl, maybe the same age as us. Her hair is light brown, and her arms and legs are quite thin, exactly like Katrina's.

"Her name was August," Katrina says. "She was my best friend. I wanted to know for sure if she was ..." She can't seem to bring herself to finish.

The capsule-drone releases a small amount of gray sand onto the rubble.

Katrina wipes her face with the back of her hand and takes note of a nearby soldier who has just opened a hatch on the ground.

"Come on," Katrina says to me.

We follow the soldier down a ladder and end up in a narrow hallway. Ahead of us, I see movement: a woman in a soiled white dress.

The soldier flips open a small compartment strapped to his forearm. Tiny drones zoom into the air. One races to the woman. It lands on the back of her head and she instantly falls to the ground. Then the drone lifts off into the air again, and goes looking for its next victim.

"They're hunting for survivors," Katrina says.

"How come they didn't find you?" I ask.

"I ran through a tunnel that goes into the forest. When it let us out, I kept running until we got to our rally point," she says. "I never looked back. I figured we were on our own. I figured everyone except us was dead. I was pretty much right."

Katrina's wounded eyes look into mine. I've never known anyone as brave as Katrina. No one in our box ever really had to be brave; our box was very safe. Katrina lived her whole life up here above the sky. Where wars kill people. Where the people who were supposed to be protecting my family hurt hers.

Katrina rests her head against my shoulder.

I stay strong while she cries.

FRIDAY, JULY 8
1803

SEVEN

After work, Ten and I head to the brig. We only have about a half hour before dinner, but Ten feels that will be plenty of time to meet with his mother. He intends his meeting with her to be quite short, just long enough to get close enough to her to pull her code.

As we walk, I sense the tension in Ten's gait. His breathing is stiff and forced.

"It's probably best if you stay in the waiting area," he says to me.

"I want to come with you." I can't let Ten face his mother alone.

"She's evil," Ten whispers. "I don't want ..."

I wait for Ten to finish, but he doesn't. Finally, I ask, "You don't want what?"

He shakes his head. "She can't physically hurt anyone anymore, but I have no idea what she'll say, what she'll do."

I close the distance between us and press my palm to his. "Whatever happens, I want to be with you."

The rest of our walk is in silence. When we arrive at the steps of the brig, a soldier escorts us inside. The brig is a cold, sterile place. It reminds me somewhat of a hospital, but without the compassion. We remain in a waiting room until two soldiers retrieve us and walk us to a small room with two chairs and a window that looks into another room with only one chair.

A few minutes after we sit down in the hard metal chairs, Ten's mother is led into the other room by two soldiers. Her appearance sends an icy chill into my stomach. Her eyes are sunken. Her lips are cracked and bleeding. She wears a thick black band around her neck and a loose-fitting yellow jumpsuit. Her arms and legs tremble a little. I wonder if her appearance is due to something that has been done to her or something she has done to herself. Ten seems unfazed by his mother's haggard appearance. Perhaps she looked this way when he saw her last.

She barely looks at us as she takes a seat on the metal chair bolted to the floor of her room. "What do you want?" she croaks.

"To say goodbye," Ten says.

His mother looks up. I think I see concern in her eyes. "Why?" she asks.

"I don't plan to see you again," he says.

She looks away. "Why not?"

"Because I hate you."

His words send a jolt of shock through me. I've never heard Ten—or anyone else—make such a negative statement as this. Hate toward another person isn't something that we were ever allowed to express back home. The strongest negative statement we were allowed to utter was, "You displeased me by your actions." But hate is certainly an appropriate sentiment for Ten to have about his mother after what she did.

Ten's mother's eyes fill with tears. "I love you, Two Thousand Ten, and I always will."

Ten's mother doesn't look evil to me; she looks pitiful. It's hard to believe that she's the same woman who planned to send her baby granddaughter off to be murdered. And who tried to destroy the box where we lived and everyone inside it. But it's also hard to believe that she is the same woman who once shared a dinner table with my family. And who I once allowed to hold my child. Her words now are the words of the latter woman rather than the former one. But which woman is she? Is it possible that she is both?

Ten stands and steps toward the window. Slowly and deliberately, he puts his palms against the glass. I am instantly reminded of the times when he used to do that back home as we gazed at each other through the windows of our families' domiciles. I would put my palms on the glass of my window and imagine that my hands were touching his.

His mother rises to her feet and struggles to take the tiny step to the window. Without being prompted, she gently places her palms against the glass, and she closes her eyes.

What is she thinking? Is she imagining that she is touching the hands of her child? Is there love in her heart or hate? I wish I knew. So I'd know what to feel.

Ten lowers his hands and turns away from the window, fighting not to release the tears that are pooled in his eyes. He wipes his face with his fist and I see him glance at the navigator on his wrist. He looks at me and nods. *Mission accomplished.*

Suddenly, without warning, on the other side of the glass, Ten's mother crumples to the ground. Her soldiers step forward, but rather than dragging her back to her feet or to the chair, one of them presses his fingers to her neck, and then she shouts, "We need a medic in here! Now!"

FRIDAY, JULY 8
1819

TEN

I spin around and look back through the barred window. My mother's body now lies inert on the ground. Both of the soldiers in the room are hunched over her.

My first thought is that the soldiers must have activated her stim collar, but why would they do that? Did she make some sort of threatening move when I turned my back to her?

My second thought is that this is just one of my mother's many manipulations. Her final desperate effort to try to hurt me.

One of the soldiers in my mother's room places his hands together on the center of my mother's chest and pushes down. Then he pushes down again, and again. It takes me a moment to realize what he is doing. Professor Adam taught us to do this if a person collapses suddenly and shows no signs of life. Compressing the chest in this manner pumps blood through the body to provide oxygen to the brain until medical personnel arrive to render aid. It's called Manual Cardiac Compression.

If the soldiers are doing this to my mother, it can only mean one thing.

My mother's heart has stopped.

FRIDAY, JULY 8
1820

SEVEN

"Please return to the waiting room," one of our soldiers says to us.

Ten ignores her and so do I.

On the other side of the window, two medics descend on Ten's mother. They open her jumpsuit and slide a medical device beneath her undershirt.

"Asystole," the device announces, as if it is announcing the time of day. "Resume cardiac massage."

One of the medics slips a resuscitation sleeve around Ten's mother's chest and the other inserts a breathing tube into her throat. Soon she is covered with various medical devices and all of her vital functions are being performed by machines.

I don't want to see this.

Ten's mother is dying.

I stay only because Ten does.

FRIDAY, JULY 8
1822

TEN

None of this seems real. It doesn't seem possible that, on the other side of this window, my mother is dying.

Her room fills with medical personnel who seem to be trying hard to save her life, as if she is any other human being in need of assistance. But why are they working so diligently to save a dangerous criminal? Aren't there others more deserving of their assistance? Will the commander call off their efforts? Does he want to rid himself of this problem, just as my mother wanted to rid herself of us? Or perhaps he doesn't want her to die just yet. Perhaps he wants her to die on his terms.

It is as if I am held by some invisible force to the spot where I stand. Seven is beside me. I feel her presence, but I don't look at her. I don't know how to look at her right now. I don't know how I feel. Just days ago, the scene before me would have broken my heart, but now …

My mind draws me back to the moment when I said goodbye to my mother before I left for Up Here. I thought then that I would never see her again. If everything had gone according to her plan, I never would have. I never would have known when she died. I suppose I always would have thought of her as living, even long after she was most certainly dead. I always would have remembered her as a caring mother.

I long to think of my mother that way now, but I can't. Because I know the truth.

I wish that truth wasn't the truth.

I wish my mother was the person I'd thought her to be.

I wish—

"You're her son?" A doctor on the other side of the window is speaking to me.

"Yes, I am," I say.

The doctor exhales. "I'm Doctor Keller," she says. "Our scans of your mother have indicated the etiology for her sudden deterioration." As she speaks, she turns a screen so I can see it. I know enough about human anatomy to immediately notice that something is horribly wrong with the images before me. "Your mother suffered a massive dissection and rupture of the aorta, causing acute catastrophic loss of most of her circulating blood volume. Her condition is not amenable to resuscitation and is incompatible with life."

I look at my mother again. Her skin has lost any hint of vitality. On her heart monitor, instead of electrical impulses, there is a flat line. She is dead.

The doctor continues, "We will continue to attempt to support her vital functions until your father has been notified."

A few minutes later, my dad arrives. I half-listen as the doctor gently repeats what she already told me—the explanation of my mother's unexpected demise. Mostly though, I just stare at what is left of my mother, unable to draw my focus away.

"Son," my father says softly.

I turn toward him and he directs my attention to the doctor.

"Is there anything you'd like to say or do before we discontinue our resuscitative efforts," the doctor asks me.

I'm not sure how to respond to that. How would I have responded days ago? Before I came across my mother in the control hub, plotting to destroy us. Would I have begged the doctor to keep trying? Would I have refused to believe that my mother's life was over?

Is it wrong that I feel relief now that my mother's life is over?

"No," I say.

FRIDAY, JULY 8
1902

SEVEN

Ten's father stayed behind at the brig to complete some forms. He asked us not to tell Ten's sister what has happened. He wants to give her one final night of her childhood before he tells her the truth.

Ten and I head to the mess hall to meet up with Ryan. Ten is planning to go to the bunker with him, so he can work on reactivating the robots.

"I'm sure Ryan will understand if you don't want to work tonight," I say as we walk fast.

Ten shakes his head. "I have to go. There's a good chance that the code I pulled will only be active for a limited time. It's the last code I'll ever get from her. It could be my last chance to ..."

"Right."

Ten is trying so hard to make things right.

I just wish that was possible.

FRIDAY, JULY 8
1912

TEN

When we enter the mess hall, Ryan is the only one there. "Let's get going," he says to me.

I turn to Seven. "I'll be back as soon as I can. At least by breakfast."

Her eyes look worried, but she says, "Okay."

Ryan leads me at a brisk pace away from the mess hall. "What was the hold up?" he asks casually. "You missed dinner."

"My mom died," I murmur.

He stops walking and turns toward me. "Are you serious?"

"Yes."

"I'm so sorry."

The way Ryan looks at me makes me feel like I might lose my composure. I didn't cry when my mom died, but I feel like I might now, because of the way Ryan is looking at me. The strong compassion in his eyes burns into my heart, making it ache with pain. Pain, not because of what I lost today, but because of the loss of all that could have been.

Before I can say or do anything, we are interrupted by echoing words from the speakers above us, spoken with the kind of intensity that invokes instant dread, "All hands report immediately to your duty stations. Those not assigned report to the mess hall without delay." The same words are repeated once more, followed by dead silence.

"What's going on?" I ask Ryan.

"I have no idea," he says, and then he straightens his shoulders and starts once again toward the bunker, taking me with him.

FRIDAY, JULY 8
1918

SEVEN

My heart leaps into my throat. Minutes ago, Ten went off with Ryan to the bunker, and now there is some kind of emergency. Part of me wants to run after them, but the possible routes are numerous enough that I'm not sure if I could find them. More importantly, I need to go find our baby.

Instead of following the orders broadcast over the announcement system, I continue into the barracks, looking for Six. I find her in the jumble of people who have spilled into the barrack's hallway. In her arms is Fifty-two.

"Where have you been?" Six asks me. "I was worried that—"

"Ten needed me," I answer honestly, but I don't elaborate.

"Do you know what's going on?" she asks me, her eyes anxious.

Our former Decision Maker just died.

All of the robots are completely shut down and we can't figure out how to get them started up again.

Lots of things are going on, but I don't know what has lead to the urgent order for us to muster. "Let's just get to the mess hall," I say, deflecting her question.

Six and I join the tide of people. It isn't long before we're in the mess hall, surrounded by the worried faces of the others from our box. Most of the military personnel aren't here. I suppose they have duties during emergency situations. That leaves the mess hall filled with the people from back home, including the current and former warriors.

No one seems to know what to do. It's hard to know what to do when you don't know what you're facing. I sit down on a chair next to my sister, at a table with my family. And we silently wait.

FRIDAY, JULY 8
1922

FORTY-ONE

When adults are worried, they keep their kids close to them. Right now, my mom and dad are keeping me very close. Luckily, my parents are friends with my best friends' parents, so Forty-seven and Katrina are close to me too.

Forty-seven brought a deck of plasticards with her, so Forty-seven, Katrina, and I put our chairs in a triangle, so we can play cards. Without talking. It seems that is the rule right now. No talking, only listening.

FRIDAY, JULY 8
1924

TEN

The inside of the bunker is filled with frenetic activity. I stay by Ryan's side as he moves into the room and approaches a soldier.

"What's happening?" he asks her.

"The base is on lockdown," she says. "We have an unknown, unmanned drone bearing zero six two CBDR. If it continues on its current course, it is expected to enter our airspace in ten minutes." She gestures to a monitor that shows a small red dot that must represent the drone. The dot is traveling fast toward green borders that must represent our location.

Ryan's forehead creases. "Any additional intel?" he asks.

The soldier zooms in on a still image of the drone. "It's a military drone, but its identification number indicates that it isn't one of ours."

"So it's either a stolen drone that's controlled by the enemy," Ryan says, "or it's from another military base that may or may not consider us to be an enemy."

"The commander has already given it a warning times three," a male soldier says. "He's looking to shoot the thing down the moment it enters our airspace."

"What's *our* plan?" Ryan's voice rises over the din, and everyone in the room seems to take note of his presence now, even as they continue their work.

"If the commander shoots it down, there'll be nothing to do," the same soldier says. "They'll dissect it in the lab and try to figure out its origins."

Another soldier pipes in, "If they don't end up shooting it down, the commander's plan is to attempt to follow it home. He has escorts on it already, but there's no way the drone will go home with escorts. It will definitely do evasive maneuvers until it loses any sign of followers, so I doubt the commander is going to get any useful information about where the drone came from."

Ryan starts toward a cabinet. "Who's our best pilot?" he asks as he walks.

"Davis," everyone in the room says.

Ryan exhales. "How about someone who isn't locked up in the brig?"

"That'd be Santiago," one of the soldiers says. I follow his gaze to a woman sitting on the edge of a table.

Ryan retrieves a controller from the cabinet, synchs it with a monitor, and hands the controller to Santiago. Then Ryan opens a small gray box. Inside is the tiniest drone I've ever seen, less than a centimeter in diameter.

"Where'd you get that?" Santiago asks, her mouth agape.

Ryan gives her a tight smile. "That's classified." He deposits the tiny drone in Santiago's hand. "You've got four minutes. Think you can learn how to pilot this thing?"

"No problem." Santiago takes control of the tiny drone,

causing it to lift up into the air. She deftly begins to fly it about the room.

"The mosquito drone can attach to our intruder and follow it back home undetected," Ryan explains as he sends up a larger drone, controlling it himself with a second device. "If you can get the mosquito within three centimeters of the target drone, it can attach."

Santiago and Ryan fly their drones in the small confines of the bunker. If I didn't know better, I would compare them to two kids enjoying a game of chase-the-drone, but their mission is extremely serious. Whoever has sent the invading drone toward us may be intending to cause us harm. The unwelcome drone could be a sign that we are in imminent danger.

A soldier pokes her head out of the room that Seven and I shared yesterday. "Ryan, I need you in here," she says.

Without seeming to give it much thought—and probably because everyone else in the room is busy with their tasks—Ryan hands the controls of the larger drone over to me. Santiago has already been able to get her mosquito close enough to attach to Ryan's drone several times now, and so I guess Ryan isn't concerned that Santiago needs more practice.

I am wondering whether I should just land Ryan's drone when Santiago says, "Go ahead. Show me what you've got."

I give myself a moment to get my bearings. It isn't difficult. The controls are almost exactly like those of the toy drones back home. After a few seconds, I'm successfully zipping around the room.

"Hey, kid, you're good!" one of the soldiers says to me.

I can't see Santiago's mosquito drone on my monitor, but it hardly matters, because I need all of my concentration to maneuver around the tight quarters of the bunker and—

"Okay, show's over," Santiago says. "Time to focus on the real mission."

I land my drone on an empty table.

Santiago lands the mosquito drone on the palm of her hand. "Who wants to take the mosquito outside?" she asks.

"I'll do it," someone offers.

As Santiago absorbs herself with the information on her monitor, Ryan returns and points me in the direction of an unoccupied computer inside the small room that he just emerged from. "You can use that workstation," he says. "It's all set up with the data from the robot. I'm going to be busy for a while here, but let me know if you need anything."

Although I am interested to watch the current mission, I need to get to work. I don't know how long my mother's code will grant me access—or even if it will work at all— and I want to get back to Seven as soon as possible. It troubles me that I'm not with her and Fifty-two when a threat is in our midst.

As I work, I overhear plenty of conversation in the main room. Santiago is flying the mosquito drone toward the invader drone, and the invader drone is closing in on us. The commander is giving warning after warning to the intruder drone, but it ignores every one.

The excitement rises in the other room. The mosquito drone is very near to its target. Santiago is trying to get it near enough to attach. She got close. Close, but not close enough. Another try. No. No luck. Someone shouts that they should give "the kid" a try. My cheeks burn. *Are they talking about me?* I try to focus on my work until … cheers. *Santiago did it!*

It gets quiet after that. I wish I knew what was happening. Is the invader drone still heading toward us? It must assume that we will not allow it to advance into our airspace. What are its intentions?

I wipe these questions from my mind and return my attention to the task at hand. I've finally arrived at my mother's hidden log in screen. I slip my warrior necklace from around my neck, place it near the sensor on the screen, and hold my breath.

The screen changes.

My eyes go wide and I exhale.

The code works!

I'm in.

FRIDAY, JULY 8
1958

FORTY-ONE

It has been almost half an hour since the commander spoke to us here in the mess hall. He told us that there's a drone heading toward us and we don't know whether it is a friend or a foe. He said not to worry though. We have so many protections on this base that, even if it is a bad drone, it won't be able to hurt us. He told us that he asked us to gather here in the mess hall so that he can keep us informed of what is happening. We aren't in any danger at all. That's what he said.

After that, Forty-seven, Katrina, and I went back to occupying ourselves with our card game, but I kept my attention focused on everything going on around me. Just in case the commander was wrong about us not being in danger.

All of a sudden, I see a flicker of light. I turn quickly and see the commander—or rather a big three-dimensional image of him—hovering over the center of the room again. "Ladies and gentlemen, may I have your attention," he says, but he didn't really need to say that. He already has everyone's attention.

He smiles awkwardly and speaks again, "I am pleased to

inform you that, after providing a show-of-force to our visitor, the invading drone altered its course and it is now retreating from our location. I ask that you return to your barracks at this time. In the event of any further occurrences that require your attention, you will be provided with muster instructions. Thank you for your cooperation this evening, and have a good night."

Slowly, people begin to stand and shuffle toward the door, as if they're not quite certain whether they should go, despite the commander's clear instructions. My family, Forty-seven and her father, and Katrina's mother and siblings walk toward the barracks as one group. The adults are talking more now, but it's the nervous kind of talking that grown-ups do when they're worried about something and they don't want to let on that they're troubled.

"I'm glad that's over," Katrina says quietly. "I was beginning to think my worst fears were going to come true."

"You shouldn't worry," Forty-seven responds. "We're safe here."

I try to smile in agreement, but I can't. We're supposed to feel safe, but I don't feel that way anymore. Maybe the commander is right that one drone couldn't harm us, but what if the bad people come back with more drones, or with other things that can hurt us? I've seen that happen with my own eyes. What's to stop it from happening again?

As we exit the mess hall, a soldier reminds us to return directly to our barracks. His presence makes me uneasy. Up until recently, I thought of soldiers as people and robots who keep us safe, but when I look at them now, I feel distrust. How can I look at them as defenders when I've seen them hurt innocent children?

Once we are inside the barracks, people vanish into their dormitories. Maria quickly guides Stacy, Noah, and Katrina to their dormitory, barely giving them a chance to wish Forty-seven and me goodnight.

At the door to my dormitory, Forty-seven pauses. "Do you want to play a game before bed?" she asks me.

I glance at my parents and they nod their approval. I haven't spent much time with Forty-seven lately and so, even though I'm very tired, I say, "Sure."

I follow Forty-seven and her dad into their dormitory, something I could never do back home. But it seems to be okay here.

"Do you want to play with us, Dad?" she asks her father.

"I think I'll rest," he says.

He surely needs some rest. The skin under his eyes is puffy and his eyes are red. It almost looks like he's been crying.

Forty-seven retrieves a game as her father lies down on one of the beds. We sit atop her bed with the game between us. It's called Battleship. For a while, we just play, quietly whispering letters and numbers to each other and noting whether or not our ships have been hit, or missed, or sunken. Then Forty-seven's dad begins to snore.

"I'm glad he's asleep," Forty-seven says. "He hasn't slept much since we got here. I think he's worried about my mom."

"Have you heard from her?" I ask. The last time we talked about this, Forty-seven hadn't seen or heard from her mother since before the evacuation. Forty-seven's dad explained that she had important duties to accomplish, and that Forty-seven shouldn't worry, because her mom was safe here on the base. But that doesn't seem right. Even if she had important duties, she'd need to sleep. Everyone else sleeps in the barracks. Where does Forty-seven's mom sleep?

"I keep asking my dad if I can see her, even just for a few minutes, and he keeps saying she's busy," she says softly. "I don't understand how she could be so busy that she doesn't want to see me." Her voice quivers.

"She must be doing something very important," I say, trying to comfort her. Forty-seven's mom is an administrator, so her job is an essential one. But I've seen all of other administrators in the mess hall with their families. It doesn't really make sense that Forty-seven's mom isn't here with us too.

Tears come to Forty-one's eyes. "What could she be doing that's *that* important?"

Guilt seeps into me. Forty-one's mother has completely disappeared from her life. And I've been spending almost all of my free time with Katrina. I thought Katrina needed me the most, but maybe Forty-seven needed me more.

"I'm sorry I haven't been around much lately," I apologize.

"We're still friends, right?" she asks timidly.

"Of course we are," I say. "Nothing has changed."

"*Everything* has changed, Forty-one."

"A lot has changed, but not everything."

"What if one of us goes back under the ground, and the other one stays up here?" she asks.

"You think they'll let us stay up here?" I ask.

"My dad said they might let people decide for

themselves," she says quietly.

"Does your dad want to stay here?" I ask.

"He said maybe," she says. "Do *you* want to stay here?"

I consider what will happen to me if we are given that choice. The answer is simple. My parents will choose for our family to be together. Them, Six, Seven, and me. Six will surely choose to return to our box. Seven and Ten will probably want to go back to our box too, because it's safer for their baby. If Six and Seven go back to the box, my parents will surely follow, and that means I will too. I must do as my parents wish.

But if I could make my own decision, what would I want? To return to the security of our box or remain among the wonders of Up Here? It's scary up here, but it's also amazing. I think I would like to live up here. But would I choose Up Here if it meant losing Seven and Six and my parents?

"I don't know," I say.

Just a moment, even though it bothers me to think it, I wish I had the Decision Makers to tell me what's right.

FRIDAY, JULY 8
2035

SEVEN

I have just finished settling Fifty-two down for the night when there is a knock on my dormitory door. It is a bit late for visitors but, considering the events of this evening, I imagine that my parents or Six might have come to privately discuss everything that is going on.

I go to the door and open it as quietly as possible, so as not to disturb Fifty-two. Instead of my family, I am surprised to find Thirteen and Nineteen standing there in the hallway. Back at the old warrior compound, the three of us would occasionally visit one another's quarters, but this is the first time either of them has visited me at the new base.

"Can we come in?" Nineteen asks.

"Yes, of course," I say, but as I move aside to let them enter, I feel unnerved about allowing them inside, because I know they will see Fifty-two sleeping here in my dormitory. That will no doubt invite questions.

As I suspected, their gazes immediately go to Fifty-two's box.

"Oh, how precious!" Thirteen says, smiling at my sleeping baby.

Nineteen looks at me. "Why do you have a baby in here?" she asks.

"It's her niece," Thirteen says.

"Why isn't she with Seven and Nine?" Nineteen asks.

Her question is a good one, and I suppose it was inevitable. Fifty-two has spent every night here with Ten and me, rather than with my sister or Nine. Eventually someone was bound to discover this.

Thirteen's gaze is more curious than challenging. Is that just her nature, or does she somehow know why Fifty-two is here with me? Over the past few days, she and Nine have been spending a lot of time together. I wonder for a moment if Nine has told Thirteen the truth about baby Fifty-two, but something inside me feels certain that he hasn't. Nine would never tell my secret.

I look into Thirteen's eyes and then Nineteen's. Not long ago, the two of them helped Six and me switch places, although they had no idea that they were doing so at the time. They risked their safety for my sake, even when they didn't know why they needed to do so. They knew only that I needed their help. And they willingly gave it.

I used to think that secrets were safest when they were known by only a few, but I am beginning to believe that sometimes secrets are more secure when they are known by many. Some secrets are safest when they are surrounded by a protective circle of trust.

And so I ask my friends to sit and, very softly, I tell them the truth, "On our Assignment Day, *I* was paired with Nine, and *my sister* was assigned to be a warrior. But I came up here, and Six stayed in our box."

"You switched identities," Thirteen says, her jaw slack.

I nod and continue, "Up here, Ten and I mated, and I became pregnant. I went back to our box to deliver our baby. To ensure that she would be safe. Then I came back up here, so my sister could remain in the box. To ensure that she would be safe too."

"So you're *Seven*?" Nineteen asks, incredulous. "And this is *your* baby?"

"Yes," I say. "And I need you to keep my secret."

They give their response with a look of utter shock, but without any hesitation at all, "Of course."

FRIDAY, JULY 8
2319

SIX

I haven't felt this alone since I woke up in The White Room for the very first time. *This* is a different kind of alone though. Back then, my aloneness was imposed upon me because I was a prisoner of the Outsiders. Now, I have a choice.

I go across the hall and tap on Jose's door.

"Come on in," he says.

My heart quickens as I slide open the door and find him in bed, reading by the light of his flashlight. He's wearing an undershirt, and his lower half is hidden under the covers. His blue jumpsuit is neatly folded on an empty bedframe.

"I'm sorry," I say. "I guess it's kind of late. I shouldn't be disturbing you."

He shakes his head. "You're not disturbing me."

"I just … I couldn't sleep," I explain.

"Me neither." He puts his book down on the bed. The book's cover is so tattered that I can't make out the image or title.

"You found a new book?" I ask.

He nods. "It's called *The Hunger Games*. It's pretty intense."

"As intense as real life?" I ask.

"I guess not."

"Do you … want to play chess?" I ask him.

He props himself up a bit more in the bed. "Let me put some clothes on."

"Okay."

I start to leave, but he adds, "You don't need to go. It'll just take me a few seconds."

And so I shut the door and remain in the room with him, keeping my back to him as he dresses.

Seconds later he says, "All set."

I turn and find him standing beside his bed, now wearing his blue jumpsuit. I still can't get over how strange it is to see him dressed just like the people back home.

Jose is so unlike everyone back home. That's part of what I like about him. He sees life differently. In a lot of ways, I like the way he sees life.

Jose straightens his bed and places the chess set on top of it. We sit on either side of the chessboard and begin to set out the pieces.

"Aside from the *event* this evening, how was your day?" he asks me.

"Good, I guess," I say. "When I'm working in the hospital, I feel like I'm back home, enclosed in a safe little space where everything goes the way it's supposed to."

"It must be nice when everything goes the way it's supposed to," he says.

I instantly regret what I said. Life must seem so unfair to Jose. Over the past few months, he lost his father, his friends, and his entire community. "I'm sorry, I—"

"You have nothing to apologize for." He gestures to the

chessboard. "You go first."

I slide my king's pawn to the center of the board. "How was *your* day?" I ask.

"I answered a bunch of questions about the Outsiders, mostly the same ones I've already answered, probably so they can see whether my responses are consistent," he says. "Then they brought in some 'artifacts' they'd recovered from my community and asked me about them."

"That must have been painful."

He shrugs with a hint of resignation. "I need to earn my keep."

I suppose he's right. While Jose isn't technically a prisoner here, he is at the mercy of the military. If the military were to release him, he would face certain death. There is no way anyone could survive on their own. But then again, I suppose we are all in that position. The military could forsake any one of us.

Even under the protection of the military, our safety is far from assured. Who knows what is out there, planning its attack on us? The drone that was spotted tonight could be the first sign of a massive assault on us. We are so weak that we might not be able to put up enough of a fight to survive an attack.

The future of *all* of our lives is precarious.

"Your move," Jose says, breaking me from my thoughts.

I move a bishop forward. "Do you think we're going to survive this?"

"All we can do is try to keep living." He looks down at the chessboard, but I can tell that his thoughts are elsewhere. "You can't spend all your time thinking of the horrible what ifs. You've got to do what's important to you.

Do what makes you happy."

"What makes *you* happy?" I ask him.

"This." He finally looks up and into my eyes. "Playing chess ... with you." He swallows and looks away again.

"This makes me happy too," I say and, although I'm not sure why, tears come to my eyes.

TEN

A collective groan breaks me from my concentration. I fight the urge to go to the door and ask what's going on. There is so much information in front of me that it will take days to pour over it all.

Ryan comes into the room and sits down beside me.

"What happened with the mosquito drone?" I ask him.

"Our mission was a partial success," he says. "We were able to attach to the invader drone. After our military fired a warning shot as a show-of-force, the invader took off in the opposite direction. We hitched a ride on it halfway across the country, but then we lost contact. We know the direction it was heading, and we have the coordinates of where we lost contact, but—"

"Coordinates?" I ask.

"The latitude and longitude on a map," he says. "For the past few days, the military has been combing the United States using surveillance drones, looking for other compounds like ours, but we haven't explored the area where we lost contact with the mosquito as of yet. Santiago works with that team so, when she goes on duty today, she's going to arrange to look at …"

Ryan stops speaking and focuses a screen that I've opened up for him. A map that I found in my mother's files. On the map are tiny red dots that I think represent other compounds. Our compound is marked in blue.

"Where did you find *that*?" he asks as he begins to explore it.

"When I saw my mother today, I pulled her access code," I say. "I logged in as her, and I found a ton of information. I don't know how long we'll be able to view it though. I think her codes are temporary ones; the code I pulled from her in the control hub doesn't work anymore."

"I'll get everyone here working on this right away," Ryan says, but he's preoccupied. He's zooming in now on a specific spot on the map.

"What are you looking for?" I ask.

"This is where we lost contact with the mosquito." As he zooms in, a purple dot appears. It is the only purple dot I've seen on the map. Ryan touches the dot and four capital letters appear. "P, E, O, C," Ryan says, sounding concerned.

"What do those letters mean?" I ask.

"I believe it's an acronym for Presidential Emergency Operations Center," he says. "There are rumored to be at least a dozen of them in various spots throughout the United States. Their locations are highly-classified."

I still don't understand. "What's a Presidential Emergency Operations Center?" I ask. "What do they do there?"

"It's where they take the ultimate Decision Maker—the President of the United States—when they think the world is coming to an end."

SATURDAY, JULY 9
0056

SIX

Jose wins our chess game, but I don't think either of us played at our best. My thoughts kept drifting elsewhere, but not to where I would have expected them to go. Not to my fears and worries about the dangers all around us. My thoughts kept drifting to Jose.

To his eyes. And his lips. To the way it felt when we kissed a few days ago. When I close my eyes, I can still experience that feeling inside me: a feeling that takes over everything else, and makes me happy.

"I think I might finally be able to get some sleep," Jose says as we return the chess pieces to their storage box. It feels like this is goodnight, but I don't want it to be.

"Can I sleep here?" I blurt out.

He glances at me and then looks away. "Yeah, sure," he says, as if I asked him something far less odd. "I can help you bring your mattress—"

"Or we could sleep on the same mattress," I say. "Together."

He nods uncomfortably. "Okay."

Jose doesn't undress and neither do I. He just clicks off his flashlight and we crawl into his bed, under the sheet.

The mattress isn't very big, so our bodies are touching a little. The touching feels both energizing and soothing at the same time. I close my eyes, letting my body feel his touch. Jose is breathing a bit fast.

"Are you nervous?" I ask him.

"A little," he says. "Are you?"

"I don't know," I answer honestly. "This just … feels good."

"It does." Jose reaches over and gently strokes my face, starting at my forehead and slowly running his fingers across my temple and my cheek, and down to my neck. His fingers start to drift lower, but then he lifts them from my skin.

"Why did you stop?" I ask.

"I wasn't sure if …" he starts, but he doesn't finish.

"Do you want to do more?" I ask.

Jose withdraws his hand completely. "Are you asking because you're afraid that I do or afraid that I don't?"

"I'm asking because I want to know the truth," I say.

I feel him inhale. "When I helped you escape from my people, I knew it meant I'd never see you again. I never imagined I would get *this*."

"This?"

"To be friends," he says. "Not because we were forced to be friends, but because we *want* to be. I want to be with you, but only in whatever way feels right for both of us."

"I want to be close to you," I say. "Closer than we are now."

"Physically or emotionally?" he asks.

"Both," I say.

I lift my hand and bring it to the zipper at the neck of

Jose's jumpsuit. A jumpsuit just like mine, but different because it hides the secrets of Jose's body. I hold my hand there, frozen in space, and I look into his eyes, searching for his consent.

His hand meets mine at the top of his jumpsuit and, hesitantly, he reveals his body to me. Slowly, cautiously, I reveal mine to him. In the gentle light that glows through the window, his hands and fingers and lips explore my body, and mine explore his. When I did this with Three, it felt so right, but doing this with Jose feels right also. It feels almost completely different, but no less right.

I wonder what it would feel like to mate with Jose.

Someday.

But will there be a someday? Who knows what tomorrow will bring, or even the next few hours? Tonight could be our last chance to be together, or it might not be. I can't be sure of anything, except for what is here and now. And here and now, I know exactly what I want, even though maybe I shouldn't want it.

"I want us to mate," I whisper.

"Right now?" he asks quietly.

"Right now." My voice trembles a little. "If you want to."

He looks deep into my eyes and then he nods. "I do."

Our bodies are already undressed, so it doesn't take much effort to prepare for mating. I let Jose fit his body into mine. It hurts, but only a very little. The discomfort is overpowered by a much greater feeling. A feeling that I have no words to describe. It's as if the piece of our friendship that has been missing all this time has finally come into place. Suddenly, I feel as if I can remember every moment that we ever spent together, not the details of what we said and what we did, but *all* of the feelings. I feel how much he cared for me, and how much I cared for him. I feel the pain of losing him, even though I don't remember how it happened.

Jose and I are moving together now like we are one person … walking, then running, then flying. Higher and higher into the night sky … until we reach the stars.

And then the sky bursts open. And Jose empties into me. And his lips find mine again.

We drift down out of the sky, gripping onto each other tightly. Our bodies so very close together. Closer than ever before.

Perhaps afraid to let go.

SATURDAY, JULY 9
0137

TEN

Everyone in the bunker is now tasked with looking over my mother's data. Backups are being created, as well as backups of the backups, because we know we might never be able to log into this system again.

Ryan and I focus on trying to use my mother's information to research what he refers to as "The Utah Compound." Santiago and her team discovered it a few days ago, using the military's surveillance drones. As far as they could tell, the compound is almost exactly like ours. Except that there are no people there. The people seem to have vanished without a trace. Ryan is trying to figure out what happened to them.

Using coordinates, Ryan locates The Utah Compound on my mother's map. The compound has another name there: KSLC. When I search my mother's files for that name, I am presented with numerous results. The first few contain mundane data that isn't very helpful, but then I find a timeline that begins many years ago, back when our own underground compound was established. Based on the countless entries after that, everything was running quite smoothly at Compound KSLC. But the last entry is dated just over two months ago.

I read the final entry aloud, "KSLC Retired."

Ryan turns and looks at my screen. "That's promising."

There's a file attached to that notation, and so I open it, but instead of displaying the file contents, a message appears:

Ready for synch.

"Synch with what?" I ask.

Ryan takes over my monitor for a moment and, after pulling up some information about the file, he answers, "It's a sim."

"A sim," I repeat. "So we can 'experience' it?"

"Apparently," he says.

I rise from my seat. "I'll get some helmets and sim suits."

Ryan puts his hand on my shoulder, stopping me. "Way ahead of you."

He disappears for a moment and returns with a box containing two sim jumpsuits and helmets. He sets down the box and starts putting on a jumpsuit. I grab the other one.

"You don't have to come," Ryan says to me.

"These are my mother's files," I say. "I want to know what's in them."

As I don the jumpsuit, Ryan peppers me with information. "Because of our space limitations here in the bunker, I'll run the program in auto mode. That forces the sim to show us what it considers to be the most important details. You won't be able to walk around and decide where to go, but you can turn and look in any direction."

"Who decides what are the 'most important details'?" I ask.

"It depends," he says. "Sometimes it's automated based on a set of criteria; sometimes an operator edits the footage after the fact."

He pulls on his helmet and I pull on mine, then Ryan puts a gloved hand on my arm. The menu before me disappears, and my screen goes dark.

When the light finally returns, it is dim and blue. I feel as if I am in the restricted hallways back home. But these are likely not the hallways of back home. I assume they are those of The Utah Compound.

I am not stationary. I'm traveling fast … flying … as if I'm riding on a small drone. Clustered in the air around me are what appear to be delivery drones, at least a half-dozen of them. We zip through empty hallways, down one, then the next, and then we approach a large corrugated tunnel. I recognize it instantly, because I spent many hours in a structure that looked exactly the same as this one: the drone tunnel.

I've never been in this part of a drone tunnel before, but the walls here are the same as the walls in the portion of the drone tunnel that Seven and I once used as our retreat, back when we were children. Our private perch high in the sky.

Now, I fly through the tunnel at a dizzying speed, as if on an important mission. Numerous delivery drones emerge from branches of the tunnel and join me on my race, until we burst out beneath the nighttime sky—or, more correctly, a make-believe nighttime sky: dots of light on a tremendous screen.

Below us is the plaza of The Utah Compound. It almost matches our plaza back home, but there are small differences in the layout, just enough that I know that it is not our former home. We don't spend much time here. Our drone makes a quick turn and enters a smaller tunnel.

This tunnel is much darker than the main drone tunnel, but a stripe of blue light on the floor guides our way. We turn this way and that before we come to a stop, and the drone door before us slides open.

We are in a control hub. Like the one back home.

The computer monitors here are alive with activity, but there are no humans or robots in sight. A clock on the wall explains the lack of people; it is after midnight. This place is quite serene with the mesmerizing glow of the monitors and the absence of any sound, but I can't help feeling tense. My only memories of a control hub are bad ones.

The drone that provides our vantage point stays close to the walls—as drones always do inside of public spaces to avoid becoming a nuisance. It finally settles atop a desk in the corner, and spins to face a monitor. The monitor screen goes to black. Then a single word appears on it, so small that I can barely read it:

Synching.

After a minute or so, two words take its place:

Synching complete.

And then the screen goes dark again.

When words appear once more, my heart nearly stops:

Nitroxoflurane flow initiated.
Gas flow: 100%

Nitroxoflurane is a sleeping gas. I know that because I've seen its name before—and I've felt the effects of it—on the day that my mother released it into our box via the drone tunnels, on the day that my mother tried to murder us.

Someone sent this drone to The Utah Compound. They programmed it to kill them.

And I have a horrible feeling that I know who sent it.

This is exactly how my mother planned to exterminate us. But, unlike when this happened to us, there is nothing I can do to stop this. This has already happened. Its outcome is assured. The people here are no doubt in their bedroom capsules, asleep. The gas will ensure that they never wake up.

After a few minutes of staring at the deadly screen, an arrow appears in the lower right of my vision and time appears to race forward.

"What's happening?" I ask, in a daze.

Ryan answers, "I'm jumping ahead. I need to find out a few things."

I don't ask what he's trying to find out. I just watch as the drone that brought us here takes off and makes its way back into the main portion of the compound. Soon, it's daytime and the robots begin to set up for their morning tasks. They take their places in front of the restaurants, waiting for people who will never come. They dutifully hold their positions for a while before they finally abandon them and go to the domiciles, likely searching for answers as to why the people haven't emerged.

A bit later, we find robots carrying lifeless humans through the hallways, to the hospital. There are so many patients that the robots have to lay out the casualties on the hospital floor. Robot nurses attach their patients to IVs and give them oxygen, but none of this seems to help. The nurses appear to be at a loss as to what to do. But they don't stop trying.

A day ends, and then another comes and goes. The people remain comatose. The robots continue to try to remedy the situation, but nothing they do seems to have any effect. Still, they try and try until, suddenly, without warning, the robots become inert.

"Their robots shut down," I say. "Just like our robots."

"Let me check something." Ryan raises one of his hands in the air and makes a swipe, then time moves backward. Once the robots come back to life, time stops and begins to move forward again. "We need to figure out what time it is," Ryan says.

I look around at what is within view. On the corner of a monitor, I spot a timestamp: "Twenty-three fifty-six."

"Four minutes before midnight," Ryan says.

We watch as the robots go about their duties, monitoring and caring for their patients until, abruptly, they stop.

I look back at the monitor. "Midnight."

I can only watch in horror as Ryan speeds through the time that follows. Urgent alarms begin to sound from the medical pumps and equipment, but no one attends to them. I watch, powerless, as the humans die, one by one. It takes days for it to happen—from dehydration, I assume. They don't seem to suffer; they just slip away. But watching their deaths fills me with an unspeakable pain. To think that my mother might have caused this is unbearable.

Finally, something new happens. For the first time, security drones enter the hospital. I am puzzled as to what they might do here, until one of them opens its doors and collects a body. The others follow suit. Our drone travels with them as they leave the hospital and parade through the main hallways, and into the restricted hallways. They stop at a wall and the wall slides open, revealing a space unlike any I've ever seen before.

The walls, floor, and ceiling of this room are made of silver metal. There are three large silver horizontal tubes here, each with a circular door that is open. One at a time, the security drones release their cargo into the tubes, and they close the doors. Minutes pass and then the doors are reopened. The bodies are gone. Only bones remain. A wave of nausea grips my throat as the drones retrieve the bones and drop them into a transparent vertical tube and close the lid. Then I hear a horrible high-pitched grinding sound. And the bones disappear into dust.

The process is repeated over and over again.

Each body is turned to bones. And then the bones are turned to dust.

I close my eyes, unable to watch anymore.

A few minutes later, I hesitantly open my eyes and find that we are now in a different restricted room, a very small one. A security drone is gently tucking an inert robot into a docking station; the scene is almost reminiscent of a parent putting a child to bed. Once the robot is secured in its station, the drone backs out of the room and shuts the door.

Ryan takes us further forward in time. All that is left

now are drones patrolling the hallways—security drones, cleaning drones, maintenance drones, and delivery drones.

And then my vision goes dark. Either the sim is over, or Ryan ended it.

"Apparently nothing shuts those drones down," Ryan says as I take off my helmet. "They were still roaming around when Santiago's team discovered that compound a few days ago."

"And the robots were still inactive?" I ask.

He nods. "They were all in their docking stations." After a moment, he adds, "Whatever shut down these robots must be the same process that shut down our robots."

"Why do you say that?" I ask.

"*These* robots stopped functioning at midnight on the third night after the humans were put to sleep. *Our* robots shut down at midnight on the third night after we evacuated our compound."

"It has to be a dead-man's switch," I say. "It must have been set off when the robots stopped receiving their inputs. In this case, the inputs stopped because the person who administered them was incapacitated by the sleeping gas. In our case, there was only one person who was 'incapacitated' when we evacuated our compound ..."

"The Decision Maker," Ryan murmurs.

"Right."

And right now, as far as the system is concerned, because I am logged in using my mother's access code ... I am the Decision Maker.

SATURDAY, JULY 9
0530

SIX

An alarm rips me from a dream I can't remember. When I open my eyes, I find myself in a bed with Jose, both of us still undressed, our bodies touching.

"Good morning." Jose gives me a shy smile. "How are you feeling?"

I give him a smile back. "I'm glad we're still here."

"We'd better get ready for breakfast," he says.

"Right," I say.

Very gently, he touches my forehead—doubling my heart rate in an instant—and then he climbs out of bed. As he hands me my underwear and jumpsuit, I avert my eyes, but not before I catch an accidental glimpse of his undressed muscled body in the daylight. Even the momentary look at him like that makes my insides tingle with energy. I dress quickly, keeping my body hidden by the sheet. It seems strange to feel so modest with Jose after what we did together just a few hours ago, but last night feels like it was a fleeting dream. Something that happened once, but maybe never again.

After a minute, I hear Jose sit on an empty bedframe. I look over and he is fully dressed.

"Are you okay about what we did last night?" he asks.

I look into his eyes. "I wanted to be with you like that, more than anything."

He looks relieved. "Me too ... Even back when you were with us."

His statement sends a shiver of curiosity through me. "Did I want to mate with you back then?"

"I don't know," he says. "I didn't want to know because, if we mated, that would have given you a reason to stay, and it wasn't fair to give you a reason to stay."

I try to swallow away my unease. "What about now?"

He shrugs. "None of us have any choice about where to go now."

"But once the box is safe again ..." My words fade away.

Jose's gaze meets mine. "You want to go back *there*?"

The way he says that makes me wince. I hadn't really considered that, even if we survived the night, I could lose Jose still. I guess I thought that he and his family would come live in the box with us. His mother grew up in that box. And Jose is wearing a blue jumpsuit, like he's one of us. I thought he wanted to live somewhere safe. But based on what Jose said just now, it's clear that he wouldn't even consider living in our box.

"It's *safe* there," I say, trying to make him understand.

Jose just looks at me. "It's a *box* ... under the ground."

Tears obscure my vision. I can't clearly see Jose's face anymore, but I don't want to see it. I don't want to see the way he's looking at me right now. I don't want to know what he's thinking.

"It's my home," I say and then, without another word, I

leave Jose alone.

SATURDAY, JULY 9
0542

SEVEN

As promised, Ten returns to me before breakfast, but he seems deeply troubled by something. Before I can ask anything at all, he launches into an update of what he learned overnight. He tells me that, using his mother's code, he was able to access a map of the United States that shows the locations of more than two dozen other military compounds. Ryan's team tracked last night's invader drone to a special compound that he believes controls *all* of the military compounds, including ours. The military is going to attempt to make contact with the control compound today.

When I ask about the robots, Ten's shoulders fall. "I was able to find the system where my mother controlled the robot's inputs. There was a very simple code that she sent out daily. I tried copying the code and sending it to the robots, but nothing happened. After that, we tried a system restore and ... nothing. I wish I knew what else to do."

I can't accept that Miss Teresa and all of the other robots have been inactivated forever, but it sounds like maybe Ten has. "There must be something you're missing." Frustration seeps into my voice, even though I try hard to stop it. "Miss Teresa knew that I switched places with Six, and she overrode that truth to protect me. I didn't see any of that in all the data they downloaded from her."

"That programming has to be there," Ten says. "Robots can't make decisions on their own."

I want to believe that there is more to Miss Teresa than her programming. "There has to be something more inside her."

For a moment, Ten appears to be deep in thought, then his eyes widen and he looks at me with an excitement that I haven't seen from him in a long time. "Maybe there is."

SATURDAY, JULY 9
0551

TEN

Without giving much of an explanation, I borrow a tablet from Ryan. I'm going to need it in order to test my hypothesis.

With Ryan's tablet in hand, Seven and I head to the hangar where the deactivated robots have been stored. I'm surprised to find it devoid of any human soldiers, but I suppose I shouldn't be. Why bother wasting valuable resources to watch over a bunch of inert robots?

I activate the tablet and make my way to the hidden log in screen.

Then I log in … as my mother.

SATURDAY, JULY 9
0559

SEVEN

Ten is bent over Ryan's tablet, everything in him focused on his task. He isn't doing any talking. I have a feeling that the thoughts in his brain, coupled with his sleep deprivation, make talking impossible right now.

I silently walk the rows of robots. Our baby is strapped against my chest in her carrier. She is quieter than usual. I'm sure she senses the distress that I feel as I gaze at the scene before me.

The robots are positioned on their backs. Each one is covered by a thin layer of clear plastic—to protect them from debris, I suppose. Through the plastic, I can see that their eyes are open, staring lifelessly at the hangar ceiling. It is eerie, like walking among the dead.

My heart squeezes painfully tight when I spot Miss Teresa under a sheet of plastic. I kneel beside her and lift the sheet, almost expecting her to take a gasp of air and come back to life but, of course, she doesn't. Her face is frozen in time. Her expression seems ... curious. Yes, she appears curious. That comforts me somewhat. Apparently she wasn't distressed when she died ... I mean, shut down.

It's hard to imagine that I will never again see the

kindness in Miss Teresa's smile. That I will never hear her soothing voice again. That I will never get to tell her thank you. For protecting me. I should have told her that when I had the chance.

Ten kneels beside me. "I'm going to try to do another download on her." His voice is soft and gentle. "Maybe with my mother's access code, I can pull up something more."

He places his tablet over the center of Miss Teresa's chest. Instantly, the screen fills with information. The data scrolls so fast that I can't read it, so instead I return my focus to Miss Teresa's face. Her hair is a bit mussed. *I can't let her hair be mussed. Miss Teresa wouldn't want that.* Lightly, I smooth her hair back down. It is something I never would do if she were functioning. It is much too intimate a thing to do. As I finish, my fingers accidentally brush her forehead. Her skin feels unnatural, like robot skin does, but now it also feels cold. Dead. Tears pool in my eyes.

"It's done," Ten says.

He sits on the ground with the tablet and starts reviewing the data.

After a few minutes, he sighs. "It's exactly the same as what they downloaded from her before," he says. "I ran a side-by-side comparison just to be sure, and—"

"That can't be all there is," I say. "Unless she really can think for herself. In which case—"

"Wait … what if …?" Ten doesn't finish his thought. Instead, he holds his tablet in front of Miss Teresa's face. Another download begins to scroll down the screen.

"Is that the same information you just downloaded?" I

ask.

"I don't know," he says, but he sounds hopeful.

The download seems to take longer this time. After the confirmation message appears, I look over Ten's shoulder as he examines the data. This is most definitely not the same information I reviewed in Ryan's bunker, but I don't really understand most of what I'm seeing. After a moment, Ten looks at me and shakes his head.

"There's a secondary memory bank in the robot's head," Ten says. "It looks like that's where the sensitive programming and information is stored, but I can only access bits and pieces of it ..."

"And you can't restart the robots." I read from his tone.

"Actually, I think we might be able to."

His words should make my heart leap, but I sense from the sadness in his eyes that there's a serious problem. "What's wrong then?" I ask.

"There's a code that's infiltrated into the secondary memory bank. You could call it a 'permanent kill command.' It tells the robot not to resume operation. The code is repeated over and over, hundreds of times. It's overwritten most of the information in the secondary memory bank. It probably happened when the dead-man's switch was activated."

"But you think you can restart the robots anyway?" I ask.

"If we're able to erase the secondary memory bank, then the kill command would be eliminated. After that, we might be able restore the robots to their original settings. We could give them the three days of memories that we downloaded from their primary memory bank but, because all the information on the secondary memory bank would be lost, they wouldn't be the same as before."

"You should tell Ryan what you found," I say numbly.

"I will," he says. "But there's something I need to do first."

SATURDAY, JULY 9
0632

TEN

Seven and I are able to convince one of the soldiers to give us a bit of breakfast, even though we arrive after everyone else has collected their food and taken their seats. We find my father and sister and Seven's parents and brother sitting at one large table. It's good to see them together. My dad and sister will need the support of friends to help them through the loss that they have suffered, although my little sister has no idea yet of the permanency of that loss.

After a subdued breakfast conversation that leaves me convinced that I'm not the only one who didn't get any sleep, I get the attention of my father. "We should talk after breakfast," I say, giving a quick glance toward Forty-seven. We need to tell my little sister what happened to her mother. I don't want my dad to have to do it alone.

My father inhales deeply and nods. "All right."

I tell Seven that I'll check in with her later, and I follow my father and sister to their dormitory. When I shut the door behind us, my sister looks at me with a childlike enthusiasm that reminds me of how young she really is. Far too young to have lost a parent.

"Hey, Ten, we're all in the same domicile again," she says, smiling. Then her smile fades, "Except for Mom."

My father looks as if he might break down into tears. He doesn't seem ready to have this conversation. I realize now that the weight of it will fall on me.

"Let's talk about Mom," I say, gesturing for Forty-seven to sit on her bed.

Forty-seven sits. My dad sits beside her. I sit across from them.

"What about Mom?" Forty-seven asks brightly. It's hard to see Forty-seven's innocence, knowing that her innocence is about to be destroyed forever.

"There's something we need to tell you, and it is going to be very difficult," I say.

Her brightness fades. "What is it?"

My dad finally speaks, "Your mother had a medical condition. She had a weakness of one of the large blood vessels deep inside her body. That blood vessel burst open and ... she died."

Forty-seven's eyes fill with horror. "No! She *can't* be dead! She *can't* be dead!"

There's nothing that I can say that will comfort my little sister now, but I need to try. "I know that Mom would want me to tell you that she loved you very much." I know that because those were her last words to me, even after I told her that I hated her.

"We've been here for days, and she was too busy with her job to let me see her for even a few minutes," Forty-seven says tearfully.

"I ... wasn't quite honest with you about that ..." My father's lower lip is trembling violently. It's clear that he won't be able to continue.

Of what we need to tell Forty-seven, telling her of her mom's death was the easier part. There is something much worse that must be said. Forty-seven must be told the truth about her mother's horrific actions. As much as I wish she could remember her mother only as she knew her, someday she may learn the awful truth about what her mother did. She deserves to hear it first from people who love her.

"There's something more you need to know," I say quietly.

Forty-seven's watery eyes focus on me.

"Mom was in *isolation* when she died." I use the term "isolation" because it is the closest thing to prison that we have back home.

Forty-seven's eyes narrow with indignation. "Why did they put her in isolation?"

I force back all the anger I have against my mother. I can't let Forty-seven feel that. This must be done gently. "She harmed people."

"Mom wouldn't do that," Forty-seven protests.

"She wasn't ... thinking right," my father forces out.

"She didn't harm people," Forty-seven says, but it's more of a plea than a statement. In the pain underlying her words, I feel my own pain. The pain of knowing that the woman who gave me life—someone who will always be a part of who I am—callously caused harm to others. *My mother killed people.*

"That's the truth," I say. "I'm sorry, Forty-seven."

She wipes away her tears with her fist, taking slow, deep, angry breaths.

"It's okay to cry," I tell her. "It's okay to be angry." And then I admit, "I'm angry too."

"I need to go to morning PT," she says.

"Why don't you skip PT today?" my dad suggests, but Forty-seven is already heading toward the door.

I think I know what she's feeling. She wants to do something normal. She needs to. "I'll walk you there," I say. "Okay?"

She gives me a half-shrug that I take as acquiescence, and I follow her out of the room.

SATURDAY, JULY 9
0653

FORTY-ONE

Forty-seven arrives for morning PT with her brother, Ten. Even more strangely, at the entrance to the mess hall, he gives her an embrace before he says goodbye. Forty-seven's eyes are red and watery. They looked normal at breakfast.

Katrina and I are sitting on a mat on the floor. When she notices that I'm looking at the door, she stops talking and turns to see what I'm looking at.

"I'll be right back," I tell her. I get up and go to the door, where Forty-seven is lingering, looking as if she is unwilling to enter the room further.

"You're early," I tell her. "Do you want to go for a walk?"

She glances over at Katrina, who is watching us. "What about Katrina? You shouldn't leave her for me."

"I'm not leaving anyone for good," I say, although maybe I will have to someday soon. I don't know who will still be in my life once the box is ready for people to live there again.

Forty-seven follows me into the chilly morning sunlight. Her shoulders tense and her arms hug her body. She stays a step or two away from me. Unspeaking. Something is clearly bothering her very much. I wonder if she is still upset that I'm spending so much time with Katrina.

Suddenly, Forty-seven turns to me. Her face is streaked with fresh tears.

"Can you keep a secret?" she asks me.

I nod.

"It's a dangerous secret," she says. "You can't tell anyone."

"I won't," I say, feeling apprehensive now. "I promise."

"Our Decision Maker is dead," she says.

SATURDAY, JULY 9
0705

TEN

When I message Ryan with a request to share some information with him, he asks that I meet him at a ruined building on the far side of the base. As soon as he arrives at our meeting place, he gives me a quick gesture to follow him and he takes me back to the bunker. It isn't until we've closed the door on the tunnels that Ryan begins speaking, "The team found information regarding a few more of the military compounds on your mother's map."

"And?" I ask.

"They've been 'retired,'" he says.

My jaw clenches tight. "How?"

"It happened exactly the same way each time," he says. "With sleeping gas."

I wonder if the same person "retired" each of these compounds. Could it be that the actions of *one* person caused the deaths of hundreds—maybe even thousands—of innocent men, women, and children?

"So what is the information you had to tell me?" Ryan asks.

I force my brain to focus. Quickly, I explain how I downloaded data from a secondary memory bank in Miss

Teresa, and I tell Ryan my idea for restarting the robots.

He pulls me into the smaller room with one of the soldiers on his team, and he asks me to tell her all that I told him. When I mention Miss Teresa's secondary memory bank, her eyes narrow. "That's strange. I went over there myself and tried scanning for an accessory memory bank. I scanned those robots all over. Arms. Legs. Head. Everything."

"I used the restricted access code." I haven't told Ryan's team that the code came from my mother. I don't want to see the way they'll look at me when they find out that my mother was the source of all that has gone so horribly wrong.

The soldier smiles. "When I go on duty this morning, I'll share this new data with my robotics team. I bet we'll have the robots up and running again by tomorrow," she says as she transfers the data I downloaded onto her tablet. "Strong work, Hanson."

Suddenly, the noise level in the main room rises. Ryan moves into the room and toward a set of monitors that seem to have captured the team's interest. Two of the monitors are dark. The others show an aerial view of a forest that goes on as far as I can see.

"What happened?" Ryan asks one of the soldiers.

"Santiago got Klein to send a bunch of unmanned surveillance drones to get eyes on the PEOC. Two of the drones were downed. They didn't detect any enemy fire or countermeasures. They just fell out of the sky inexplicably. Her team couldn't remotely control them."

A soldier who has been monitoring a listening device adds, "The commander ordered the other drones not to proceed further."

"Likely the same thing would happen to any unmanned drones we send," the first soldier says. "We need to fly there in a manned drone and see what's going on."

"That could be a suicide mission," Ryan says.

"What's a 'suicide mission'?" I ask.

"It means that, anyone who goes on the mission would have to be willing to die," Ryan answers distractedly.

"We've gotta do something," the first soldier says. "The PEOC already knows our location. They confirmed that with their drone yesterday. But they didn't initiate friendly contact. That means they don't intend to play nice with us. They're probably already making plans to destroy us."

"I'll do it," I say. "I'll go on the suicide mission."

Ryan turns and gives me a pointed look. "No, Hanson," he says forcefully.

The other soldiers don't acknowledge my offer; they continue their discussion as if I hadn't spoken at all. "The commander would never approve a manned flight," one soldier says. "There's no way he'd risk it."

"He might if the right person volunteers," another soldier says.

The first soldier cocks his head. "Who's going to volunteer for that?"

This time, I keep my mouth shut, for Ryan's sake. Instead it is Ryan who speaks.

"Davis," he says.

Jackie.

SATURDAY, JULY 9
1220

JACKIE

I spend most of my time with my memories, both good and bad. The memory that occupies my mind most of all is both good and bad. It is the memory of Ryan's visit to my quarters just a few nights ago. I remember how he sat a few feet away from me, on my bed, as I shared the intel that I'd gathered at his request. He'd come to my quarters because I'd felt that it was no longer safe for me to bring my notes to a drop-off location; there were too many suspicious eyes watching me.

I remember how I longed to lean close to him and feel his lips rest against mine. How I longed to feel his touch—strong, but gentle—against my skin. How I longed to feel him love me.

But I knew that I was undeserving of his love. Undeserving even of the friendship that he gave me. And so I stayed a safe distance away. Ready to draw back if he moved forward. But he never did.

And now he never will.

SATURDAY, JULY 9
1207

FORTY-ONE

At lunch time, Katrina and Forty-seven and I all eat at the same table, just like we have ever since our first day at the military base. I like it when we're together like this. Katrina and Forty-seven are different, and I am different with each of them. And when the three of us are all together, I feel different still. I like feeling different.

Forty-seven doesn't seem to care anymore about what the kids from back home think about us being friends with Katrina. She is once again displaying the kind of fierce loyalty to our friendship that we've had ever since I can remember. *Us against everything else.* That's what we used to whisper to each other whenever life seemed unfair.

Life must seem very unfair to Forty-seven. It must have seemed that way for a while, but she didn't tell me until today. She was too afraid.

She has suspected for a few weeks now that her mother was the Decision Maker—the only Decision Maker. She didn't know for certain, but she was pretty sure. She overheard her parents arguing one night. She said that it sounded like her mother was doing bad things, and her father was trying to stop her.

She was afraid to ask any questions about it, because bad things happen when we ask questions. At least that's what we've always been told.

But bad things happened anyway. Her mom harmed people, and then she was sent to isolation, and then she died.

"Maybe I should have asked questions," Forty-seven told me this morning. "Maybe then all those bad things wouldn't have happened."

"None of this is your fault," I said to her. "You don't even know if she was really the Decision Maker."

"She was," she said. "I asked Ten and he told me she was." Then she looked at me with the saddest expression I've ever seen and she said, "I'm glad she's dead, because I was scared of her. Do you think I'm a bad person?"

"No," I told her. "You're my friend. Us against everything else."

Forty-seven and I will always be friends. Even if I have to go back into the box and never see her again.

We might only have a short time left together—me and Forty-seven, and me and Katrina—and so I'm glad that the three of us are sitting at the same table. Together. For now.

SATURDAY, JULY 9
1211

JACKIE

I have a visitor. That's all the guards have told me. They don't tell me much. It just one of the many ways they ensure my discomfort.

I am told to stand and walk. Two soldiers flank me.

I don't dare not to follow their orders. The uncomfortably-tight stim collar around my neck is a constant reminder that I am at their mercy.

The soldiers direct me into a small room that faces a barred, black, opaque window.

"Sit," one of my guards orders me.

As I sit, the window becomes transparent. On the other side is Ryan. His gaze meets mine and I immediately feel his hatred for me.

This hurts far more than anything here has hurt me yet.

"Ryan, I'm sorry," I croak out. I haven't heard my voice in a while. It sounds tight and pained, the way I feel inside. I try to put everything in me into this apology. It is likely my last chance to offer it to him. And he at least deserves that. "I'm so very sorry."

Ryan stares at me for what feels like an eternity. I wish he would say something. Whatever it is. I just want to hear his voice. One final time before I die.

His lips part.

I hold my breath, so as not to muffle his words by the sound of my breathing.

Finally, he speaks, "I'm sorry too."

SATURDAY, JULY 9
1225

TEN

I am sucking the last bits of peanut butter out of a plastic packet from an MRE, sifting through my mother's files, when I hear some grumblings in the bigger room of Ryan's bunker. I poke my head into the main room. "What's wrong?" I ask one of the soldiers.

"Davis said no," he says. "Ryan said she's not going on the mission."

"Who is going to go then?" I ask.

"Nobody," he says. "Unless they come up with someone else whose life is expendable."

"Let's clear out," someone else says.

Lunch is almost over. The soldiers have to get back to their duty stations, so they don't arouse anyone's suspicions. I follow them to the exit door. Ryan told me to leave the bunker when lunchtime was over and go back to the barracks. He said he'd see me at dinner.

All conversation ceases as we make our way into the tunnels. We exit the hatch in singles, triples, and pairs so as not to invite attention. I leave last, because I am not supposed to have anywhere important to go.

Except that I do.

SATURDAY, JULY 9
1312

JACKIE

For the second time today, I have a visitor.

It could be the same visitor as earlier. But I hope that it isn't.

I don't want to see Ryan again. I loathe looking into his eyes and seeing the revulsion he has for me. It makes me disgusted with my own self.

But if Ryan has requested another visit with me, I must accept it. I must sit in the chair opposite him until he is through with me. There may not be any worse way to spend my time, but that isn't my decision to make. My time is no longer mine to own. It never will be again.

I take a seat in the chair that faces the black barred window. It takes a bit longer this time for it to go transparent, but finally it does.

I am shocked to see Hanson sitting opposite me. He looks at me with heartbroken eyes, like those of a lost child. I wish I could sit in the empty chair beside him and offer him comfort, but I have a horrible feeling that he doesn't want any comforting from me. No doubt Ryan has told him what I did to deserve my imprisonment. How I hurt his colleagues and esteemed instructors. How I might have killed *Murphy* if I hadn't been thwarted.

"I suppose you've heard some pretty terrible things about me," I say.

He shakes his head. "I saw them with my own eyes."

Then it's worse than I thought.

"I can apologize and try to explain," I say, "but I have a feeling that won't change how you feel about me."

He nods. "You're right."

For a while, he just sits there quietly. The silence presses in on my ears. If he's not here for an explanation or apology, then why has he come?

"Why did you say no?" he finally asks.

"What are you talking about?" I ask.

Hanson exhales. "When Ryan came to see you today. Why did you say no to him?"

"I didn't say no," I reply.

Hanson looks at me, his eyes narrowed with distrust.

I'm not sure why Ryan came to visit me here. Was it to tell me without words that he despised me? To stare at me, his eyes burning into me, until he finally told the guards to take me away? That could have been it. But maybe there was something more. Something that he wanted to ask but didn't.

"Ryan didn't ask me any questions," I add.

"What did he say then?" Hanson asks.

I think back to our conversation. Ryan said just one thing. "Only that he was sorry."

SATURDAY, JULY 9
1334

TEN

I march off to Ryan's station, unsure of exactly what I'll say when I get there.

Weirdly, I have a feeling that Jackie was completely forthcoming with me just now. But if Ryan didn't ask Jackie to do the mission, then why not?

Ryan's team feels that someone needs to go to the PEOC before it destroys us. Maybe it should be me. It is my mother's fault that we are in danger. She said she told the other warrior programs that we were a threat. That is no doubt why the PEOC isn't trying to establish friendly contact. They want to destroy us before we cause any additional harm. I can't let that happen.

I arrive to find Ryan faithfully carrying out his military duties as if he doesn't spend all of his free time in a secret underground bunker questioning the military's every move.

"I'm here to see Lieutenant Commander Ryan," I tell a soldier who questions my presence. "It's important."

The soldier calls Ryan over.

As soon as Ryan turns and sees me, his shoulders stiffen. He nods to the soldier and walks me outside. "What's going on?" he asks me.

"I went to see Davis," I say. "She told me that you came to visit her and all you did was apologize. I thought you were going to ask her to do that mission."

"Did you mention the mission to her?" he asks.

"No," I say, "I wasn't sure if—"

"I can't talk now," Ryan says. "We can discuss this after dinner."

"No!" I say as forcefully as I can without calling attention to us. "Did you ask her to do the mission or not?"

"I did not," he says.

"Then I'll volunteer," I say.

Ryan grabs my shoulder far too tightly. "Listen to me, Hanson. I didn't ask her. I couldn't make myself do it. But it turns out that the commander's team came up with the same idea on their own. He hasn't told Davis about the mission yet. He didn't want to give her any time to prepare a plan to ruin ours. The mission is a go for eighteen thirty hours today. Are we good now?"

"I guess," I say.

"Good," he says.

I leave Ryan to his work and head back to the barracks. I should probably rest, but I don't feel tired. There is too much adrenaline running through me to fall asleep.

I find Seven reading on her tablet. Fifty-two is asleep in her little box.

Seven puts down her tablet as I enter. "Any updates?" she asks.

I nod. "They're going to try to reactivate the robots. They should be running again by tomorrow."

"Without their secondary memory banks," she says.

"Yes," I say.

But instead of expressing the sadness that she surely must feel, Seven holds out her arms to me. I join her on the bed, and she pulls me close. Instantly, everything else falls away, leaving only me and her. She presses her lips to mine and I breathe her in. I see and hear and feel only her.

Her hands slip over my chest and arms, then they grab me desperately. Wanting me to be closer to her. Needing me to be closer to her. Our clothes come off fast, but they don't seem to leave us fast enough. Our bodies need to be together.

I plunge into her and my body melts. I'd almost forgotten how good it feels to be with her like this. We shouldn't be doing this now. There is too much happening. Too much to be done. Too much to worry about. But with our bodies together, everything feels right, if only for these moments.

Seven lets out a soft sound and her body grips mine. A moment later, it happens to me too, and then I hold her as she catches her breath and I catch mine. As we come back to reality, a horrible thought creeps into my brain: *What if that was the last time that Seven and I will ever mate?*

But rather than weaken me, that thought makes me even stronger and more certain of my goals. I must ensure that we are safe from those who wish to destroy us. If not, Seven and Fifty-two, and all of us, are doomed. And so I will do whatever it takes to prevent our destruction.

Whatever it takes.

SATURDAY, JULY 9
1804

JACKIE

The stim collar around my neck feels tighter than before, but it shouldn't. No one has tightened it. I suppose it just feels that way because my pulse is pounding so frantically in the arteries beneath it.

I am surrounded by at least a dozen guards as I walk through gleaming hallways that I've never navigated before. I was just given a fine meal of herb-crusted salmon, roasted asparagus, and black coffee, and I am now dressed in a typical military jumpsuit—like the one I wore before I was locked up in the brig. These are not good signs. When it comes to life as a prisoner, change generally isn't a positive thing, especially if no one is telling you why things have changed.

Today, two of my former friends came to see me. Likely the others don't care to look upon my face ever again. I'm sure they were all told that tonight I would be sent to Terminal Transfer.

That is the most likely reason for my relocation. I figured this would happen at some point, but I didn't think it would happen so soon. Back home, there would be a trial. A counsel would hear the evidence against me and I would be allowed to state my defense, but that isn't how things work here. I knew that going in. The purity of this society is too precious to allow anyone unfit to remain. The unfit are sent away.

My guards take me through a secure door and, suddenly, we are outside. My eyes squint involuntarily against sunlight I haven't seen in days, but I tilt my face to the sky to feel the warmth of the sun against my skin. The ocean breeze is gentle. I hear the distant crash of the waves and the call of a seagull. It seems unimaginable that my time on Earth is nearing its end, but I know that soon my life will extinguish into darkness.

I won't fight it. I deserve my fate.

We enter the hangar and my guards lead me into the aerial drone that will transport me to the Terminal Transfer facility. Strangely, aside from my guards and me, the drone is completely unoccupied. Even more strangely, the guards bring me to the *pilot's* seat.

"Sit," one of the guards says to me. "I'd strongly advise you not to try anything stupid."

I sit, my mind racing.

What the hell is going on? Why am I being seated in the pilot's seat of a drone?

"Lieutenant Davis." It's the commander's voice, coming from behind me.

I nearly leap to attention, but I decide that a sudden move such as that would be ill-advised. And so I remain seated, facing forward. "Sir," I say quietly.

One of my guards rotates my seat so that I am facing a hologram of the commander.

"You have been assigned to an extremely important

mission," the commander says.

My pulse quickens even further. I wonder if he is toying with me, like a cat toying with a mouse before it breaks its neck. The only *"mission"* I figured would be in my future was a one-way trip to Terminal Transfer. But the commander should be far too busy to toy with a useless criminal.

"What type of mission, sir?" I ask.

"We need you to navigate this drone into a valuable area and gather intel about what you find there," he says. "The drone will be on autopilot during the first part of your flight, but there is an area surrounding the target location that will require you to fly manually. Be advised that you will be carefully monitored during this mission. If you attempt to deviate from my orders, you will be destroyed. If you do not return within five hours, you will be destroyed."

"If I choose not to go on this mission?" I ask.

"You will be destroyed," he says, matter-of-factly.

I figured that.

"Is the 'target location' hostile?" I ask.

"It could be," he says.

Well, at least he's being honest.

He looks at me, as if he is trying to read my eyes. "Prepare for takeoff at eighteen thirty hours," he says.

According to the clock on the instrument panel, eighteen thirty hours is twelve minutes from now. I listen as the commander briefs me on the details of the mission. He provides me with disconcertingly little information, but I assume he is sharing all that he will, and so I don't ask for more. When he is finished, he gives a curt smile. "I wish you a successful mission," he says, and then his hologram vanishes.

I nod at where the commander's image was, feeling an empty sense of abandonment, then I turn back to the instrument panel and examine the information there. Most of the usual data is missing from the monitors. They don't want me to know too much about where I am headed or what I am facing. I'm sure that I will be given only the information that they think I need to know in order to carry out their mission. I only hope I am given enough.

As the guards begin to file out of the drone, one of them turns to me. "Good luck, Davis," she says. And I feel like she means it. She wants me to succeed. Probably not for my benefit, but for hers.

After the drone door seals shut, I am alone. No other humans. No robots. Only the quiet sounds of the drone as it prepares for imminent takeoff.

I close my eyes and focus myself, trying to shake away the emotions of the past several minutes: relief at knowing that I am not facing Terminal Transfer just yet and fear that I might be facing something even worse. This mission must be extremely dangerous. Why else would they send me? True, I am respected for my skills as a pilot, but there are others who can fly just as well as me. And, when it comes to those other pilots, the commander is fairly certain where their loyalties lie.

The commander must be counting on my motivation to survive to carry me through. Regardless of the outcome of today's mission, my fate will likely remain unchanged; the commander would have told me if his intentions were otherwise. So why should I try to survive this mission? What do I have to return to? Days and nights spent in a prison cell with the knowledge that my eventual fate will be Terminal Transfer? What kind of life is that to look forward to?

But this mission isn't about me. This mission is about helping those who I hurt. This is my last chance to do something right with my life.

I wipe tears from my eyes as daylight streams into the hangar through the rapidly-growing opening in the roof. The drone begins its countdown to take off. Time feels as if it is racing forward too fast, and I am powerless to slow it.

My drone ascends into the bright blue sky. It's one of those rare days when the visibility is unlimited. There's not a single cloud anywhere in sight. *A perfect day to die*, I think.

No, I can't allow myself to think like that. I can't think of this as a one-way mission. I have to imagine myself as having a future, even if it is a bleak one. I must stay alive at least until I accomplish my goals. I will only allow myself to die today if the mission depends on it.

The drone begins to travel inland. The terrain here is well-known to me, reassuring. After a few minutes, I see the site where my community once stood. The military removed all traces of what was left after they destroyed our homes and our people, apparently even going so far as to fill our extensive network of underground tunnels with dirt. Returning the land to its natural state. Before people. As if my community never existed.

I pull my thoughts away from my past life and focus on the horizon as we leave behind all that is familiar. *I wonder where we're headed. Is it far?* I've been on countless flights during my time with the military, but we never flew very

301

far. There was no need to. There was nothing out there that we needed to see or do.

Now, for the first time in my life, I fly off into the unknown. The navigation equipment is still providing me with only very basic information. We are heading northeast, maintaining our altitude. The world below me is peaceful, natural. No buildings or signs of life. Just lush green land stretching out into the distance. I wish I could stop here. Live here. All alone. With no one who hates me ... except myself.

I didn't always hate myself. I was once the kind of person who I admired and respected. I used to believe that no person was more worthy than any other. That we should all be cherished and protected. But somewhere along the path of my life, I forgot that. I let the needs of my people numb me to the needs of others. I harmed other people for the sake of my own. I killed people who could have been my friends. I nearly killed people who later became my friends. Now those people hate me. And I hate me too.

I'm glad the drone is on autopilot. I can barely see the instrument panel through my tears. Although, even if I had dry eyes right now, I would still be flying almost blind.

Still, I need to calm myself. Who knows how soon I will be called upon to take over the controls? I steady my breathing, and I direct my attention to the landscape below as we race from the last rays of the sun. Shadows darken the depths of majestic canyons that furrow the earth. Water flows in raging rivers. I've seen photos of places like this in old books and magazines, but I was never truly certain that they actually existed. What I wouldn't give to explore this place. For a moment, I let myself pretend that I will one day. That I'm surveying the world, looking for the perfect place to return to, unwilling to stop here just yet because there might be something even better out there.

As we leave the sun behind, the world around me darkens. The drone windows transition to full night-vision, so I can still see what is below me, but now my surroundings appear more intimidating—still beautiful, but ominous.

A voice makes me jump back to reality, "Lieutenant Davis, you are approaching the location where you will need to assume manual control," a female voice says. It sounds like Santiago's, but I don't ask. That way I can imagine that my former colleague is guiding me. Like this is any other mission. "I'm going to unlock your screens," she says.

A moment later, the missing information from the drone's monitors magically appears. The screens are now fully populated with data. They've given me *everything*. Either they're trusting me or they think that I'll need it … or maybe they have no idea what I will need.

"Thank you," I say softly.

Before I have time to check out all the new information presented to me, the woman speaks again, "Prepare to assume control in five, four, three …"

I take hold of the manual controls and orient myself.

And then … I'm flying. I'm in full control.

I never thought I'd get the chance to pilot a drone ever again. I'd almost forgotten how much I enjoy it. I'll never forget the time I got into an aerial drone for my first actual flight. Even after all of my hours of practice in the simulators, I expected it to be difficult to manage the drone,

303

but it wasn't. It was like the drone was an extension of me. Like it was a tool that allowed me to do what I was born to do. To roam the sky, like a bird. Defying gravity—

The drone makes an unexpected descent. *We must have hit an air pocket.* We've encountered at least a half-dozen air pockets so far on this flight—back when the drone was on autopilot—and I barely registered them but, given the uncertainty I am facing right now, this one unnerves me. To be safe, I pull up bit, increasing the distance between us and the ground.

And then, suddenly, without warning, everything— every single display in the cockpit—*everything* goes dark.

SATURDAY, JULY 9
2103 MST

TEN

Something is very wrong.

Up until a few moments ago, Jackie's flight was proceeding exactly as expected, but now we are at a critical point in the mission. Close to the spot where the military's surveillance drones inexplicably fell from the sky. And now *this* drone is bouncing around violently, making random jerky movements up and down, side to side, as if it is trying desperately to stay aloft.

Inside the drone it is oddly silent. No one is providing Jackie with information or instructions. Or asking her what is wrong or if she needs help. But maybe they can't.

I poke my head out of the hiding spot I made for myself beneath the drone's seats. When I see the cockpit, my heart flies into my throat. Jackie is sitting there with her back to me. In front of her, the entire instrument panel is *completely dark*.

"Why did you turn off all the screens?" I ask Jackie urgently.

She spins around and her eyes widen, but then she quickly returns her attention to the drone's controls. "I didn't do anything," she says. "It might have been an

305

electromagnetic pulse or … what the hell are you doing here, Hanson?"

"I came along to help," I answer honestly.

Jackie shakes her head. I've never seen her this troubled before, especially not when she's flying. *Jackie doesn't have this under control.* I wonder for a moment if we are going to die, but I try to chase that thought from my brain.

"Get over here," Jackie says.

In a split-second decision that I hope not to regret, I leave the weapon that I brought with me under the seat, and I race to the front of the drone.

"Have you ever flown anything before?" she asks as I approach.

"I used to fly toy drones all the time when I was a kid," I offer.

"Okay, good," she says, obviously trying to force a reassuring tone into her voice. "This is a lot like flying those toy drones. The controls are almost exactly the same. Focus on the artificial horizon. It's right there." She points to a small circle near the center of the dark instrument panel. The top half of the circle is bright-blue and the bottom is blood-red. Dividing the two halves is a thin white horizontal line that wavers uncertainly. "Try to keep us level with the horizon. We're in manual reversion, so the controls are extremely stiff. You're going to need a lot of force to adjust them but, still, you have to be gentle. It isn't going to be easy." As she speaks, she guides me into position, letting my hands take the place of hers, one at a time, until I am controlling the drone.

It *is* quite a bit like flying a toy drone, but yet not, because I can feel the dizzying motion, and I know that our lives depend on my ability to keep us airborne. As Jackie warned me, the controls are exceedingly stiff. I try to be strong, but gentle.

"You're doing great," Jackie tells me as she yanks open a panel below the instrument panel and starts working furiously. She's either trying to kill us or save us. I hope it is the latter.

Suddenly, our shaky drone drops fast toward the ground. I yank back hard on the lever to my left—probably too hard—but our descent continues.

"Pull back on the lever!" Jackie shouts at me.

"That's what I'm doing!" I shout back. I can hear the intense fear in my voice.

"Okay, all right," she says, speaking fast, even though she doesn't seem certain of what to say. "Direct us to the right with the stick, but keep us level with the horizon. When you feel the force against us weaken, then pull back."

I do as she says, urging us to the right as gently as I can with the uncooperative stick. We tilt sideways and I have to correct, but my correction sends us too far in the other direction. I try to correct again, and the controls suddenly loosen, as if something inside them has broken free. We tilt hard to the right. I move the stick to the left and pull back on the lever, and we surge up fast into the night sky. Way too fast.

"Level off! Level off!" Jackie's hands wrap over mine, guiding me into doing as she says, leveling us off, as the drone's monitor screens come back to life.

After a moment, she says, "You can let go now."

My shaky hands relinquish the controls to her. Putting my fate back into Jackie's hands.

She nods toward the copilot's seat. "Sit down and buckle your safety harness." And then she adds, "Relax and try to enjoy the rest of the flight." The sarcasm in her tone is evident, but I'm glad it's there. It's mildly reassuring.

I move to the copilot's seat, thinking that maybe I can trust that Jackie wants to keep us alive. Apparently, she wants this mission to succeed, although I'm not exactly sure why.

"Is there any more trouble that I should look forward to?" Jackie asks me.

"I don't know," I answer honestly. "I don't think anyone back at the base knows."

I half-expect someone back at the base to say something to us. But the communication system seems to be down. If it wasn't, I'm sure someone there would have said something by now.

"So are you going to tell me what this mission is all about?" Jackie asks me.

I suppose I might as well.

SATURDAY, JULY 9
2109 MST

JACKIE

It's hard to believe that what Hanson is telling me is true, but why would he lie? By coming on this mission, he has put his life in my hands.

And so, apparently, we are heading to the current Presidential Emergency Operations Center. Yesterday, someone here sent a surveillance drone to our base to gather intel. We have come to try to establish friendly contact with them before they return and obliterate us.

I've never seen a defense zone as sophisticated as the one we just passed through, so I do believe that, at least at some point in time, this was a fairly-sensitive government location. But if we really are heading toward a PEOC, there should be additional defenses. They certainly know that we made it past their "wall of death." They should be focused on destroying us or, at the very least, preventing us from proceeding further. But, as far as I can tell, they are allowing us to fly freely now. I can only come up with two reasonable explanations:

Either the PEOC isn't here anymore.

Or they are *letting* us come.

SATURDAY, JULY 9
2113 MST

TEN

"We're almost at the target location," Jackie says softly as she points to a monitor.

On the screen, the number of nautical miles to our destination has dropped to less than twenty. I look out the drone windows, trying to spot something that could be the PEOC. We're close enough that we should be able to see it if it is a building or a—

"Look at that." Jackie is pointing to a mountain just to the left of us. On the far side of it is a large irregular oval of black. Cautiously, she brings us closer, and then she hovers.

I squint my eyes, trying to get a better look at the strange black spot on the mountain. And then I realize that it's actually a *hole*. A tremendous gaping hole large enough to fit hundreds of aerial drones like this one inside it. And it isn't *just* a hole; there is a structure inside it. A structure not unlike the box where I once lived. But *this* box appears to have been ripped open by an unimaginable force.

We get closer and closer, as if the structure is drawing us into itself—but when I glance over at Jackie, I can tell by her demeanor that she remains in complete control of the drone. We are drawn not by physical force, but by human curiosity.

As we move deeper into the structure, I watch in horror as the magnitude of the destruction is revealed. Walls are split in half. Pipes jut out at abnormal angles, their broken ends reaching into the empty air.

And in the destruction is even more horror …

"Bodies," I breathe.

I want to turn away, but Jackie brings us in closer. I suppose that is what the commander would want her to do. She was sent here to gather information. Apparently she is taking her duties seriously.

"Do you think *we* did this?" I ask quietly.

Jackie shakes her head. "The kind of force necessary to cause something like this is more than your entire military could muster with every weapon in your arsenal."

I stare at the bodies now in full view before us. Some are human, some robot. They are frozen in uncomfortable-looking positions, as if they were thrown there, probably by whatever force destroyed their box. The flesh of the humans is shriveled, the blood dried. I suppose, their deaths weren't recent. My mind takes me back to the beach where our warrior compound once stood. In my memory, I stand there with Seven, looking at the bloodied bodies of those who perished in the explosion, knowing that the blood was shed at the hands of my own mother. I feel as helpless now as I did back then, but for a different reason.

I was hoping that, by coming here, I would be able to help everyone back home. I thought that if the people at the PEOC believed we were the enemy, they would need more than just a message broadcast by a drone to convince them otherwise. They would want to meet the person behind that message. I didn't trust Jackie to be that person.

But it turns out there's no one here to convince.

"Why did you agree to go on this mission?" I ask Jackie.

"I didn't have much choice," she says, pointing to the stim collar around her neck. "But that isn't the only reason," she adds. "I wanted to try to right some wrongs, even though that will never be possible."

I stiffen at her last statement. Because it could have been spoken by me.

"Why did *you* come on this mission?" she asks me.

It takes a while before I find my voice. "I wasn't going to let you do this alone."

"Because you don't trust me?" she asks, and then she quickly adds, "Never mind. Don't answer that. Of course you don't trust me, Hanson. Why should you?"

"You tried to kill Murphy." I probably shouldn't have said that given that my life still rests in Jackie's hands, but in all my exhaustion and shock and sadness, it just comes out.

"I didn't know her back then," Jackie says. "I had no idea what kind of a person Murphy is. She was just an obstacle to a goal. I despise myself for thinking of another human being in that way, especially someone like Murphy. I wish I could undo the trauma I caused. Maybe then I could forgive myself."

Burning pain rushes into my heart. What I wouldn't give to have heard my mother utter those words. For her to show some remorse for what she did. My mother's last words to me were words of love, but not of regret. I only wish that, instead of telling me that she loved me, she'd told me that she regretted what she'd done. Maybe then I could have released the anger I still feel toward her. Maybe then I could have forgiven her.

"I forgive you, Davis." I say those words so softly that if it wasn't for the dead silence inside the drone, there would be no chance she could hear me.

But I know she does hear me, because when I look over, I see silent tears slowly begin to run down her cheeks.

SATURDAY, JULY 9
2125 MST

JACKIE

Hanson forgives me. Maybe that is enough. If I die today, at least there is one less person in this world who despises me.

But I can't die just yet. I need to get Hanson safely back home.

"I assume no one knows you stowed away on this mission?" I ask him.

"Right," he says, "and I need to keep it that way. Ryan would be furious if he found out ... The commander would be too, probably. Ryan said this was a suicide mission."

It is. Even now. But if Ryan told Hanson that this was a suicide mission, why would he decide to go on it? "Do you understand what a suicide mission is?"

"It means if you go on it you have to be willing to die," he says.

"It means that it's highly unlikely that you'll make it back alive," I say. "That's why they sent me. They figured if I didn't come back, it would be no great loss."

Hanson quietly inhales and doesn't breathe back out.

I have a feeling that he didn't understand the immense risk that he was taking by coming with me today.

"Hopefully we've survived the worst part," I say, wishing that, by saying it, I could make it true. In case we're not through the worst of it, in case I don't make it out of this alive, there's something more I need to say. "If you hadn't come along, I wouldn't have made it this far."

Hanson finally exhales, but he doesn't speak.

Our conversation has become far too morbid for my taste, besides we need to focus on the task at hand. "So you said a surveillance drone came from this location yesterday," I say.

"We don't know *exactly* where it came from," he says, sounding even more subdued than before. "We followed it back to somewhere around here, but we lost contact with it."

"Well, I don't think it originated from this structure," I say. "I ran tests for radiological, chemical, and biological contamination, and for signs of biological and electronic life. All of my testing indicates that this area is cold."

"Then we need to keep looking," Hanson says.

He's right. If I don't return with something useful, who knows whether the commander will let me come back at all? I need to ensure that I am allowed to return to the base, for Hanson's sake as well as my own.

I fly out of the tremendous hole, and we continue our search for life. As I evaluate the surrounding area, I find it disappointingly dead. Not even a deer or coyote or mountain lion. It seems the defense shield is extremely effective in keeping out all types of intruders. But somehow, months ago, *something* was able to pass through. Something horrible.

I'm starting to become more conscious of my shrinking

time window. I have less than three hours left before the commander's deadline, and it will take an hour and a half to fly back to the base if we encounter no obstacles. To be on the safe side, I need to ensure that Hanson and I are on our way within the next hour. I'm not sure how the commander plans to destroy me, but there is a risk that my destruction could result in collateral damage to Hanson. I won't allow any harm to come to—

I get a hit. Something electronic. Deep inside a mountain not far from the destroyed one. This mountain, though, appears intact.

I stare at the glowing spot on the monitor screen. "There's some kind of chamber inside that mountain." It's hard to tell exactly what's in there, because the monitor images are faint and fuzzy. The rock is too dense to allow adequate penetration of my equipment.

I circle the mountain, looking for an entry point to the chamber. Strangely, I don't see one.

"Where's the entrance?" I wonder aloud.

I descend so we're a little closer, but still I see nothing.

"What about that?" Hanson asks, pointing.

I see what he's talking about. An opening so well-camouflaged that, at first glance, it looks like a mere irregularity in the rocky mountainside. But when I carefully direct my equipment to examine it, at just the right angle, I see that it is actually the mouth of a tunnel. The tunnel turns and then disappears inside the mountain. I can't see the ending.

It would be useful if I had a surveillance drone to send into the tunnel, but the commander didn't provide me with those. I doubt he thought I'd get this far. If I want to know who or what's inside the mountain, I'm going to have to find out the old-fashioned way.

"I need to explore that tunnel on foot," I say. "I'll set us down and—"

"What if they attack us?" Hanson asks, concerned.

"If they were going to attack us, they would have done it by now," I say. "Our equipment isn't picking up any signs of landmines or other defenses. I have a feeling that this structure's primary defense is camouflage. Apparently it's worked well so far." There may be additional defenses inside, but I don't think that needs to be said. I'm sure Hanson understands that this is still risky. It's no more dangerous than anything else we've done so far.

Hanson nods, and I set down our drone on a patch of dirt.

I pull on a helmet and synch it with one of the drone's monitors. "You can watch what I'm doing on this monitor," I tell Hanson. "Do not exit this drone under any circumstances. If anything happens to me, you take the drone and go home. Once you're out of this area, you should be able to reestablish contact with the base. They can guide you—"

"Stop," he says. "We're going home together. That's how it's going to be."

I nod at him. "Right."

I open the drone door and step out onto solid ground. The terrain here appears similar to the land back home, but different too. The plants and trees are comparable to those I know from days spent in the woods surrounding our community. The flowers, however, have floppy petals that form gentle curved shapes. Even though I can't see their colors, they fascinate me. I wish I could summon the daylight, just for a moment, so I could see them in their full splendor. But I have much more pressing things to concern myself with right now.

I avoid trampling the flowers as I head toward the tunnel entrance. I feel naked without a weapon, but I suppose it would offer little protection. If whatever is inside the mountain wants to destroy me, it won't be difficult. If I am attacked, I am as good as dead.

I take a deep breath and enter the tunnel, staying close to the wall. The tunnel is lined with metal and who knows what else. I advance slowly, my hands kept visible at all times. If someone is watching me, I need them to know that I mean them no harm.

The tunnel twists deeper into the mountain. Whether in reality or my imagination, it grows colder and colder. I assume that eventually I will find a hatch or a door. I'm not sure yet how I'll get through it, but I suppose I can deal with that problem when I get there. *If* I ever get there. It seems that this tunnel might go on forever.

As I round a bend, I stop short, and my jaw falls slack.

I have found a door.

And it is already open.

SATURDAY, JULY 9
2149 MST

TEN

I grab the weapon that I'd stowed under the seats, pull on a helmet, open the drone door, and start running toward Jackie.

Seconds ago, I was watching as she walked through the mountain tunnel. And then, the video feed went to static.

She's probably just out of range, I tell myself as I race toward the mountain. *She's going to be livid that you disobeyed her orders to stay inside that aerial drone.* But Jackie isn't in charge of me. I'm here on my own accord. If I'm willing to risk my own safety for this mission, that is my choice.

The inside of the tunnel is silent aside from the muted sounds of my shoes against the ground. The tunnel seems longer than when I watched Jackie pass through it. For a moment, I wonder if she has been captured. If this is a trap.

But then, far up ahead, I see Jackie's silhouette. Her back is to me. She's standing just outside a shredded metal doorway that is missing its door. She's looking at something, but I can't see what. And then Jackie steps forward, out of view.

I hold my weapon ready, and I move ahead slowly.

Jackie hasn't noticed me and apparently neither has whatever is ahead of her. I keep moving forward until I spot Jackie standing in a room that is reminiscent of the control hub back home. Aside from Jackie, there are no people or robots here, not even bodies. It's a control hub without any controllers. Data scrolls eerily down some of the monitor screens. On the others is a decidedly simple screensaver—just large white words scrolling across a plain blue background: Welcome to the Cheyenne Mountain Command Center.

My foot slips against the ground, making a small noise. Jackie spins around and cowers. For an instant she looks so vulnerable, but she quickly recovers. "Hanson!" she says, quietly. "What the hell? You nearly gave me a heart attack. I told you to stay put."

"Your helmet stopped transmitting," I explain.

She looks at my weapon. "And you came to defend me?"

"I came to ensure the success of this mission," I say.

She gives me a small smile. The first of our trip. "All right then. Let's proceed."

Jackie starts walking toward a wall of small metal doors, each covering doorways only big enough to permit a small child to enter, and only if the child were to crawl through on hands and knees. "What do you suppose is behind those doors?" she asks.

"I can try to open them," I offer.

She looks at me and her forehead furrows. "You think you can pull an access code *here*?"

"If this place really is the PEOC, then it was once responsible for us. There could be some overlap in the technology," I say. "It's worth a try."

I suppose Jackie decides that it is, because she steps aside and permits me to try to pull a code. A minute or so later, I have an access code made up of letters and numbers on my navigator's screen. I transfer the code to my warrior necklace.

"I'll open the door," Jackie says. "You stand back and be ready with your weapon. Just in case."

I hand Jackie my necklace, and I hold my weapon ready as she cautiously opens the door, but nothing worrisome happens. Beyond the door is a small gray drone. It powers up quietly, and its little colored lights flash, indicating that the drone is still at least somewhat functional.

"That looks like the drone that came to our base yesterday," I tell Jackie.

She gives back my necklace and examines the drone. "It appears to be more-or-less identical to your military's surveillance drones." She returns the drone to its cabinet and heads toward the computers. "I'm going to see if I can figure out who sent it."

I use my necklace to open another one of the small doors.

Jackie gives me a quick glance. "They're probably all the same."

"Maybe not." I open door after door, looking for proof that we've found what we've been searching for. And then I find it. As the surveillance drone activates its lights, I take it from its resting spot and run my finger over its belly. A tiny mosquito drone is tightly attached to it. "*This* is the drone that came to us."

I head toward Jackie, and she turns away from the

computers. Her gaze immediately goes to the belly of the drone. She walks over and twists the mosquito free. "This is mine. How'd it—?"

"Ryan had it," I explain. "Santiago flew it up to the drone. That's how we tracked it here."

Jackie references one of the computer monitors. "From what I can tell, it looks like the drone got an automated alert regarding suspicious activity at the Santa Monica base. It appears that the surveillance drone sent itself to gather intel and bring the information back here. Even though there's no one here to care."

"You think these drones are just surviving here on their own?" I ask.

"Drones are like cockroaches," she says, moving to another monitor. "If you don't literally stamp them dead, they survive. Sometimes they even survive despite that. They'll probably still be surviving here on Earth long after humans have gone extinct."

Jackie is now staring at a screen of twelve squares of video footage—views from security cameras here in this bunker, the tunnel, and the area just outside the entrance. Jackie and I are visible in two of the squares, but when I look at the locations where the cameras should be, I see nothing. The cameras must be nearly undetectable.

Jackie brings up a log in screen. "Can I borrow your necklace again?" she asks me.

I hand over my warrior necklace. Once Jackie is logged in, she scrolls back through the video footage until we see some activity, then she sends the footage forward again.

In three squares, about a dozen soldiers in black jumpsuits occupy the same tunnel that I walked through moments ago. They carry weapons larger than any I've ever seen. Jackie zooms in on one of the squares.

"No way!" she breathes. "I know those guys. They're from your base."

I feel as if my heart has stopped and my eyes have frozen open. I watch as the soldiers—our soldiers—destroy the door and enter this room. I watch as they forcibly take control of the four terrified people who were here.

"So we *did* do this," I say.

Jackie shakes her head, more in disbelief than dissent. "Your military couldn't have done all of this alone. It's just not possible."

Our soldiers lead their four prisoners through the empty doorframe and into the tunnel. One of the remaining soldiers goes to the monitor just to our right. After a minute, he rushes back to the tunnel to catch up with the others, leaving this room as abandoned as it was when Jackie and I found it.

Jackie has moved to the monitor next to me—the same one the soldier interacted with just before he left. Suddenly, she says, "Oh, that's not good!"

Before I can look to see what has concerned her, a disembodied voice from a speaker overhead makes every hair on my skin prickle to attention. "Self-destruct resumed. Evacuate in fifty-two seconds ... fifty-one ... fifty ... forty-nine ... forty-eight ..."

Jackie grabs my arm and starts toward the door. "Run!"

I run with her as if my life depends on it.

Suddenly, the frigid tunnels go hot. It feels like the heat is getting closer and closer. I look behind me and I see why. Fire is chasing us through the tunnel. Jackie pushes me ahead of her. "Go! Go!" she shouts.

We're almost at the exit. I can see the moonlight streaming in. I give one final push of energy, and I feel the cool air from outside slice into me.

I keep running straight into the night. Jackie shouts at me not to stop until—

BOOM!

SATURDAY, JULY 9
2203 MST

JACKIE

My ears are ringing like never before. My helmeted face is against the ground and a torrent of rocks and debris is raining down on me. My body aches as if I've been badly beaten. I can barely catch my breath enough to cough. But at least I'm not dead.

When I look up, I find the area around me engulfed in flames and thick black smoke. I can hardly make out the mountain that I just escaped from.

Where's Hanson?

"Hanson!" I shout. My voice comes out as a cough and a whisper.

I scan my surroundings, but the fire and smoke prevent my helmet from detecting any signs of life around me. About a hundred yards away is our aerial drone, with flames closing in on it. Between me and it is the surveillance drone that Hanson had with him when we ran out of the tunnel.

"HANSON!" I scream with everything in me.

Maybe he can't hear me. I can barely hear myself. Or maybe he's unconscious. Or maybe he's … No, I won't allow myself to even consider that.

And then I see movement on the other side of a wall of flames. *It's Hanson!* He is standing up, still wearing his helmet, but he looks completely bewildered.

"HANSON!" I raise my hands to try to get his attention, sending waves of pain surging through my arms, shoulders, and chest.

I need to get him out of there. As I assess the situation, I see that he is trapped by the fire on all sides. The only way out is *through* the fire.

The military jumpsuits are supposed to be able to withstand a limited amount of direct exposure to fire, although I've never personally tested this out. If Hanson puts his hands in his pockets and runs, he might be able to make it out of there completely unscathed. If it were me, I'd put my faith in the jumpsuit and make a run for it. But perhaps Hanson doesn't know that the jumpsuit is designed to protect him like this. Or if he does, maybe he's too disoriented to remember.

"THIS WAY, HANSON!" I shout. "COME ON!"

He stumbles toward me, toward the flames, but then he backs away.

I look back at our aerial drone. The fire is getting closer to it. There's only one way to get Hanson out of here. I need to go and get him myself. If the jumpsuits really can withstand fire, getting *to* him should be no problem. Getting him out could be a problem, though. I'm not sure if my jumpsuit will be able to withstand a second trip through the flames.

But I don't need to survive this. I have nothing left to live for other than this mission. And I have accomplished all of the goals of this mission, except for one: I must send

Hanson back home.

The only way he will die today is over my dead body. And I won't allow myself to die until I know he is safe.

I tuck my hands into my pockets, take a deep breath, and I run into the fire.

SATURDAY, JULY 9
2208 MST

TEN

Jackie must have lost her mind. She's running toward me, straight into the wall of fire that separates us. A wall that feels hot enough to kill. On her side of the wall is our aerial drone. She could get into it and leave without me, but instead she's choosing to join me here. To sacrifice her life with mine.

But after she passes through the thick wall, somehow she's still standing.

She survived running through the fire.

"How did you do that?" I ask, incredulous.

"Hands ... pockets," she says in a strange garbled voice.

I'm not sure what she's trying to say. "I don't understand," I shout.

She shakes her head and unzips two of my pockets. Forcefully, she shoves my hands inside. "Keep ... hands ... there," she yells, still sounding like her mouth is underwater. She grabs my left arm and pulls me back the way she came, toward the fire. "Run!"

All of my survival instincts tell me not to do this. I should find another way out. But I don't see any other way. And Jackie just ran through the fire, and she seems perfectly fine. Maybe fire isn't as dangerous as I was told.

And so I let Jackie lead me, running, straight into the fire.

SATURDAY, JULY 9
2211 MST

JACKIE

My body spasms violently as flames engulf me. My jumpsuit is definitely not protecting me this time the way it did last time. It feels as if it's barely protecting me at all. My right hand hurts the most, because I have left it largely unprotected. I need to use it to keep hold of Hanson's arm. I can't risk letting him fall behind, because I won't be able to go back for him if he does.

Over and over again, I tell my brain, *Don't think. Just run.* I can't allow myself to stop running until Hanson and I are inside that aerial drone.

Even though all I can see is fire and smoke, I focus on a mental image of that drone.

I keep my thoughts fixed on that image … until I finally see the real thing.

I feel like the heat is subsiding. I'm not sure if that's because I've gone numb to it, or if we're through the worst of the flames.

Hanson pulls his hands from his pockets. I want to shove them back in, but I physically can't. My body doesn't feel as if it's completely under my control.

He grips onto my arm. "COME ON!"

Hanson is leading the way now, to the aerial drone. Out of the corner of my eye, I see him grab the banged-up little military surveillance drone off the ground. And then he shuts us inside the aerial drone. He takes off his helmet, and he takes off mine too.

"Are you okay?" he asks.

I look down at my hands. The back of my right hand is burned quite a bit, charred black in some spots and blistered in others—second and third degree burns. Most of my body throbs. I don't dare to fully assess the damage, because I'm afraid of what I will find.

I force what I hope looks like a casual shrug. "I think I'm good enough to get us home."

"Good." Hanson gives me a smile, but there's a worried tone to his voice.

I'm worried too. I'm not sure how long it will be until these burns get the best of me.

I hope we make it home before they do.

SATURDAY, JULY 9
2149

SIX

I'm not sure exactly why I am drawn back to Jose's dormitory, but I feel that I must go there. I tap on the door.

"Come in," Jose says.

As I open the door, he looks up from the damaged book—*The Hunger Games*. He's still wearing his jumpsuit. Maybe he was expecting me. Or at least hoping I'd come.

"Did I catch you at a bad time?" I ask with a formal politeness that shouldn't be necessary given our history together.

"Any time is a bad time when it comes to this book," he says, but he clicks off his flashlight and puts the book down anyway.

I slide the door closed behind me, but I stay close to it. Jose meets me there. He stands so close that I can feel him near me, even though we aren't touching at all.

"I'm sorry for being upset with you this morning," I blurt out.

"I'm sorry too."

"It's just …" I swallow and force myself to continue, "I'm just so afraid."

"Of what?" he asks.

"Of losing you," I whisper.

"I'm scared of losing you too." Jose pulls me into his arms and everything changes. All the sadness and fear and frustration just dissolve away.

And then I say something I never thought I'd say, but I say it now, because I feel it with every bit of my heart, "I don't care where I live. I just want to live with you."

Jose kisses my forehead, and then my cheek, and then my lips. We fall into bed and he holds me so close. I feel completely calm in his embrace. Touching him. Feeling him touch me.

All I want is this. A life exactly like this.

But I don't know if that's even possible.

SATURDAY, JULY 9
2315 MST

JACKIE

Hanson is nestled under the drone's seats again, the way he was when we left the base earlier this evening. Before he went into hiding, he helped me bandage up my hands with soothing burn dressing that makes them feel almost normal. I also took a tablet of W10 107 which has dulled the pain from the rest of my burns down to a gentle ache that I can successfully push from my consciousness, without affecting my ability to fly.

When I think of Hanson, my heart fills with intense gratitude. His reasons for coming on this mission were probably many. It is highly likely that none of them had anything to do with saving me, but save me he did. If he hadn't joined this mission, I would have died before it really began. Earlier tonight, Hanson saved my life. And just now, I saved his. We're not even. We never will be. But I feel like I have become, once again, the kind of person who I was back when I was a kid. Someone who does what's right for all rather than what's right for some. Someone deserving of respect. Someone who I respect.

As I anticipated, the "wall of death" that surrounds this place is only deadly in one direction. It seems there are no obstacles to leaving the defunct PEOC. And so we get on our way in record time. We will be cutting it close to the commander's deadline though.

A few minutes after we've left the restricted airspace, the autopilot automatically engages. Since I didn't initiate its engagement, it is clear that the base has now regained control of the aircraft. I suppose that's a relief. Now I don't have to worry about my fading ability to keep us airborne and on course.

The sudden sound of the commander's voice makes me jump. "Lieutenant Davis," he says in a subdued tone. "I'm pleased to see you again."

"You didn't think you would, did you, sir?" I ask, but then I remind myself that I should hold back on the sarcasm, especially because I am still responsible for Hanson's fate in addition to my own.

The commander ignores my question. Instead he asks, "What the hell happened to your hands?"

I suppose that means he has no idea what occurred once I entered the restricted airspace. He can't see the rest of my body, so he doesn't know that I'm significantly injured there as well. I decide to hold off on revealing the extent of my injuries for now.

"It's a long story, sir," I say. "Ultimately, though, I would say the mission was a success."

"Do tell," he says.

"I found this, sir." I lift the surveillance drone that Ten left sitting on the floor next to the empty co-pilot's seat, so the commander can see it. The drone looks a bit worse for wear, but it seems to have survived the trauma it endured. Its little lights are still blinking and glowing. I'm guessing it's probably still able to fly just fine.

"What is the identification number on that drone?" he asks. I hear the eagerness in his voice.

I read off the number imprinted on the body of the drone.

"I see." The commander knows now that I have the drone he was looking for.

"But I'm afraid I have some unfortunate news, sir," I say.

"What news is that?" he asks.

I don't answer.

For the remainder of the flight, I will feign loss of radio contact. I have told the commander enough that he knows I will be of value when I return. This will ensure that I will be allowed to land safely. Once I deposit Hanson back home, I will tell the commander everything that I've discovered.

And then I will allow him to dispose of me as he wishes.

SUNDAY, JULY 10
0625

SIX

At breakfast, the commander announces—via his
gigantic hologram—that the robots have completed their
maintenance updates and have returned to duty, a fact that
is already evident because those serving our meal this
morning are robots. The other major announcement comes
as a bit of a shock, even though I've been anticipating it.
Our box has been cleared for rehabitation. The shocking
part is that whether or not each individual returns to the box
will be *their choice*. Anyone who once lived in the box,
along with their offspring, may return to it. Or not. We
don't have much time to decide though. We must make our
decision by twelve hundred hours today, less than six hours
from now. The commander ends by telling us, "I trust that
you will come to a swift and satisfying decision." That's a
lot to ask from these people, most of whom have never
made a life-altering decision in their entire lives.

A few tables away, I see Seven holding Fifty-two tight.
Seven looks over at me, no doubt wondering about my
decision. If our decisions aren't the same, will she be able
to keep her daughter? Babies and children will be allowed
to stay up here, and those now in power seem not to care

who lives with whom. And so maybe our decisions don't need to be the same.

"They certainly aren't giving us much time to think about this," I say to Jose.

"Sometimes it's better that way," he says. "That way you go with your gut. Your first instinct is probably the right one."

My first instinct is to go back home.

Jose continues, "What are you thinking?"

Before I can answer, his gaze shifts to something behind me. I turn and find Three standing there. She looks into my eyes anxiously. "Can we talk?"

"Of course," I say, my heart accelerating.

Jose rises from our table. "Come find me later," he says to me.

"I will," I say.

Jose leaves Three and me alone. But we can't talk freely here in the mess hall, and so we go to my domicile. I slide the door closed behind us, and Three sits on my bed stiffly.

"Have you made your decision?" I ask her.

She looks at me, her eyes certain. "Yes," she says. "Have you?"

"I think so," I say, and then I add, "But I need to tell you that, wherever we decide to live, even if we end up in the same place …"

Tears pool in her eyes. They pool in mine too.

"You love Jose," she says.

How do I respond? I can't deny the truth of what she said. I won't lie to her.

"I love you both," I respond honestly.

"I'm going back home," she whispers.

I couldn't have been more certain of that. "I know," I say softly.

"And you're staying here," she says as if she knows it to be true.

"Yes," I say. "I'm going to stay up here."

I have a feeling that Three knew my decision before I did. Sometimes I think she knows me better than I know myself.

"It's okay," she says quickly. "I want you to be happy. *Please* be happy."

I take her into my arms, and I feel her begin to sob.

I love Three. I love her with everything in my heart.

I always will.

SUNDAY, JULY 10
0635

SEVEN

Last night, Ten joined me in our bed very early in the morning. I slept much better once he was beside me. We didn't talk much before breakfast. He said only that he had something important to show me.

After our meal, he leads me away from the murmuring people who are trying to decide their fates. "The robots are going to be transported to the box at zero seven hundred hours," Ten says as we walk. "Do you want to see Miss Teresa before her flight?"

Part of me does, and part of me doesn't. "I guess I should," I say.

Inside the hangar, robots are lined up in neat rows. Unlike the last time I saw them, they are upright, and they are no longer covered in plastic. Now, they appear as they normally do. With their pleasant smiles. Waiting to assist us.

I walk down the rows of robots, and see many familiar faces. If my gaze lingers long enough on any of them, they smile responsively. The way robots do.

And then I spot Miss Teresa. I stop and turn toward her, but I can't make myself look at her. I can't bear to gaze upon the face of a stranger who used to be my—

She presents her right hand, palm facing up. *She wants to scan my chip.*

I place my left forearm over her hand, and I wait for her response.

"Good morning, Six," she finally says. "How can I help you?"

My heart sinks. *She has no idea who I am.*

I shouldn't have come to see her. But now that I have, I need to finish this interaction.

"I … I came to say goodbye." I stare hard at the floor and force out the rest of what I have to say, "I won't be seeing you again."

She doesn't respond for long enough that I am impelled to look up. When my gaze meets hers, I see something change in her eyes, although I am sure that it is only in my imagination.

"*Fue un placer conocerte*," she says.

It takes me a moment to translate what she said: *It was a pleasure knowing you.* But even more important that *what* she said was *how* she said it … in Spanish. Miss Teresa never spoke in Spanish to Six.

She must know that I am Seven.

"Who do you think I am?" I ask, hopeful.

It seems to take far too long for her to answer, but finally she says, "My friend."

I nod my agreement, and then I turn away, so she doesn't see my tears.

I guess I was hoping that she would say that I am Seven. But I have a feeling that she can't or won't say it. Although Miss Teresa hasn't given me the answer I was hoping for, in a way her answer is more than I could have hoped for.

I won't ask her any more questions, because I don't need any more answers.

I will always believe in my heart that Miss Teresa was more than just a robot.

And I will always know for certain that she was my friend.

SUNDAY, JULY 10
0649

JACKIE

My body is weak and my thoughts are cloudy. When I open my eyes, it takes me more than a moment to realize where I am: in a hospital room.

A nurse is watching over me. She smiles the type of reassuring smile that only a nurse is able to give to someone as injured as I am. "How are you feeling?" she asks.

"I won't complain." I'm still alive, and it seems I am being cared for. At least for the moment.

A man's shadow appears just outside my doorway. I wonder at first if he is the doctor, but when he steps into view I see that he is the commander. I've never seen our new commander in person, only in hologram. His presence commands my attention. I attempt a salute, but the bandages that cover nearly all of my body prevent me from doing so.

Apparently the commander notices my efforts because he says, "At ease."

"Sir," I say with a nod.

The commander takes a seat in the chair beside my bed. He looks quite tired. I suppose he didn't have a very restful night either. "I reviewed the data and footage from your mission," he says, "and I wanted to personally thank you."

I'm sure the shock is evident on my face; this is not at all what I expected him to say. I wonder whether he is referring to the data and footage that I recorded for him or if there was additional information that was recorded without my knowledge.

He continues, "Your actions yesterday are a testament to your character."

I don't know which actions he is referring to, but I suppose it doesn't matter. "They don't excuse my previous actions," I respond.

"No, they don't," he says. "However, *those* actions occurred during a time of war. That war is over now. It's now a time of peace. Hopefully that peace will last indefinitely."

"I hope so too," I say.

"Later this morning, I will send specialists here to fully debrief you." The commander rises from his chair. It seems our short visit is already coming to an end.

I'm not sure if it's the pain medicine or something else that makes me ask, "And after that, sir?"

"I'll leave you in the capable hands of our medical staff until you fully recover," he says.

My heart speeds. Why would the commander bother allowing me to recover if his goal was to send me off to die? Is he just trying to give me hope so that I cooperate with the debriefing? Or is he telling me that something has changed?

I decide to ask one final question, promising myself that, regardless of the answer, it will be my last on this subject, "And what will happen to me after that, sir?"

The way he looks at me, with compassion rather than contempt, tells me that perhaps I will have the chance to do some more good in this world before I die. Perhaps I will be given a chance to live a little more life.

And then the commander speaks the words I'd already inferred, "We'll see."

SUNDAY, JULY 10
0703

TEN

After she says goodbye to Miss Teresa, I take Seven to Ryan's bunker. When I left the bunker very early this morning, I told Ryan's team to expect us, and so we are granted access. When we enter, everyone is working busily.

I wonder how long Ryan will maintain this bunker. I suppose he will maintain it until he is confident that those in charge can be trusted. I wonder if that day will ever come.

I take Seven into the smaller room and pull up copies of my mother's files. My mother's access code stopped working at midnight last night, but it doesn't really matter. Ryan's team has copies and backup copies of every file. They are currently hard at work pouring through the information contained in them.

They haven't reviewed this one yet. I'm sure Ryan would have told me if they had. I found it very early this morning, when I searched my mother's files with the name that I saw on the PEOC computers: Cheyenne Mountain Command Center. When I did, only one file appeared in the results. This one.

As far as I know, only two people have ever laid eyes on

the words that fill the screen.
Only me and my mother.
Until now.

SUNDAY, JULY 10
1425

SEVEN

Today was like Assignment Day and Departure Day all in one. At this very moment, everyone who decided to live out their lives in the box is on their way home. The rest of us will live our lives here.

It surprised me how many people chose to go back to the box; nearly everyone chose to return. A few former warriors chose to return as well, but only very few. None of my warrior classmates chose to go back.

My mother and father—and therefore my brother—chose to stay here. My parents talked to me about it first. I think they wanted me to reassure them that it was safe up here. I didn't, because I couldn't. But even boxes under the ground can be dangerous.

Six chose to stay as well. She said she wanted to be with Mom, Dad, Forty-one, and me, which makes sense. She told me privately afterward that there was more to her decision, though. She said she would explain later.

Ten's father and sister are staying up here as well. I think Ten's father is hoping to leave behind the memories of the past. I know Ten is too.

As I expected, Maria and her family are going to remain

up here.

Perhaps the decision that surprised me most of all was Nine's. He's going to stay up here. I have a feeling that his choice has a lot to do with his newfound friendship with Thirteen—the person who he used to dream of being paired with. Back when we were all classmates in the box, Nine and Thirteen weren't even friends, because he was too shy to really talk to her. But seeing them together now, I can easily picture the two of them as a pair. I know they would be content.

This morning, just before we left Ryan's bunker, Ryan told us that Jackie will be pardoned by the commander. Considering how strongly Ten felt about her betrayal, he seemed to accept this news surprisingly well. On the way back to our dormitory, he told me that, although he will never forget what she did, he does forgive her. I wonder if his change of heart has something to do with his mother.

Also this morning, Ten showed me a classified file that he discovered just hours ago: his mother's personal log—a journal she kept from her earliest days as the Decision Maker up until her final day in the box, the day she tried to execute us.

It explains so much.

A few months ago, our box was in grave danger. The President of the United States was considering ending the all of the warrior programs. He felt they were a waste of precious resources. The Decision Makers did not want their programs to be terminated. And so, the United States became a place of rebels. Ten's mother was the biggest rebel of all. She encouraged the warrior programs to band together to overthrow the President.

And they succeeded. The President of the United States is now dead, along with everyone who stood beside him.

After the President was destroyed, there was turmoil. The individual warrior programs competed for power. Ten's mother crafted a plan to systematically destroy the other programs, one by one. And that is exactly what she did. One by one, she "retired" every single warrior program in the United States of America. The last one was retired twenty-one days ago. And so, when Ten's mother told us in the control hub that she had notified the other warrior programs that we had been fatally compromised, it was just another one of her many lies.

In the United States of America, the states are no longer united, because there's nothing left to unite. It's just us and scattered bands of Outsiders.

We are all alone, but few people know this. Ryan's team will know soon, through Ten's mother's journal. The military will figure it out eventually, through their explorations. Once the military realizes the truth, they might share that knowledge with all of us. Or maybe not.

Is it better to wonder if you are alone or to know for certain that you are?

I believe it's better to know for certain. It's better to live with painful truths than dangerous lies. My life was once a life of lies, and those lies nearly destroyed us.

I think now there are far more truths than lies.

This is a future that I never could have planned, but it may be better than any I'd imagined. Ten and I and our child will live lives that are our own. There is no longer a Decision Maker to decide our fates. We will make our own choices, right or wrong.

My life has become a life beyond my wildest childhood aspirations.

A life of both dreams and nightmares.

A limitless life far beyond the sky.

About the author

J.W. Lynne has been an avid reader practically since birth and now writes inventive novels with twists, turns, and surprises. In the science fiction series THE SKY (ABOVE THE SKY, RETURN TO THE SKY, PART OF THE SKY, and BEYOND THE SKY), an eighteen-year-old fights to survive in a dystopian future society founded on lies. In THE UNKNOWN, eight children are kidnapped in the middle of the night and transported to a frightening and mysterious world full of secrets. The romantic contemporary novels LOST IN LOS ANGELES and LOST IN TOKYO follow a young woman's journey after a horrible betrayal. KID DOCS dives into the behind-the-scenes action at a hospital where children are trained to become pint-sized doctors. In WILD ANIMAL SCHOOL, a teen spends an unforgettable summer working with elephants, tigers, bears, leopards, and lions at an exotic animal ranch.

CPSIA information can be obtained
at www.ICGtesting.com
Printed in the USA
LVHW041107221219
641386LV00002B/576

9 781985 100671